Eleanor Limprecht spent her childhood in the US, Germany and Pakistan but now lives in Sydney, Australia. Eleanor's previous novels, *What Was Left* and *Long Bay* were both published by Sleepers Publishing to critical acclaim.

THE PASSENGERS

ELEANOR LIMPRECHT

ALLEN&UNWIN

SYDNEY•MELBOURNE•AUCKLAND•LONDON

Allen & Unwin
83 Alexander Street
Crows Nest NSW 2065
Australia
Phone: (61 2) 8425 0100
Email: info@allenandunwin.com
Web: www.allenandunwin.com

 A catalogue record for this book is available from the National Library of Australia

ISBN 978 1 76063 133 8

Internal design by Sandy Cull, gogoGingko
Set in 13/17.5 pt Adobe Garamond Pro by Bookhouse, Sydney
Printed and bound in Australia by Griffin Press

10 9 8 7 6 5 4 3 2 1

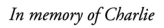

In memory of Charlie

Up ahead they's a thousan' lives we might live,
but when it comes it'll on'y be one.

JOHN STEINBECK, *THE GRAPES OF WRATH*

CHAPTER 1

I watch her at the railing, looking out to sea. Skin so soft it slopes from her cheeks, fine white hair billowing around her face. I like to imagine her—the same age I am now—making the opposite journey, with no idea of what is on the other side. I've seen old photographs, curling at the edges, of her lounging in a chair on an upper deck, shading her eyes from the sun with a hand. Shorts and a halter top, hair wild from the wind, mouth open in laughter. I hold her coffee now and wait for her to turn, studying the rough, wrinkled skin on the backs of her elbows, the veins which bulge behind her knees.

Grandma turns and her bright blue eyes blink away the water from the wind.

'Hannah.' She smiles and steps towards me, taking my arm. 'You've brought coffee. Aren't you a doll.'

We walk the deck in the early sunshine, the yellow hulls of the lifeboats above us. The only sign the ship is moving is the vibration of the deck. Hardly anyone gets seasick now, Grandma says, because they put stabilisers on all the cruise ships.

'Good for you,' Mom said when I told her I wanted to travel back to Australia with Grandma. 'She'll need your help—she's not exactly spry these days.'

'I know. That's why she asked me. And I need to get away. Come with us?'

Mom had sighed, a rush of air in the phone, and I could hear the turn signal in her car ticking, the low murmur of the radio news.

'Can't afford to take that much time off. But this is something she's talked about forever. Since before Grandpa died. I'm glad one of us can go. You need to be strong, though, to help her. Up stairs, in and out of cars once you're there. Are you being healthy?'

'Yes,' I said. 'You forget I'm a nurse—at least, training to be one.'

'Like I'd forget.'

Now the deck has grown busy with passengers making their way to breakfast.

'Are you hungry?' I ask.

'I will be when I see the food.' Grandma threads her arm through mine and we turn around to walk to the dining room. 'Let's go see what's on offer.'

Once we've chosen from the heaped fruit and pastries, the bains-marie of bacon and potatoes and eggs, we find a vacant table beside a window, on the starboard side of the ship. There are two dining rooms that serve breakfast and I've already forgotten their names. They both sound like Italian mobsters.

Food is everywhere—I can't escape it. For an extra cost we can eat Japanese, Brazilian, pizza in the fake Italian piazza or Ben and Jerry's. Just swipe your room card to eat more calories than you'd ever consume on land.

I can tell the cruise regulars because they have lanyards for their key cards—ranging from the simple kind they got for free at a work conference to the bling-laden version that screams bridge-playing retiree. Grandma has a tasteful lanyard of blue and white beads—they're plastic, she says. I don't have one, and don't have a pocket on my dress, so I've stuck the key card in my bra. Plenty of room in there.

Ash says he doesn't mind my lack of boobs. Says he prefers it, which I find hard to believe. Was it only yesterday we drove down together from LA? Already it feels like weeks ago. We picked up Grandma from her retirement villa near San Diego among the glaring green golf courses and electric carts, the Lincoln Town Cars and permed ladies in perma-creased pants with white-soled shoes. Grandma hadn't met Ash yet. I had only mentioned him once or twice. I worried she'd say something to embarrass me—she loves to remind me how at my age she was married. As we sat in traffic Ash tapped his fingers on the wheel. Grandma was surprisingly quiet though, her head nodding to the jazz playing low on the radio.

'What do you normally do on cruises to pass the time?' Ash asked her as he drove us to the dock.

'Play a lot of bridge, go to the shows. I dance if anyone asks me. Walk the decks. I've never been on one this long, one with a destination. I always bring something to read but I never seem

3

to find the time. Mostly, I plan to enjoy the company of my granddaughter. Did you bring a book, Hannah?'

Grandma reached back from the passenger seat and patted my knee with her manicured fingers, and I put my soap-dried hand on top of hers.

'Did I ever. I have a stack of textbooks I'm meant to read.'

'Don't tell me you brought *all* your nursing textbooks,' Ash said, looking at me in the rear-view mirror. He was wearing his Ray-Bans. It was hard to tell if he was joking when I couldn't see his eyes.

'I did.'

'It's a vacation, babe. You're not going to want to study.'

'If I don't ace the exams I probably won't get the clinical internship I want. Paediatrics is super competitive.'

Grandma pointed out the window then, changing the subject. 'I think I see it. There, that huge one. That's our ship.'

It was so big sitting there at the wharf it looked fake. It dwarfed everything else; the other boats looked like small toys beside the gleaming white beast.

'A floating mall,' Ash said, and I kicked the back of his seat. He had made plenty of comments about the environmental ethics of cruises, and at home I'd agreed, but I didn't want to seem ungrateful now that I was here.

Ash hugged us both goodbye at the passenger terminal, where we joined a snaking line of tourists in fanny packs and bright t-shirts. We were different from them, I'd decided. We had a purpose to our journey. While Grandma got her passports out—she had both, US and Australian—Ash put his hand on my cheek. I pushed his sunglasses up to his forehead. In his pupils were tiny reflections of me.

'Will you miss me?' I asked.

'More than you know.'

He kissed me. I watched him walk away, turning back to wave when he stepped off the kerb. I had forgotten to say that I'd miss him too.

•

I move the food around on my plate, cut it into smaller pieces. I find the salt shaker and smother the two teaspoons of egg. Laughter explodes at a table near us, a woman raises her voice to be heard over the cackles of the others at her table. The room is broken up with railings and drapes but it is still cavernous, ornate like a cheesy Italian restaurant where the waiters sing.

Most people in the dining room are in Grandma's age bracket but there are also families with small children, wide-hipped mothers wiping maple-flavoured syrup from the hands of their wriggling toddlers, counting down the minutes until they can send them to kids club. Middle-aged couples who spend their days by the Calypso Reef pool, skin already peeling from sunburn, drinking mimosas and bloody marys with breakfast. Teenagers moving in small packs, carrying plastic soda cups and avoiding their parents' table. The only demographic missing seems to be mine.

My friends are spending their spring breaks backpacking in South America or snowboarding in Vermont. Even drinking margaritas in Cancun. But this is Grandma's trip home. She said she could use my help: getting around, the suitcases, the travel. But I suspect there's something more. I watch her lay her napkin carefully on her lap. The way she eyes mine. She has always had these perfect manners; she takes her fork in her left hand, her knife in her right. In this way she carves every little bite, even the bacon, and brings it to her mouth in dainty, careful portions.

She has kept so many of these habits she grew up with, in spite of being so far away. How easy it would have been for her just to give up and eat like the rest of us, using her fork as a shovel, her knife only when necessary, ignoring the different forks and spoons and the order in which they are used. But she's hung on, and it makes me think it is out of longing as much as habit.

'Grandma,' I say, pushing my plate away, 'you must be so excited to be going back to Sydney. How many years since you've been home?'

She pats her mouth with her napkin, lipstick smearing the linen pink.

'Sixty-eight,' she says. 'But Sydney isn't home, love. Never was. Home is the farm we lost when I was sixteen.'

CHAPTER 2

I remember leaving like it was yesterday. The sky breaking open with rain, Blackie's howls fading the further we drove away.

Up until that point my life had been defined by milking.

Waking before dawn while the sky was grey, my limbs heavy, I pulled a dress and apron over my nightclothes. In the kitchen the sounds of my two brothers scratching, blowing their noses, Mum passing us cups of tea, too early for actual words. Smoke from a twig fire in the stove. Our boots from the verandah and we walked to the shed, rocks and sticks crunching underfoot, the first greenish light visible beyond the bush to the east. There Dad waited for us with the buckets, milkers already tied by one leg with a rope, the damp, sharp smell of urine-soaked hay. Cows snuffled, lifting their heads from the trough of bran. Some lowed at the sight of us, glad for the prospect of relief from the weight of milk in their teats. I dragged my stool beside one and ran a hand along her side gently, the warmth and silkiness of her hide. Then, both hands on her full udders, I began to pull and squeeze, smelling the milk as it came, leaning my head against her flank. Her long tail swatted me, her untied back leg quivered and stamped. Sometimes I wondered if the cow pretended I was her calf, her sweet gangly-legged thing, come back to nurse. Mostly my mind wandered other places though, for my hands knew this motion as my lungs knew to breathe, and I went from cow to cow, passing filled buckets to my dad. He put the milk into the hand separator—the cream would be delivered up the road to the butter factory, and the skimmed milk sent to Sydney in a big truck with steam-driven refrigeration to keep it cold. Some farms had milking machines now, but not small ones like ours.

On their stools my brothers farted and muttered and gradually woke, their rowdy movements frightening the cows. Dad once said I was the best milker of us three, the only compliment he ever gave me. I just loved the cows, their clumsy movements and wide wet noses, whiskers beaded with dew. Slow-blinking eyes with long lashes, mouths always chewing, tongues rough and surprisingly dry. A dairy cow is a gentle beast, a predictable thing, a creature who can stand in a paddock all her life with the sun on her back, munching grass, raising her tail to release wet, black, damper-sized stools. From when I was six I woke every single day before dawn to milk, coming back to the house for breakfast as the birds were chattering in the trees, the whipbirds calling like slingshots, slow tension and release, the black cockatoos hinges that needed oiling.

Mum had fed the poddy calves who still called for their mothers, then fed the dogs and let them off their chains, and they would run to meet us, tails wagging low, pink tongues out the sides of their mouths. Blackie always stayed at my heels; I had rescued her when my dad was going to drown her in the dam because she was a runt pup, so she thought she would always be safe with me. She was the smallest and ribbiest of the kelpies, but clever and cunning. She could round up the cows with the strongest and fastest because she knew whose heels to nip. I saved her scraps from the Sunday roast, crusts of bread, a stale biscuit. Her tongue on my hand was wet and warm. Her eyes were gold-flecked green lined with black, as though she had painted them like a film star.

We kicked off our boots again on the verandah—it was Jack's job to clean them—and went into the kitchen, where Mum had bowls of porridge ready for us, slabs of bread thick with butter. The dogs panted behind the flyscreen, and beyond them the sun broke up the fog which collected overnight in the valley, until only little patches remained in the coldest corners of shade. Dew sparkled on the spider webs and blades of grass glowed as the sun lit them from behind.

After breakfast we got ready for school. The only benefit of being a girl was that I got to use the washhouse first. I scrubbed my face and hands and combed my hair, plaiting it so it swung heavy to the small of my back. Then, back in the house, I changed from my milking clothes and nightdress into my school clothes, the chemise and stockings, the pinafore and blouse, everything grey from having been washed so often and coarse and scratchy. An hour after the sun rose we were saddled up and on our way to the Yatte Yattah school, around a three-mile ride to the south, across Yackungarrah Creek and through Myrtle Gully. Blackie came as far as the creek most days, then sat on her haunches and whined when I told her to go home. She was always there, waiting, in the afternoon. I rode Big Bill, who was called that because he was the smallest of the three but thought himself grand. He had a way of striding with his head high, his step quick, as though he were leading a parade. The kids nearest the school walked or cycled, and a few from larger farms came in cars, but there were still many of us who rode horses and ponies, and there was a long post to tie them to in the shade and a trough for their water.

I had been going to that school since I was seven, and the teacher only changed once in that time. There was possum-faced Mr Buckland, with his hard metal ruler and lunchtime flask, and when he left we had pudding-faced Miss Wren. She could not control the older boys, but she would read stories to us and showed me how to write in a beautiful hand.

The school had one large room, the youngest pupils sitting closest to the coal stove while the eldest sat at the back. It smelled of damp socks and pencil shavings, chalk dust that made me feel on the verge of a sneeze. We washed the chalkboard, cleaned the erasers, used our pencils until they were just nibs and filled every blank space on a piece of paper. After lunch we were allowed outside for half an hour to feed and water the horses, play cricket on the grass; the little ones played hopscotch or swung from the lowest branches of the trees. Then a fly-drowsed afternoon of trying to keep my eyes open while the others droned their recitations. For the first four years I sat watching the creases of dirt on the back of Thomas Ryan's neck. Then he drowned at sea, swept off his father's fishing boat, and only when he was no longer there did I wonder how it was he sat in front of me for four years and we never once spoke.

I loved school and I learned quickly, craving the praise I received. It was also my only chance to see my friends Evelyn and Ada. Evelyn lived near the school—her father ran the post office—and Ada was on another dairy farm along Little Forest Road. She had hands like mine, rough from milking, and the same difficulty keeping her eyes open after lunch. We stood beneath the scribbly gum together at lunch, trading pictures of film stars cut from magazines, pictures of dresses torn from mail order catalogues which we could never afford but dreamed we'd buy one day. I wanted Evelyn's blonde hair rather than my own muddy brown, Ada's small and perfect feet. They envied the blue of my eyes. They told me if Ellis Jones had been staring at me. Ellis was the other reason I loved school. He sat at the very back, as the eldest, and rode a motorbike from the butter factory his father owned. He was taller than my father and brothers. He lived only a mile or two from our farm and was friends with my brother Fred. I felt his eyes on me sometimes, his amber eyes, and there was a place on my waist he had held when he helped me down from my horse, a place where I imagined his handprint to be still, hot against layers of cotton and wool. Unlike the dead Thomas Ryan, Ellis and I spoke sometimes, though it was often awkward and stilted.

'How is your mother, Sarah?'

'Fine, thank you, Ellis, and yours?'

'She has had a bad cough this winter but she is recovering.'

'Oh dear.'

These conversations frustrated me; we had talked easily as children. Ellis would come with his father to inspect the dairy and he and my brothers and I fell into one of a hundred games. He taught us rude words and silly songs and kissed me when I was only eleven, behind a paperbark while we played hide-and-seek. His lips were dry and hot, the skin peeling off them like bark, and before I could ask what he was thinking Fred shouted, 'Ready or not, here I come,' and Ellis ran off towards the dam.

Ellis was often absent from school, and I wondered if it was his choice or his father's. I never missed school on purpose, but I could not go if a cow was calving or the neighbour's sheep were being shorn, or if my brothers were away, for it took three times as long to milk the cows. If my mother had a spell I could not go, for then it fell to me to clean and cook and do the washing. Oh, how I longed for school on those days.

'What are they teaching you, anyway?' my father said when I complained one morning. 'You know how to read and write already.' He was rolling tobacco from his pouch into a thin cigarette.

'I'm learning to be faster with my sums,' I replied. 'And she's teaching us biology, geography.'

He struck a match on the verandah post, cupping it and sucking in until the tip of his cigarette glowed red. He squinted at me, exhaling, a cloud of smoke dissipating around us.

'Fat lot of good that'll do you. Who needs to know where Africa is if you can't find your own arse?'

Jack rescued me then, saying that Mum needed my help in the kitchen. When I went she wasn't there, but he rolled his eyes and sat on the bench, crunching an apple. 'Avoid him if you can, he's cross about Fred.'

'Why?'

And that was how I learned that Fred was moving to Sydney, and I admit my first thought was for myself and how there would be more cows to milk when Fred was gone. I would be the eldest child and the most responsible, and Dad was unpredictable. We knew somehow to blame it on the war. He had fought in France. Of the men he was over there with, one had an amputated leg, one a disfigured face, one a hand blown to bits. Some of the men hadn't returned. Dad's injuries were the less visible sort; the sort which made him drink, and snap into a rage at something as small as a button missing from his shirt. We cowered like dogs when he'd been drinking, doing our best to stay out of his sight.

Dad had burst capillaries in his cheeks and nose, his eyes dripped and his nose watered. There were blisters on his lips from the sun and his yellowed thick fingernails were split and broken. Sometimes I looked at him and wondered if my mum had ever desired him. But if I came across him splitting firewood, snigging logs with a chain, shovelling out the yards, I saw his strong back, his thick neck, his capable arms. I saw from afar what made no sense up close.

Milking was not just mornings but afternoons as well. On school days I rode the half-hour home to milk again, Blackie at my side, and then finished in time for tea. Afterwards there were dishes to wash, then schoolwork, until I could no longer keep my eyes open and went to bed. Weekends were no break from work, but Sundays there was Mum's roast to look forward to. Pumpkin skin blackened and flesh melting into the juice of the lamb. Gravy thickened with flour and stretched with water from the kettle, always a splash of sherry or brandy from the cupboard to the left of the stove.

Mum wasn't the sort for hugging or cuddling my brothers and me, but her eyes lit up when she watched us eat. Dad at one end of the table, Mum at the other, my brothers and I either side. The nice cloth and napkins, the polished silver, crystal salt and pepper shakers, different to the everyday.

Butter in the blue dish, Dad blowing his nose with a trumpet sound and Mum passing the green beans. The thin line of her mouth, the worried crease in her forehead, which softened as she drank the single beer Dad always poured her on a Sunday. She was funny, my mum. Soft and hard all at once. Who could say what went on inside her head? She had painted before we were born, there were the watercolours framed and stacked against the wall in the shed: flowers, chairs, bowls of fruit. I never once saw her paint, even when I was small and my brothers and I were given brushes, her old paintboxes, precious paper and smocks of Dad's old work shirts to wear over our clothes. 'Why did you stop?' I remember asking, maybe as a young woman, maybe a big-enough-to-wonder girl.

She shrugged. 'I wasn't any good.'

I thought maybe she was, though. Dad told a story sometimes about a prize she won, an art prize sponsored by Milton Presbyterian Church. Ten pounds, and they had just met, and she had bought the fabric for a dress (cream silk taffeta with a lace trim) that made him think she must be from such a fine family she would never want him. Imagine his luck, he would say. Imagine his luck that her family were not so fine after all. Her father was an honest working man, like his own, from farming stock. Salt of the earth. It was just her hands that were fine, her eyes. Her figure—before the children, that is. The wattle yellow of her hair.

As Dad told this story she would brush her greying hair from her temples with the back of her veined hands and retreat to the kitchen, carrying stacks of plates. *Before the children, that is.* I wondered sometimes if we ruined her, the three of us. Ruined her for him.

The sun came through the lace curtains in the dining room at two o'clock in the afternoon, a fly buzzing around the bone of the roast while Dad and Jack had the chequerboard out. I washed and dried the dishes while Mum sat with her knitting; she was making a blanket for a baby born to a family at church. I looked at her fingers grasping the knitting needles and tried to picture them holding a brush. Holding my father's hand. Her wedding ring no longer fitted, and she kept it in a red cedar box in her chest of drawers. Later we would turn on the wireless and I would get out my schoolwork. Dad would go to the pub in town. He would come home for milking before dinner: cold lamb sandwiches with lettuce from the garden. My mouth waters now at the thought: white bread Mum baked herself. Salt, pepper, butter. And curling slivers of cold leftover lamb, sliced so thin the light shone through.

•

I was eating one of Mum's lamb sandwiches at a school picnic when Ellis brought me a glass of lemon cordial. When it began to rain he pulled me under the branches of a nearby tree while the other students ran towards the schoolhouse. The foliage was dense and gave off an astringent-smelling heat from the dampness; the very ground steamed. He touched his finger to a raindrop suspended from the tip of my nose.

'It's raining,' I said, or something similarly stupid.

'I've always wanted to kiss you.'

'You did. When we were little, playing hide-and-seek.'

'Has anyone since?'

I shook my head. I felt like a fairy wren who has hit the window and lies stunned but still alive in the grass.

His breath was warm and his mouth seemed to take over my own. How was I meant to breathe? It was suffocating, too wet and soft and slobbery. I pulled away, gasping for breath. It wasn't what I had wanted after all. I ran through the sheets of rain towards the school, hearing him call after me, 'Sarah, wait! Sarah!'

That evening my mum came into my bedroom, which used to be the pantry off the kitchen, where I slept away from my brothers' smells and snores.

'Your brother said Ellis has been paying you some attention,' she said, sitting on the edge of my bed while I hung my dress from the nail in the wall beside my hat and jacket.

I nodded, keeping my face turned away.

'It would be wise to give it time. You're still young. Just keep yourself in check. Some things can't be undone.'

I fussed with the belt of my dress, my face burning. 'I don't even know if I fancy him.'

Mum reached for my hand, pulled me down to sit beside her. 'What he wants is worth nothing once you have given it.'

How is it you tell people things without words? In looks, or the lack of them. In waiting behind when school finishes, or not. Tethering your horse as far as possible from where he parks his motorbike. Hurrying off after church as fast as you can in your too-tight shoes.

•

After Fred left for Sydney it was just Jack and me to help Dad with the milking, and the work was such we could never catch up to it, it was always just beyond our grasp. Dad had a crease between his eyes as deep as a furrow in soil. I wanted to smooth that crease, to take some of the worry and ease the work which woke him hours before the sun rose, long before the milking was due to begin.

One night I was woken by a distant neighing and went outside to check, thinking perhaps a fox was trying to break into the chook shed or bothering a new calf. I walked across the grass in my nightdress and bare feet. The pale moon made the trees glow silver and the corrugated iron of the shed roof ripple with light. Dad was standing beside the shed in shadow, smoking, and I jumped when he stepped towards me.

'What're you doing?' His voice was hoarse and cracked.

'I heard the horses and came to check. Remember that fox last year who dug under the chicken coop?'

Dad nodded, crushing his cigarette into the dirt. 'It's just me they're whickering at. Can't sleep. Thought I'd get a fence mended rather than lie in bed awake.'

'I'll help.'

He shook his head. 'You'll need your strength for milking come morning. Go back to bed 'fore your mum sees you're gone and starts to fret.'

I stood there a moment longer looking up at the whole moon, the stars dim beside its light, feeling as safe as I ever would with my father there beside me, before turning back towards the house.

Later I learned that he had reason not to sleep, for Ellis's father had told him the cream from our dairy was too unreliable, our cows didn't yield enough, our equipment was too old. It turned out Jack and I alone were not sufficient. It would cost my father too much to hire labour, to buy milking machines, and there were debts already: the separator which was never paid off, the bills from the vet, the grocer in Milton. So he decided to sell. He announced it at dinner one night.

'We're moving to Sydney. We'll stay with Mum's sister in Glebe until we find our feet.'

And so it was that in September 1939, only days after Germany invaded Poland, and England and France declared war, we left the only home I'd ever known and moved to the city. I was sixteen, with calloused hands, an understanding of cows, with more education than either of my parents had ever received.

'Think of how it'll feel to not have to wake before dawn every morning, not to have to milk those beasts every single goddamn day of your life,' Dad said.

We sold the farm to a fellow who'd run a fishing boat from Batemans Bay, further south, and he bought the herd, the horses and the equipment too. Dad told him he'd throw in the dogs for free, and though I wanted to keep Blackie he said I could not; the Chevrolet truck bought with money from the farm was full as it was with our trunks of clothes and pots and pans, the radio, Mum's sewing machine, the butter dish and Bible. We sold the furniture to a man who came in a truck and haggled with Dad out front for an hour before they loaded on the bedsteads, the bureaus, the table and chairs. What he didn't want we burned: piles of old catalogues, a broken chair, Mum's paints and canvases. The rocking horse from our childhood. My papers from school. The fire was still smouldering the next morning as we climbed into the Chevy.

'Maybe you can fetch her when we're settled,' Mum whispered.

Blackie cried and strained at her chain as we drove out of the valley, her painted eyes seeing, her nose pointed towards the sky. The cows bellowed and the clouds were low and dark. They opened as we shut the gate behind us, the world itself wet with sorrow. Blackie haunts my dreams still, her soft, nudging muzzle, her shining black coat, the way she stayed on my heels, expecting me to protect her. Years later I saw Ada at a YMCA dance and asked her what became of our farm. She said the man didn't know what he was doing; he lost the herd to tuberculosis, sold the place to Ellis's father and went back to fishing.

'And the dogs?' I asked, but she just looked at me blankly, then laughed with her bright lips, lifting her skirt to show a stockinged leg and a small, perfect foot. 'Will we dance, then? Couple of milkmaids like us—look at us now!'

But I was in no mood to dance. I was pining again for Blackie. For the smell of milk in the morning and wood smoke in the valley, the mist rising from the dam as she bounded across the grass towards me, tongue sideways, body low.

CHAPTER 3

We are the only people left in the dining room besides the waiters. They push cartloads of dirty dishes back into the steam-filled industrial kitchens. I watch Grandma blink away this old sadness.

'Is this the valley where my uncle lives?' I ask. 'Where we're planning to visit?'

She nods. 'They say it now only takes three hours to drive there from Sydney. I don't think we'll find Blackie though.' She smiles.

'Maybe her grandpups,' I say. 'Or her great-grandpups. Remember Pip, that dog you had when I was a girl?'

'With the black-and-white face? The owner left her at the clinic when he learned she was blind in one eye.'

'She ate bananas.'

Grandma laughs now, her face a frond of wrinkles. 'She was a funny dog.'

'Remember how scared I was of her at first, because she'd put her paws on my shoulders and lick my face?'

'I do, and I remember how, by the end of the visit, I'd find you curled in her bed with her in the early morning. You would make me promise not to tell your mother.'

I stand, for there is a man with caramel skin, an apron and checked pants hovering behind us and I can see that he needs us to leave. I feel lightheaded but blink the dizziness away, offering my arm to Grandma.

'What are your plans for the morning?' I ask her.

'It's made me tired, remembering. I might lie down for a spell.'

'Will you tell me about Sydney later?'

'Of course, my love.'

I walk her back to our cabin and then go to explore the many layers of the ship—the restaurants, the gym at the bow, the spa and bars and hundreds of closed cabin doors. All of it man-made, artificial, and so different from what Grandma's been speaking of: the land, the animals and birds, the work which suited her, which felt right. I feel the same when I am on the wards, finding veins, adjusting cannulas, shifting a patient to place a bedpan beneath. I feel like I know this work of bodies, as though my hands were made for it. If only the other parts of life came so easily, were so simple to achieve.

I think of Grandma in her single-room schoolhouse and I think of myself in school, always trying to please, collecting ribbons at races, in spelling bees, folders filled with certificates and awards. I was desperate for any recognition. Mom always told me that life was different for me than it was for her generation. They'd fought for the freedoms we had: girls weren't expected to just be teachers or nurses anymore. I could be anything: lawyer, scientist, astronaut, president. I thought that meant I had to be everything. Dad loved to say that second place is the first loser.

Ash doesn't get what he calls my 'perfectionist streak'. Because I haven't told him the history.

Already I feel like the oldest sophomore in the nursing program at UCLA. What the other students are interested in—keg parties, pep clubs, streaking the quad drunk—holds no appeal to me now. I prefer staying in the library until it shuts, waking up early to run in the grainy light before dawn, going to extra study sessions with my pack of multicoloured highlighters.

'A lot of us took a while to figure out what it was we wanted to be,' Ash told me when I complained about their lack of focus. 'I spent more time on a skateboard than studying. I was directionless too.'

I nodded as if I agreed, but at that age I wasn't directionless. I had a very specific purpose.

I wanted to disappear.

CHAPTER 4

The smells and sounds of Sydney were a shock. There were cars everywhere, throwing up dust or mud—depending on whether it had rained or not. The smell of dunnies in the heat, grease and steel, rotting fish by the harbour and stale beer outside the pubs. In Glebe everyone lived in each other's laps, except those in the fine, grand houses on Glebe Point Road. The narrower the street, the narrower the terraces lining either side.

Mum had always had spells every few weeks, meaning she would have to lie down for an afternoon. I'd thought that being away from the work of the farm would help them, but in Sydney they grew worse. The doctor said it was her nerves and that she simply needed rest. We were too many of us in my aunt Joy's terrace: a skinny house with floorboards so mouldering that sometimes they gave way. They were patched with flattened kero tins. Joy also had her husband Alf and her boys, who were nine and six, streetwise kids with missing teeth and freckles as thick as fleas. With the truck, Dad found work as a delivery driver for a bottling factory and he took Jack with him to help out. I was stuck at home every day with Joy and Mum. Luckily the boys went to school and so I had some relief from them catching frogs and worms and slugs and sticking them beneath my pillow and inside my boots. I helped Joy with the housework and brought Mum her headache powder, and at night after dinner and washing up and listening to the news about the war on the wireless, I lay down beside Mum on the bed we made on the living room floor while Jack and Dad slept outside on the verandah.

Fred came to visit, wearing his khaki shirt, shorts and boots with white canvas gaiters. He had a slouch hat with a puggaree, and a strap which came across his chin in the front; I always wanted to tuck it beneath. He was army now, staying at the barracks and finishing his training, and Dad had something to be happy about. He thumped Fred's back and said, 'Jack'll join up soon too,' though Mum said, 'Hush, he's not yet old enough for that.' Fred did look smart in his uniform, and he told me Ellis had come to Sydney and was joining the navy, and Mum watched me across the table to see how I reacted. I did imagine Ellis in a uniform—how handsome he would look with his height and broad shoulders—but then I remembered his large wet mouth.

What I wished more than anything was that we could leave that stinking, stifling place and go back to the farm. I thought I would be glad for a break from the work, but the truth was I missed it. Every morning before dawn my body woke and told me it was time to trudge across the paddock to the shed and lean my forehead against some warm flank and milk the cows.

One morning, try as I might, I could not go back to sleep. I tiptoed out of the room, past my father and my brother, to sit on the verandah steps and watch the sky lighten. There were still plenty of birds but they were the common kind—magpies and sparrows, sometimes a wren. Jack stirred and came to sit beside me. He was a year younger but taller than me now, fair-haired with Dad's dark brown eyes. 'Strange, isn't it, not having to wake at this hour?'

I nodded, turning my face away so he couldn't see the bare emotion on it.

'What are we doing here?' I asked.

'It'll be right, Sar. It's not so bad. We just need to find our own place.' He draped his arm loosely around my shoulders. He still smelled like he did as a boy, of haystacks and rust, even in the city.

'There's no room to breathe.'

'I can't say I miss all the work, but I miss the horses. What I wouldn't give to saddle one up and go for a ride, that way.' He pointed towards the south.

'I miss Blackie,' I said. 'It doesn't feel right, does it?'

'No. It don't.'

•

Dad found us a place on the other side of Glebe, in a suburb called Forest Lodge. I had no idea why it was called Forest when there was no forest anywhere near, but maybe it was named by someone who missed the forest so much they thought a word could conjure it. Our new home was five rooms and an outdoor loo and a verandah choked by oleander, and Dad parked the truck in the front yard. But at least Jack and I had a proper room to sleep in and Mum perked up as soon as we were out of Aunt Joy's. The only problem, it seemed, was that there were two pubs in less than two blocks and so Dad never had to travel far for a drink.

I began to look for work, as we were all meant to have a job—to do our bit. I was glad. I had no intention of spending the rest of my life fetching Dad home from the pub and mixing Mum's headache powders. My skills weren't particularly useful, for there were no dairies which needed an extra hand with the milking, but then our neighbour Mrs Thompson said she had a typewriter and could teach me to type in exchange for help with the housework. And so I would do the housework early and then, in the stifling heat of midday, sit in front of the Remington learning where the letters were on the keyboard. Before having children (three, and another on the way), Mrs Thompson had worked as a typist, and after explaining the intricacies of the machine while I cranked the mangle or scrubbed the kitchen floor, she told stories of the larks she'd had with the other girls in the office, the speeds some of them would type and the relief at seeing the tea cart at ten when their fingers began to cramp. She made it sound as though her office days were the best days of her life.

At night, back home, while the rest of the family sat outside waiting for the southerly to bring cool air, slapping mosquitoes and smoking cigarettes, I would sit with a dummy keyboard and practise typing the pages from a book. Sometimes Jack would come inside and dictate to me, putting on silly accents so I couldn't help but laugh.

'Don't look at your hands!' he would snap in a German accent. 'Vat a naughty girl.'

My silent typing became fast. There are no errors when you can't see what you've typed.

At Mrs Thompson's my fingers flew across the keys with a satisfying sound, that jostling *click click click click* then *ding!* when you reached the end of a line. Every week she timed me, and when I could type sixty-five words per minute she said I was ready to try out my skills in the world.

'I wish it were me,' she sighed, putting the dustcover back on the Remington.

A man Dad worked with had a daughter who was a typist for the Americans, and he set up an interview for me.

The Americans had entered the war at the end of 1941, when the Japs bombed Pearl Harbor, and it wasn't long before their khaki uniforms spilled into the streets, bringing a new energy and purpose to what had so far seemed like a distant war. By the early months of 1942 the streets were overrun with Yanks. The war seemed closer than ever when Darwin was bombed by the Japanese on 19 February. I saw photographs in the newspaper of aeroplanes bombing ships in the harbour, of families fleeing town. Two hundred and thirty-five people were killed and no one had expected or prepared for it; everyone said we'd been caught on the back foot. So the sight of more uniformed soldiers on the streets gave us a sense of security, as well as a secret, belly-deep sort of thrill. They seemed so confident, so certain of their place in the world, that we let ourselves be convinced of it too.

Dad and Jack dropped me near the Grace Building on York Street on a sunny day in March. I was wearing my neatest belted peplum skirt and blouse, dove-grey silk stockings and my blue felt hat with a daisy on the brim. I had twisted my hair into rolls and pinned them either side of my head.

'Knock 'em dead,' Jack shouted out the window as they drove off.

I stood still for a moment, letting the human traffic flow around me. I could see the building from where I stood, a solid block of stone with tall narrow windows reflecting the sun, making my eyes water as I gazed up at the towering monolith. Down at street level, I was surrounded by smartly dressed women, some in uniform, some in skirts and blouses, others in dresses and heels, nearly all of them wearing lipstick and stockings, their hair in fringes and curls. There were men in uniform and men in suits with hats and ties. Shoeshine boys, paper boys in front of stands on the corner selling drinks and cigarettes and matches and fruit. A serviceman caught my eye and winked and I shut my mouth and looked away, remembering I shouldn't stare.

I began to walk, and for the first time, perhaps because I was on my own, I felt a quiver of excitement about the city rather than just disdain, a quiver like the shudder that runs through a horse when you're putting on his saddle. I walked through the crowd as if I belonged and I went into the Grace Building and caught my very first lift to the very first job interview of my life.

The office of the Quartermaster Corps was filled with the clicking of machines, ringing phones, the murmur of serious voices, a sense of purpose. A secretary took my name and told me to sit and wait.

I must have smoothed my skirt fifty times before a young woman with a pageboy haircut approached and introduced herself. Her name was Dot and she was the daughter of my father's workmate. She had a pointy chin and a wide smile and put her hand on my arm, and I hoped we would become friends. She took me to a row of typewriters where eight or nine women sat working, their backs pencil-straight and their eyes on their pages. There was the whir of fans and fingers flew. Dot introduced me to the oldest-looking woman, a Mrs Faber, who had a pair of gold-rimmed spectacles hanging around her neck on a thin gold chain. Mrs Faber said she would test my speed, and so we went into another room where there were not so many distractions. We walked past dozens of men in uniform, all wearing pinkish-beige tailored pants and jackets with epaulets. These, of course, were the American army officers, and even the way they spoke caught me by surprise. Their voices were loud, nasal; they pronounced their a's and r's but seemed to swallow their o's and l's. I was glad it was Mrs Faber rather than one of them testing me. Luckily she didn't ask many questions about what I'd done or where I'd worked before, but she wanted to see my speed both taking dictation and typing directly from a handwritten page.

The typewriter she sat me in front of was large and well oiled, newer than Mrs Thompson's, but as soon as I placed my fingers on the keyboard I found my rhythm. As I typed I thought about how our hands can be trusted to know the way, both with cows and with keys. These machines were not going to breathe their warm, grass-scented breath on me, but they still responded to my touch. After twenty minutes or so we were done. Mrs Faber took off her specs, folded them, and let them dangle against her flower-patterned bosom.

'You'll do just fine,' she said. 'And excellent spelling with the dictation. There aren't many girls who make so few mistakes. Come with me and we'll get you to sign some papers, put together a few training days and you're set to begin.'

·

And so I became a clerk with the Quartermaster Corps of the US Army, working five days a week in the city, learning to dress and talk and type like an office girl and not the bushie I had been. I became confident, at least on the outside. I laughed as loud as the other girls and chewed gum and varnished my fingernails with Glazo nail polish and wore Mitcham Lavender. I made just over two pounds a week, and while most of it went to Mum and Dad, I still had enough to buy pretty things— those I could get with ration coupons; I made do and mended those things I couldn't. Some evenings and weekends I went to coffee houses and picture shows with Dot and her friends. Watching them, I learned how to act around men, how to be mean or nice at the drop of a hat, how to bring them in and then hold them at arm's length.

If we were friendly, the officers at work had ways of getting around the rationing. They brought us nylon stockings, tinned fruit, boxes of chocolates which you had to eat quickly before they turned sticky and soft in the heat. I learned how to hold a few drinks without acting too silly, and not to mix spirits and beer. Dot teased me when I drank a beer, because it wasn't something many women did, but I always thought of Mum's single Sunday glass and it seemed something that brought us closer, like a part of her which was now my own. I learned to dance, how to let go of my stiffness on the dance floor, what it meant to have a good lead, what it meant to follow.

I learned that most men did not kiss like slobbering puppies, that a real kiss didn't mean you had to wipe your face afterwards. And that it was the beginning—a kiss—rather than the end, and you had to hold their hands to keep them from wandering, unless that was what you wanted. My first proper kiss was with one of Jack's friends after he took me to see a matinee one Sunday. I can't even remember what we saw, because the pressure of his hand on my shoulder made everything else seem like a distraction. His knee touched mine and his body was narrow and tall, folded into the cushioned velvet seat. In the dark at the back of the cinema he leaned over and kissed me as the credits rolled, and his mouth was soft on mine, his lips as tender as a horse lifting the apple from your palm. His black curls brushed my cheek as he bent to kiss my neck, and his scalp smelled yeasty like bread. He had lashes like a girl's and long thin fingers, high cheekbones. We went to the beach the following week—to Coogee—and walked the promenade while foamy waves crashed, the colour of the water muted by clouds. Afterwards he bought me a shandy and himself a beer in the Coogee Bay Hotel, and then he held my hand and told me he loved someone else. He died in the Pacific the following year. He wrote me a letter once, but I lost it. I can't recall his name.

CHAPTER 5

I kiss Grandma goodnight on a cheek made slippery with face cream. I watch her lower herself into bed. She lifts her loose-skinned legs onto the mattress slowly, one by one, and pulls the sheet over them. I resist the urge to tuck her in. She has kissed men who have been dead more than seventy years. She has been around my entire life, holding my hand to cross the road when I was a girl, reading me stories in her low, melodious voice, then telling me to hop into bed, 'quick sticks', before she got in trouble for letting me stay up late. When my parents had parties I sat at the top of the stairs, watching her talk and drink cocktails with the other grownups. I could pick her perfume, the certain sound of her laugh. I've taken for granted that she will always be here. But she won't. We might have five more years if I'm lucky, perhaps fewer.

She accepted me when no one else did, sat beside so many hospital beds, tried her best to understand.

I turn off the overhead light and slip between my own sheets.

I pull out my phone and open the calorie tracker I keep in a hidden folder. I list everything that has gone into my body today.

Breakfast
1 slice honeydew melon: 36 calories
2 tbsp scrambled eggs: 46 calories
½ cup orange juice: 56 calories
1 slice dry wheat toast: 79 calories

Lunch
Bowl vegetable soup: 98 calories
3 saltine crackers: 39 calories
¼ cup ice-cream: 90 calories

Dinner
½ chicken breast: 142 calories
½ cup vegetable stir-fry: 65 calories
1 light beer: 104 calories

Total intake: 755 calories

Exercise
½ hour treadmill: 250 calories
½ hour elliptical: 270 calories

Total output: 520 calories

I feel the familiar bile of self-loathing rise. I should have skipped the beer and the toast. Then I'd be closer to even.

Lying there beneath the sheet I feel the knobs of my hipbones, elbows, wrists and knees. They comfort me. They keep me going. If I had taken the time I spent thinking about food and used even half of it productively, I might be a concert pianist or a brain surgeon or have discovered the cure to a rare genetic disease. I could be a lawyer and an astronaut. I think of Ash and his music, his skateboarding, how food occupies such a tiny fraction of his thoughts. How he doesn't know any different, could never understand.

In treatment they said you cannot be in a relationship until you have learned to love yourself, so for years I avoided boyfriends. Sure, I had one-night stands, but more than one night was too many. Six months into nursing school I went out for sushi with a girlfriend and complained that since moving to LA I hadn't so much as talked to an interesting guy. The demographics of nursing school are skewed towards female, and the other students were five years younger than me; the few male nursing students were still figuring out how to shave.

Right then and there she pulled out her phone and set up a Tinder profile for me. I could tell she was dying to do it; she was still with her college boyfriend. We giggled at the men's photos and looked for someone I'd be halfway willing to date. Plenty of the guys were good-looking, it was just that they all seemed to know it, and I couldn't stand the smug posing beside a list of demands for girls they might want to fuck.

Straightaway I decided what would rule them out:

1. Shirtless selfies.
2. Bad spelling.

3. Any of the following descriptors: hot, casual, sexy, buxom, tight, classy, hook-up, no strings attached, boo, kinky, sugar mama/daddy, MILF, booty.
4. Anyone who specified an age limit for women significantly lower than his own age.
5. Anyone who specified an age limit for women significantly higher than his own age.
6. Anyone wearing sunglasses in their profile pic. How can you trust a guy when you can't see his eyes?

This narrowed the field considerably. 'What *do* you want?' my friend asked, and that was harder to communicate.

'I don't know . . . Someone who's going to make a playlist of songs he thinks I'll like. Who's sensitive. Sweet.'

'Oh God,' she said, typing away with her thumbs. 'You're going to end up with such a loser.'

'Why?'

'Sensitive means mama's boy, doesn't it? Like he'll make you a playlist, but he'll wait for you to do his laundry and he'll leave all the dishes in the sink. And he'll want you to talk about the playlist he made for, like, the next week at least. Here, let's use this photo—you look hot.'

I moved the sushi around on my plate, leaning in to look. 'I hate that picture.'

'Look how tiny your waist is!'

'Yeah, and look how my face is all squinty.'

'It was sunny. You've got a good tan.'

'Fine.'

'Are we done? Let's get a drink. I'll tell you if we get any interest.'

Maybe I shouldn't have had three slivers of fish for dinner and four glasses of wine, because we did swipe right later plenty of times, giggling in the corner of the bar where we had planned to shoot pool but ended up hunched over our phones instead.

The subsequent chatting ruled out most of them, but I ended up with two coffee dates and one of those morphed into drinks. It took a month, maybe two, before I could figure out within the first words of a chat whether or not a guy was just looking for someone who was DTF. Sometimes that was fine, but after one or two I stopped. It felt dangerous. A precipice above the past. I became good at using emojis, and I realised that a sense of humour is a fairly difficult thing to communicate via text.

It was—admittedly—a shallow reason that drew me to Ash's profile at first. The photo showed him on stage but was taken from close up, so his green eyes and dark, close-cropped hair were evident. It sure as hell wasn't his interests that caught my attention: he listed playing drums, downhill skateboarding and hanging out.

When I showed it to my friend over brunch she said, 'Oh no. Hell no. Not the musician-slash-skateboarder, please.'

I ignored her and swiped right.

'You're going to regret that one, honey,' she said, dumping another creamer into her coffee.

I still don't know if she was right.

The first time we met was in a bar Ash suggested in Santa Monica, the kind of place that tried to look older than it was, with tables made of reclaimed railway sleepers and wooden whiskey barrels lining the walls. I walked in with my phone in one hand and my purse in the other, ready to bolt if he wasn't there. I was fifteen minutes late. Walking into a bar by myself is right up there as one of my least favourite things to do.

I spotted him right away, sitting at the end of the bar, looking up at the TV screen rather than towards the door. Leaning up against the bar was his skateboard. This would be a first. Would we skate off into the sunset together at the end of the night? I felt all wrong in my jeans and loose tank top, my hair pulled into a ponytail. He was way too cool for me. I walked over and when I drew near he looked away from the TV.

He stuck out his hand. 'Hannah?'

'Ash.'

'Have a seat. You look great. I mean, I've never seen you before so that's kind of a weird thing to say, but you do. I'm really glad to meet you.'

He was like that, I realised as soon as I sat down. He said what was in his head, he talked about whatever he was thinking or feeling at the time. He grew up on a commune in Marin County, so I guess it isn't surprising. He's the kind of person who'll tell you his life story straight away, and he did, smiling at me, his knee bumping against mine every so often as we sat on adjoining bar stools.

His parents were hippies and he was the last of their six children, born on what he called an 'intentional community' where they grew soybeans from which they made organic soymilk, tofu and tempeh.

'Go on, laugh,' he said. 'Everyone does.'

I had been holding back a snort of laughter but I let go.

'Do you even like tofu?' I asked.

'I eat it sometimes, like when I go home to see them, but I'm not a vegetarian anymore.'

We talked about music we liked, about nursing school, about the difference between the east and west coasts. He was too easy to talk to; I had to remind myself that I didn't really know him.

'So you ride that everywhere?' I asked, nodding at his board.

He grinned. 'My friends said it's the wrong way to get to a date, but I had to prove them wrong.'

'Or right, maybe.'

'Ouch.'

'So what's the downhill thing? Explain.'

'I'll show you.'

He pulled up a clip on his phone. There were whole YouTube channels, it turned out, devoted to this. People on longboards slaloming down the steepest hills they could find, winding across the black asphalt, knees bent, arms behind them, heads forward as they gathered speed. They wore gloves and used them to gently touch off the road, the leather skimming the hard tar. The speeds they reached, with nothing between themselves and the street but a thin board and four wobbling wheels. Madness. It made my heart sit high in my chest to watch.

'Have you hurt yourself?'

He showed me some of his scars.

We stayed at the bar for hours, drinking, eating the kind of greasy bar snacks that made me feel like I'd have to run twice as far the next day to make up for them. Before the night even began I had decided not to go home with him. We walked along the promenade by the beach when the bar closed, and the night was warm, the water slapping against pylons.

'Have you ever ridden?' he asked.

'Not since I was, like, ten.'

The board felt precarious beneath me. He ran beside me as I rolled, unsteady, with the courage alcohol brings. I went faster, pushing off, positioning my feet. There it was: the knife edge of balance. I understood. But I couldn't stop, and there was the grass and I tumbled, landing free, the dull thump of damp earth. He brushed me off, both of us laughing.

There was a man packing up his fruit stand beneath a street-lamp and Ash asked if he could buy something. He gave the man three dollars for two peaches, and we ate them without even washing them, the juice running down our chins, the brush of fuzz and wet bright flesh beneath. There are seventy calories in a large peach. We threw the stones in the sea. I was telling him about growing up in Virginia and needing to get away from what I'd always known when he put his hand on the back of my neck and his sticky fingers through the hair above it.

'Can I kiss you?' he asked, and that question was what undid me. Instead of answering, I kissed him. I tasted peach, and sun on leaves, and thought about creamy white blocks of tofu quivering on trays. When I felt his tongue against my lips I thought of how a man had come into the university hospital the other day who had bitten his tongue clean through, and the threads of flesh and tissue it hung by. The way the surgeons stitched the tongue back into place. Ash's fingers traced the hollow behind my ear, the curve of my cheekbone, the tenderness of my temple where you can feel an echo of pulse.

In the months since moving to LA I had not once felt my body want something my mind had decided against. I stopped to catch my breath, regain control.

'Are you okay?' he said.

'Yeah,' I lied. 'I'm fine.'

•

Ash doesn't know about the years I was in and out of treatment facilities. I can't bring myself to tell him. I don't know why. Or I do. Because he'll watch me more closely, like my mom does, like everyone who knew me then. He'll see my body differently. With pity. Less desire.

The thing is, I think he might get me. Because I get him: I get why he wants to fly downhill. I stand on the verge to watch him sometimes, whooshing past, the carve and scrape of his wheels, the movement all danger and grace. A wrong turn. A bit of gravel. A fast car. That is all it would take.

It's: how close can I get to the edge of this? How deep before I must go up for air?

Is this a life?

It has to be. I don't know another way to exist.

CHAPTER 6

Jack lied and said he was eighteen in order to join the army. While he was in training, Fred's unit left for the Pacific. Mum spent her days glued to the radio, as if it might somehow communicate his demise. Dad stayed out drinking more and Mum's anxious state seemed to worsen. Her eyes were often bloodshot and puffy from crying.

With Jack gone, I had the bedroom to myself and when I wasn't at work I was holed up in there, reading fashion magazines, trying out new hairstyles or taking up the hem on one of my skirts. I had packed all of Jack's books and form guides and jars of stinky hair pomade into the trunk at the foot of his bed. I only missed him late at night, when we used to talk about the future if neither of us could fall asleep.

I liked to daydream about leaving home, walking down the aisle in white with a fluttering veil, having a husband and a place of our own. Not long after I got the job at the Quartermaster Corps I put a wedding dress on layby at Grace Bros. Wedding dresses were becoming scarce, and I didn't want to miss out. It was cotton organza with a long skirt and a lace bodice, puffed sleeves and a square neckline. The lace was a pattern of love knots. Dot knew about it but not Mum and Dad; I was afraid they'd laugh at me.

One night I was sitting up in bed, fixing a button on a bouclé suit jacket, when Mum came in. She sat on the edge of Jack's bed, her thighs straining the seams on her dress.

'You could leave those little repair jobs for me, now that you're working,' she said. Even in the lamplight I could see loose skin sagging beneath her chin. I wondered when she'd last worn make-up or visited the hairdresser.

'I don't mind, Mum.'

I had used a longer length of thread than I needed for a simple button, but she watched quietly, not commenting on my ineptitude.

'Could you pass me the scissors?' I pointed with my chin to the pair lying on the windowsill. I had used them to cut my fringe earlier.

She stood and retrieved them, holding them out to snip the thread for me, then sat back down.

'Thanks.'

I hung the jacket back in the narrow closet, which was getting quite stuffed now with my things. I would have to see if I could fit Jack's shirts into his trunk as well.

Mum cleared her throat. Her hands were clasped in her lap. 'Would you tell me, Sarah, if you saw anything funny?'

'What do you mean?' I didn't look at her, but stood brushing the snipped bits of thread off my coverlet.

'Your father—if you saw him with another woman, would you tell me, or would you keep a secret for him?'

I looked at her now, trying to digest what she had said. It was several long moments before I could reply. 'Surely you can't be serious, Mum. Dad? What woman in her right mind would want him?'

Mum blinked and her eyes filled with tears. 'There's no need to be cruel, Sarah. I just have some—' she sniffed, pulled a hanky from inside her blouse and pressed it to her nose —'some suspicions.'

The idea was absurd. Mum must have finally gone completely batty, I decided, what with sitting beside the radio night after night waiting to hear some news of Fred. But she was right; I shouldn't be cruel. I didn't want to cause her further grief.

'Tell me why you're suspicious,' I said, humouring her.

She cleared her throat and sat forwards. 'You know how he always goes to the Town Hall or the Royal to drink, and then on a Wednesday to the harness racing and Friday the dogs?'

I nodded. I had gone to each of these places on various occasions to bring him home before he spent the week's rent, and had learned to assume a lighthearted tone to keep him from getting angry. Mum sent me because Jack would just be roped into drinking with him.

'Well, last night when you were out with your friends from the office, Jack dropped round from the barracks.'

'I didn't know.'

'I was waiting to tell you. I gave Jack some tea and told him to wait while I went and fetched Dad, because I knew your father would want to see him. So I walked to the harness racing, but he wasn't there. I asked this fellow at the gate whether he'd seen him and he said he'd left with a lady an hour earlier. So I came home, upset of course, and told Jack what the man said, and Jack went out to find him. When Jack came home he had Dad, but he had a split lip as well. Jack said he found him at the pub and Dad says of course there was no lady, the ticket collector was daft. But I can't stop thinking on it. I want you to watch him, Sarah. See if you can find out who this woman is.'

'Really, Mum? Don't you think the ticket collector just mistook him for someone else? Jack would have told you if things were wrong.'

'Do you think? He's just another man, Sar, I know where his sympathies lie. Besides, there was something off between him and Dad, I could tell. Jack wouldn't tell me how he got the split lip, either; he told me some nonsense about running into a door.'

It was mad to imagine I would somehow find this woman who surely didn't exist. The only way was to wait outside the pub and see if he left alone or in company. But to sit on my own and then slink through the shadows after dark was not only crazy, it was unsafe. Mum had worked herself into a state, though, and she was already on edge over Fred. How could I say no?

•

The following Sunday I had plans to see *Rebecca* at the Lyceum on Pitt Street with Dot. I decided to leave straight after the film rather than going on to a coffee house to chatter away about Laurence Olivier and Joan Fontaine. That way I could catch Dad in time for the six o'clock closing. He was always at his worst on a Sunday evening. He always washed his truck in the morning while Mum went to church, and then disappeared not long after Sunday lunch to one of the locals, which meant he would have been drinking all afternoon.

The film left me in an odd state—the Gothic setting and the delicacy and grace of Joan Fontaine; the strength she found to deal with that awful housekeeper. I would have loved to talk it over with Dot afterwards, but instead I made my apologies, telling her my mum was expecting me home before six.

'Oh, but that means I've got to go home now too.' Dot frowned. 'At least let me walk you part of the way.' We walked arm in arm up George Street and Broadway, talking about Fontaine's tiny waist and the impossibility of maintaining a figure that slim.

'She must starve herself,' Dot said.

'I wish I had that sort of willpower.'

Dot lived on the other side of Victoria Park in Camperdown, so we parted at the duck pond. I felt guilty for lying to her. I wished I could have confided in her, but I thought of how it would make our family seem, and since her father worked with mine, the gossip was sure to spread. I hurried through the warm evening. The streets had that quiet of a Sunday evening, with all of the shops shut and the only sound the chatter of birds in the softening light night. Why couldn't my dad be the sort who stayed home with his family on a Sunday evening?

I was almost at the Town Hall when I realised I had a problem. I couldn't go into the pub on my own, as it would draw everyone's attention, but nor could I ask one of the regulars if my dad was there. They were likely to alert him and so he'd steer clear of this lady, if she was with him. I entered the corner shop opposite the pub and asked for a pack of cigarettes, thinking I might stand outside and smoke and not look out of the ordinary. The shopkeeper greeted me and I recalled the brand of cigarettes some of the girls from work smoked.

'I'll take one pack of Lucky Strikes and a box of matches, please.'

He slid me the cigarettes and my change, and I headed outside, tearing back the paper and foil of the pack and pulling out a single cigarette as I went. I had smoked before, but I had never bought cigarettes for myself, had never even lit one of my own before; there had always been a man to do it for me. The sulphur smell of the match was quickly eclipsed by the rich scent of tobacco and I held the cigarette carefully between two fingers as I had learned to do, pursing my lips as I blew out the smoke. I looked up when I heard a swell of voices— the collective slur and shout as the patrons scattered into the street like a handful of marbles. There was a scrawny pepper tree outside the corner shop and I slunk behind it, keeping my eye on the door of the pub. I recognised the voices of our neighbour Bert, of Johnno from up the road and a few of Dad's other regular companions. Their hats were askew, their jackets worn loosely over shirts that were crumpled and stained. Several recognised me and came over to greet me.

'Good evenin', love.'

'Spare a cigarette for an old man?'

Soon my box was half empty and Dad was still nowhere to be seen. I asked one of the men whether my father had been at the pub.

'Not tonight, girl. Not sure where the old scoundrel's got to. The missus send you to fetch him, did she?'

I nodded. So I'd wasted my time at the wrong pub, wasted my money on cigarettes and made myself look like a fool to anyone watching. Shame burning in my throat, I hurried home, where I opened the door to see Dad and Mum sitting in the lounge—Dad with the paper, Mum with her knitting.

'There you are, Sarah,' Mum said. 'I was starting to worry, it being so late and all.'

•

The next morning I told Mum it wasn't going to work, that I'd had enough of spying on Dad. She nodded then turned back to the clothesline. From behind I saw her wipe her nose on her shoulder with a little shrug.

Secretly, though, I decided to keep trying; I was curious myself now. My next plan was to go to the greyhounds at Wentworth Park, where Dad could be found every Friday night. The races began around six and went until nine, and unlike the pub, plenty of women went to the dogs. Anyone could have a punt at the dogs, and with the totalisators—automated betting machines—you didn't have to put up with some grubby bookie sneering at the paltry amount you were willing to part with.

I went straight from work, though it meant turning down the officers who asked Dot and me to meet them at the Trocadero. Dot said she would ask Susan instead, and I tried to suppress my envy; it wasn't as though I hadn't been invited.

The park was at the bottom of Glebe, on the edge of Pyrmont and Ultimo, and easy enough to get to. The dog track was separated from the rest of the park with brick boundary walls, and this was to be the last month of race meetings before the Americans commandeered the site for an army camp. Dad had grumbled about this: 'Bloody Yanks come in thinking this is their country to do with as they please.' I held my tongue rather than reminding him it was the same bloody Yanks who paid my salary. The dogs were going to share the Harold Park track with the harness racing, and since it was closer to both our house and the pub, I couldn't figure out what Dad was so worked up about.

I queued up and paid my sixpence for entry, then watched the dog owners strut around the track with their sleek greyhounds on leads. The dogs were muscle and bone, not an ounce of fat on them, with long snouts and watery brown eyes. I remembered Blackie and the thump of her tail when she saw me, her cold wet nose against the palm of my hand.

I took a form guide and scanned the crowd for Dad but only met the eyes of leering young men who sat with their packs of friends, shirtsleeves rolled up, smoking cigarettes and drinking from flasks and bottles they hid beneath their seats. I could see them turn and whisper to each other as I passed. High up in the stands there was a free seat between a group of middle-aged women in housedresses and a family with three small children, and I took it, hoping I would be safe here from unwanted advances.

I was still scanning the crowd for Dad's distinctive green hat with the hummingbird wing when the starting gun went off and the dogs burst onto the track in a blur of coloured saddlecloths. It was all over quickly, and I kept an eye on the queue to collect winnings. Sure enough, I saw Dad's hat in the queue, and he was wearing the good suit he was meant to save for church. I stood up and squeezed past the housewives beside me and hurried down the steps for a better view, taking a seat close to the bottom rail, my hat pulled low over my eyes in case he glanced my way.

Even though it was the only time I laid eyes on her, I'll never forget what she looked like. She was as tall as him, broad-shouldered, wearing cream gloves, a netted pillbox hat, and a navy skirt and double-breasted jacket with gold military-style buttons. She had dyed blonde hair and dark red lips and a beauty spot to the right of her small, upturned nose. She had her arm slotted through Dad's and was laughing at something he said, showing two rows of teeth so perfect they must have been false.

I'd never thought of my dad as handsome, but I'd never looked at him as a stranger might. Now I observed the way he held himself, chest out, chin up. He had recently begun to care about the way he looked. His moustache was waxed to sharp points either side of his mouth and his salt-and-pepper hair was neatly trimmed beneath his hat. What a conflicting mess of feelings I had within me then, watching them together. I felt anger and dread and sorrow, yet I couldn't look away. Dad was enjoying himself, he was happy, and as much as I hated him for it, I recognised my own desire to chase that feeling too. What right did I have to take away his happiness? Would it relieve Mum's suffering if I told her what I'd seen, or would she only suffer more? What on earth was I meant to do?

I did nothing. I sat there with my handbag on my lap, my eyes following Dad as he collected his winnings and took this woman by the elbow, whispering something in her ear, and ushered her to the far side of the track. I watched as they stood through the next race, watched as they placed another bet and then watched as they made their way towards the front gate to leave. I got up then, squeezing past knees and shiny shoes and murmuring apologies as I pushed through the crowd, but I had lost sight of them. I stood on the street, helpless, my heart aching for my mother, with her shabby dresses and rough hands, wrinkles gathering on her face like the skin on a pan of cooled milk. While Dad was God knew where with the blonde woman, I had to trudge back to our small weatherboard house where Mum would be sitting by the radio, knitting, waiting for dreadful news.

So I avoided going home and instead wandered the streets. I didn't want to find my father. I wanted to lose myself. I sat on a bench and smelled the peaty leaf litter as I kicked at the dirt and pulled a loose thread on my sleeve and wished for the warm breath of Blackie in my lap and the strength to tell my mum what I had seen. Of course, just because I had seen him with another woman didn't make him guilty of anything. He could say she was the wife of a friend and he was showing her how to punt, doing a mate a favour by taking his missus to the dogs. He could tell us anything he pleased. But I knew the truth from the way he'd looked at her: a way I had never seen him look at Mum.

I waited until I was sure Mum would be in bed before I went home that night. It seemed to me that everything had changed.

Not so long ago, my mother had looked after me. Now it felt as though I was responsible for looking after Mum. It was up to me to protect her. How would I do that?

That night I tossed and turned for hours before sleep came, the sheets and nightdress twisted around my legs, and when I finally slept I dreamed that Blackie was being chased by a pack of bloodthirsty greyhounds, Dad cheering them on. I begged him to stop the race, but my cries fell on deaf ears.

•

When I woke it was late morning, and the smell of frying sausages was thick in the room. I dressed and did my hair quickly, for I was starving.

Mum was at the stove and Dad sat at the table, only his legs visible, the rest of him hidden behind a newspaper. Mum was in a housedress and apron, her grey hair hanging lankly either side of her face, staring into the pan of spitting sausages. She looked up when I came in.

'Morning, love. Did you sleep alright? You must've come in late last night; I'd gone to bed already.'

I kissed her dry cheek and sat across from Dad, pouring myself a mug of over-steeped tea. 'Dot asked me over to her place after the film to look at her new dress patterns,' I lied. 'She's going to let me borrow a few.'

'Oh, did you bring them home? Can I have a look?' Mum brought the pan over and slid some sausages onto Dad's plate and then mine.

Dad folded up his paper, set it beside him and began slicing the bread, one slice each for Mum and me and two for himself.

'After all that I forgot them! She'll bring them in to work on Monday, I'm sure. She's not nearly as forgetful as me.'

Dad paused with a forkful of sausage halfway to his mouth and looked at me through narrowed eyes. 'How'd you get home?'

'She walked me with her little brother, Gus.'

'Good. I don't like you coming home on your own after dark. All kinds of unsavoury characters out there. Most of them in uniform.'

'And when did you get home?' Mum asked as she lowered herself into the chair beside his. 'I thought the races finished at nine.'

Dad finished his mouthful of food, took a swallow of tea, and wiped his mouth on his napkin before answering. 'They do. George P. staked half a week's wages on Julius, who won, and though the odds weren't good he invited us to his place for a celebratory drink.'

Mum nodded, keeping her eyes fixed on her plate.

Dad looked at her. 'What's with you into everyone's business?'

'Well, I worry. As if it's not enough having two boys enlisted in the war, I have the both of you to fret about as well.'

'There's nothing to worry about here. I'm too old by half to fight.' Dad stood and took his plate and cup to the sink. 'I'll be outside working on the truck if anyone needs me,' he said, adding sharply, 'There's no need to worry—I'll stay within sight.'

The silence hung between us as Mum and I ate, broken only by the clink and scrape of forks. From outside came the sound of Dad filling a bucket of water from the outside tap and the slam of his truck door.

'You've made up your mind, then?' Mum said finally, looking up at me.

'It's not worth the worry, Mum,' I said, as gently as I could. My voice shook a little and I wondered if she could tell I was lying; she knew me so well. 'Dad just wouldn't.'

Her face contorted, and it took me a few seconds to realise she was crying. I was nineteen and I'd never seen her cry before. I jumped up to fetch a clean tea towel for her, put the kettle on again to freshen up the tea and then sat beside her, stroking her back, the way she used to do for me when I was little and had a fever, her cool hand running up and down over the bumps of my spine. I could see Dad through the window, hunched over the engine of his truck, his face obscured by the bonnet.

Mum sniffled and clutched the tea towel in her fist. I wanted to get the hell out of there as fast as I could. I would rather have been Fred in a horrible jungle, surrounded by enemies, than here lying to Mum. I should move out, I thought. Get a place of my own. I rose to freshen the teapot.

Dad stomped into the kitchen, bringing the smell of petrol with him, his voice loud. 'Have we got any more rags? Mine are all filthy.'

He saw us and stared for a dumb moment, his mouth working to chew the corner of his lip.

'I'll get them,' I said. 'Mum's just feeling a little weary.'

I went into the broom cupboard for rags.

'She ought to be lying down. Can you help her to bed, Sar?' He was still gazing at Mum. 'I think you should rest today, love. Have a lie down.'

'Who's going to cook your tea?' Mum asked.

'I'll get it at the pub.' The flyscreen slammed behind Dad as he went back out to the yard.

'I'll wash up,' I said. 'You go lie down for a bit.'

Mum shut the door to her bedroom and I scrubbed the dishes clean, washing the sausage pan twice. I scrubbed and scrubbed at the stuck-on grease, which clung and clung until finally, all at once, it fell away.

CHAPTER 7

'You never told her?'

Grandma shakes her head.

'Why not?'

'I couldn't. It was a terrible thing to be mixed up in. If I'd told Mum and she'd left him, it would have been my fault.'

'It was a lot to keep to yourself.'

'What would you have done?'

I take a sip of my red wine. I don't want to make her feel bad. We're in the Admiral's Bar and Lounge and it's happy hour, half-priced drinks between five and seven. Grandma's been nursing her gin and tonic and now it is just melted ice with a crescent of waterlogged lime. The walls are covered with kitschy maritime decorations: wooden helms and old sails, anchors and ropes, life preservers and chunks of coral. There is even an antique-looking lifeboat hanging from the ceiling. On a raised platform beside the bar, a woman in a floor-length black dress with a thigh-high slit is playing the piano.

'I don't know,' I say at last. 'It's a hard question. Probably the same as you. Remember when Mom and Dad divorced?'

'How old were you again?'

'It was just before my ninth birthday. I remember going to spend weekends with Dad, how he would ask me all these questions about what Mom was doing, who was coming over, even what she was cooking. And then I'd go back home after the weekend and Mom would want to know where we went, who was there, where I slept, what I ate, how much Dad drank. And I didn't feel like I was me anymore to either of them. I was their spy. And then finally I just said to both of them: it's none of your business. Dad shut up about it, but Mom kept asking for the longest time.'

'That was tough, wasn't it? And you didn't like Larry.'

'Larry was an asshole.'

'Whatever happened to him?'

'I have no idea.'

I think back to that year and feel the fist of my old fury. At my dad, for leaving. At Mom, for accepting being left. At Larry, the boyfriend she'd brought home one day and who moved in the next. Who left smelly ashtrays in every corner of the house. Who cut his toenails in front of the TV. Larry disappeared, thank God, but nothing went back to normal, even after he was gone. Dad had left and everything changed. It was like—*boom!* Childhood's over. The family I'd taken for granted was gone. There is no such thing as happily ever after now.

'I don't want to talk about this, Grandma. Tell me what happened next. Actually, you'd better tell me over dinner, otherwise I'll be drunk.'

I stand and hold out a hand to help Grandma out of her chair. She leans on me as we walk and it's just what I need: her weight on my arm. To be steady for someone else.

CHAPTER 8

Dot came over one Sunday afternoon and we sat on the verandah with cups of tea. Mum was lying down inside so we kept our voices low. I told her I wanted to move out and she said she wished she could move in with me. We talked about work and which of the officers we liked and which we loathed. Most of them were too old for the girls in the typing pool anyway, but it didn't stop them from trying, even the ones with wives and children. Besides the senior officers there were an increasing number of junior officers around—first and second lieutenants, younger and with less of an air of importance to them but still attractive in their uniforms, smelling of cologne rather than just soap and sweat, cigarettes and beer.

One named Roy had followed me off the lift just that week, walked me to my desk and asked what I was doing on the weekend. He was sandy-haired, freckled and tall, with a snub nose and the widest smile. But my mind had been stuck all week on the image of Dad at the races, on the lie I'd told Mum.

I said I was staying in. He'd winked and said he'd try again next week, maybe I'd change my tune.

'What'd he look like?' Dot asked, and I described him to her.

'He works on my floor,' she said. 'He's a doll, Sarah. You should've at least gone on a date with him. Given him a chance.'

I felt a little twist in my gut then. Any other time I would've. 'So I was too mean.'

'Don't worry—it'll only make him keener. I'll bet Roy's talking about you to his mates right now. What if I mention you next time I see him? I'll tell him what good friends we are and I bet he'll ask me to put in a good word for him.'

'Don't. It will seem too contrived.'

'It will not! It's what everyone does. Or I'll just tell him we're going to the Troc next Thursday. That's not contrived, is it?'

'S'pose not.' I stood and cleared away our empty mugs. 'Come see the dress I'm fixing up.'

•

Thursday was swing at the Troc, and Dot came over after work to get ready. She borrowed my blue-and-white belted dress with the full skirt and sweetheart neckline, and I wore a high-waisted red skirt with a short-sleeved black blouse. We polished our shoes and applied lipstick in front of the mirror. Dot had filled her brother's flask with her dad's rum and we sipped it, cringing as it burned our throats. It made me feel fearless, though, and warm in the cheeks, as if there was nothing in the world to worry about. I said goodbye to Mum without kissing her, so she couldn't smell the rum on my breath. I'd been avoiding her and Dad all week.

I hadn't seen Roy since I'd been short with him, but I felt suddenly certain he was going to be there, and we walked to the Troc with our skirts swishing against our legs, giddy with the freedom of being out. Inside it was full to the brim and our eyes stung from the smoke. The band played 'Ain't Misbehavin'' and the dance floor was the only space where you weren't crushed against a hundred other people. There were uniforms everywhere: Yanks and Aussies, even a few Brits. We squeezed closer to the stage on the edge of the dance floor and said no to shouted invitations to dance. I couldn't see how we were going to find anyone we knew in that crush of people.

I was about to ask Dot if we could go outside for a minute when I felt a hand on my waist, and a voice in my ear said, 'If it isn't Sarah from down south.'

I spun around and there was Ellis, his black hair cut close, in the square-necked blue top and white trousers of the Australian navy. He was a head taller than me and his hand was now on my arm.

'Hello!' I shouted. 'This is my friend Dot. Dot, this is Ellis—I went to school with him.'

'Hi, Ellis,' Dot shouted, then smiled sweetly. 'I'll keep looking for them, Sarah. You dance with your old friend.'

Ellis led me onto the dance floor and twirled me around a few times. He smelled like wet wool and wasn't a great lead, but he was trying to talk as well. He told me—mouth against my ear—he had been in training and was just dying to get on a ship to where the action was. He asked about Fred and Jack, and I told him they were both in the Pacific. Jack had just left. That last I heard they were both safe. I told him where I was working, in the city, and he asked which friends we were meeting.

'Some fellas from my office.'

'Yanks?'

'Yes. Really I'm here with Dot, though.'

Ellis was frowning at me now. He pulled me to the side of the dance floor.

'Don't tell me you're one of them girls, Sarah. You've got more sense than that. Letting them buy you with cheap chocolates and nylons.'

His face was right up against mine and I could smell onions and beer. His hand was tight around my arm and I tried to prise it free.

'I'm not stupid, Ellis. Don't be an arse. And let go of my arm, would you?'

As quick as a blink, Dot was beside me, flanked by Roy and what must have been one of his friends.

'I heard the lady ask you to let go,' Roy shouted, his face as close to Ellis as Ellis had been to me.

It all happened so fast then, the way Roy's neck snapped back as Ellis's fist hit, the dull, sick sound of knuckle and flesh and the shouts of other men as they joined in the tangle. The Yanks were with Roy and the local lads with Ellis, all of them eager for an excuse to thump each other. Dot pulled me clear and I stood gaping as more and more men, sneering with rage, leaped into the mess of limbs. The band started playing a manic tune (I later learned it was 'Stars and Stripes Forever'—Roy told me it was what they always played when a fight broke out between the Americans and the local boys). In the midst of it all the cops appeared, swinging their batons, and then the green-uniformed military police. Ellis was taken off in the back of a van and we found Roy and his friend sitting outside on the kerb, talking to an MP. Roy caught my eye. There was a trail of blood running from his nostril to the corner of his mouth and a purplish lump on his cheek. When the MP walked off, Dot gave me a little shove in his direction.

'You alright?' I kneeled beside him and gingerly touched his cheek above the bruise. 'That looks like it's gonna hurt.'

'Ain't nothing.'

'You didn't have to—'

'I heard you tell him to let go and it made me see red when he didn't. He your boyfriend?'

'No. Someone I knew from a long time ago.'

'Well, I think he wanted to know you better.'

I pulled a handkerchief out of my purse. 'Here, you've got blood on your face.'

'Where?'

'I can do it, just . . .' I tried to blot it but it was dry.

He caught hold of my wrist, nearly pulling me off balance. 'What're you doing now? You hungry?'

I shrugged.

'Let's the four of us go get something to eat. That place was way too packed anyway. No room to swing a cat, much less a gal.'

So the four of us—Dot, me, Roy and his friend Bob—ended up in a milk bar near the Cross called the Liberty Bell. We all squeezed into a narrow booth, Dot and I on the inside seats. It was not the type of place I'd ever been, full of other GIs and not many women. The few women there were particularly loud and garishly made-up.

'So this is where you boys go?' Dot asked.

'Best hamburgers we've found,' Bob said. 'I know the clientele is rough, but remember, ladies, we didn't grow up here. We don't know the city so well.'

'Some excuse,' Dot said. 'Sarah didn't grow up in Sydney either.'

Roy turned towards me. 'You're not a city girl?'

We ordered hamburgers and milkshakes and I told them about the dairy farm, and Roy told us about Virginia, where he was from, outside a place called Roanoke, where his dad farmed tobacco. Bob was from the east coast also, Massachusetts, and they told us about the different accents from various parts of the country.

'Ours aren't like that,' I said. 'I mean, some people say Queenslanders talk slow, and people from Victoria sound like Pommies, but most Australians sound the same.'

'Yeah, but you guys have the funniest slang.'

I liked how Roy and Bob talked and joked with us like we were just people. They were lighthearted, easy to be around. Different. The local blokes only had conversations at the bar with their mates and clammed up when we walked in. I watched Dot throw her head back as she laughed at something Bob said. I felt keenly aware of Roy's leg next to mine, his arm behind my back on the booth, grazing the edge of my shoulders when I leaned back. I could almost feel sparks from the touch, like when I scuffed across the rug in socks in winter.

And the way he smelled, of clove and vetiver from the cologne he wore. He was nothing like Ellis or my brothers or Dad. It was a relief.

The boys paid the bill for our meal when we were done, even though Dot and I tried to pull out our purses, and the four of us walked back towards Oxford Street. I was on Roy's arm now instead of Dot's (he had crooked his elbow at me: 'C'mon, chicken, grab a wing'), and he was making me laugh at all the dodgy clubs we passed and the drunken servicemen out on the streets. When he offered to walk me home and Bob said he would walk Dot, I raised my eyebrows at her, not sure whether we should agree. She gave me a secret little smile and a nod, and I walked towards my house with Roy.

He had his arm around my waist, and we traded stories of tobacco and dairy farms the rest of the way, and I told him how we came to be living in Forest Lodge after Dad sold the farm.

'You live with your parents?'

I nodded, wishing I didn't.

'You're sayin' I'll have to leave you here then,' Roy said, and he leaned back against the wrought-iron fence outside my house. I worried that he would or wouldn't kiss me, unable to speak with the sudden fear of both. He looked so calm, the opposite of how I felt. He had washed the blood off in the men's room at the milk bar, but the graze looked worse than it had before, ringed by yellow-tinged skin.

'I'm sorry about the fight,' I said, reaching out my hand but not actually touching him now.

'Don't be. Every time it hurts it'll remind me of you.'

It was so silly that I laughed, and then felt bad, but he was smiling too.

'Can we go out again sometime?' he asked.

'Why me?'

'You're beautiful. And this sounds funny, but you remind me of the girls back home.'

'Is that meant to be a compliment?'

'Yes.'

'Oh,' I said. 'I suppose.'

He looked down then and I could see relief on his face, not arrogance, and so I did something I'd never done before, carried away by the chaos of the night and how strange it had all been: I placed my hands on his chest and leaned forwards on my toes to kiss him. His breath caught and he kissed me back, and I could feel his lips tighten in an involuntary smile.

We kissed more and I felt dizzy from it, so different when it was at my behest. I took the lead, but he followed, and after a minute or two I knew I ought to pull away.

'Well,' he said, grinning.

'Sorry. I just . . . I've never . . .'

'Ain't I lucky then?' He opened the gate for me, waited as I unlocked the door.

There you go, I thought, embarrassed. I must be my father's daughter after all—chasing the thrill rather than thinking of the implications. But then again, I couldn't help but feel the bright fizz of it. I felt like squeezing myself into a ball and exploding out, life spilling from every part of me, so much bright and irrepressible life.

•

I tell Hannah, but I don't think she really understands: how fast everything moved then. Not fast like people run around now, constantly busy and so self-important that they need to tell the entire world what they ate for breakfast, but fast in the sense that all that had been safe and normal suddenly wasn't. The world we knew had changed. Death was closer than it had ever been, the Japanese were liable to attack at any moment, and our brothers, cousins and lovers were away, dying in trenches, firing weapons from their freckled, blunt-nailed hands. Hands which they had used to catch fish, milk cows, shoot marbles and fly kites. Hands which had held us as we danced. Hands that played piano and tickled the arch of a foot, hands that unhooked a bra, cupped us and made us cry out.

How was anyone to make sense of it? The world was upside down, flipped and spinning backwards—women working men's jobs, street and railway station signs taken down or covered in case the Japs landed, coupons needed just to buy butter, tea, sugar or meat. Blackout curtains in our houses and air-raid wardens walking around to make sure no light seeped through. Headlights on cars painted black. Petrol so hard to get that Dad put a charcoal burner on the back of the truck in order to keep deliveries going. The army and navy requisitioning anything they wanted, anything they needed for war. Japanese subs in Sydney Harbour.

When death is close, you have to live.

Roy was being transferred to New Guinea. He knew it before we kissed, but he didn't tell me until weeks later, when he took me to the cinema. I can't remember what film we saw, because we didn't really watch it; we sat in the dark room with the smell of dust burning off the projector bulb and kissed, his hands travelling up from my knee, stopping at that tender midpoint of the thigh, an impossible place to stop. I wanted to cry out. I bit his shoulder instead. Afterwards we ate dinner in a little cafe, Repins, and I could hardly swallow. My mouth felt tender, and I touched it with the tips of my fingers, wondering if I should reapply lipstick.

Roy's fork was poised in mid-air—he ate with his fork in his right hand and used it like a shovel, the opposite of how I'd been taught—when he said it.

'I'm going in a coupla months.'

It took a moment for the meaning to sink in.

He wouldn't see me cry; he wouldn't see me care. I stood up and left.

Roy must have paused to pay because I was a little way down the street when he ran up beside me. 'Sarah,' he said, grabbing my hand, pulling me towards him.

'Get off it. Leave me alone.'

'But we were having so much fun.'

'Find another girl for your "fun". I'm not interested.'

'I don't mean it like that. I mean—'

'There's girls you can pay for fun.'

'I mean, I'm crazy for you, baby. I want to stay. I want to leave them and stay. I don't want to go either.'

And his eyebrows knit in together as if a thread had caught and pulled them tight and I saw that he was scared too, terrified, and it wasn't only what he was leaving but where he had to go.

I felt selfish, then, for thinking only of my own sadness. What did I know of war? We leaned against the side of a building, out of the traffic and rush of passers-by, and I put my hand on his wrist, which hung at his side. I felt his pulse there, under the skin, like a moth banging against a paper lampshade, blind and panicked. He was fighting back tears, blinking fast, and his face was red from the shame of it. For the first time I remember thinking: how glad I am not to be a man. He was twenty years old.

I kissed him then, as much in apology as to hide his face from the street, his shame, his almost-tears. As much to save him as to bind him to me. And what did I have to offer except my body? It was clearer than words, which would have come out wrong. Muddled. Underdone. I pressed myself to him, felt the long flat belt buckle through the thin fabric of my dress, his scratchy face, his quick breath. I wrapped my arms around his neck, damp with sweat, prickling with tiny, vulnerable hairs. Would I have fallen for him if there had not been the rush, the desperation? I don't know. Was it love? It was different then. He was leaving, he might die there, and what could I give him if not myself, that which I had been told was precious—that which I was meant to hold dear?

•

I thought of little else, and even at work I saw people differently now, imagining them naked, with a lover, how they would moan, shift, kiss. The more I thought about it, the more I wanted to try. I wanted Roy and me to be as close as we could possibly be. Time stretched slow over hours of typing, filing and taking dictation. The tea cart and the lunch cart and the gossip in the ladies' toilets. Devon sandwiches and buns with pink icing sat half eaten on my plate; I wanted only to see Roy again, nothing else could sate me.

Every day he met me after work, and all we sought was to be alone together. He was staying in barracks with nine other men in his room, so there was no opportunity there. The parks were patrolled by police wielding torches, and the park benches were filled with other soldiers and their lovers. The cinema was fine for kissing, but you weren't going to let it go too far. We didn't have a car, and I certainly wasn't going to try my parents' house. So we were simmering with lust, both of us desiring and unable to find the place or the time. We went dancing (he taught me the Jersey bounce, the jig walk, the jitterbug) and to the beach (diving into the surf in our swimming costumes, lying side by side on the sand; when he closed his eyes I studied the curves and lines of his body). We drank coffee, went walking and saw films, but all of it was exquisite torture, a substitution for what it was we really wanted to do.

Meanwhile, things at home were worse than ever. I couldn't speak to Mum or Dad, having lied to one and knowing the other was lying. The tension between them was unbearable, so when I was there I shut myself in my room. The silence drove me mad. I decided it was time to move into my own place. I prepared a speech one night at dinner about why it was necessary, but to my surprise neither Mum nor Dad put up an argument. They were both too distracted by their own concerns. There was a room in a boarding house for women in Surry Hills run by a Mrs Mulligan. She kept the place respectable, with a curfew and no men allowed into the bedrooms, but she was also as deaf as a stone, so a few sneaked in after she fell asleep, and on more than one occasion my paper-thin walls let in noises I would rather not have heard. I stuffed cotton wool in my ears and buried my face under the pillow, but I never complained. After all, I considered sneaking Roy in myself. And I knew how it felt to have nowhere else to go.

My room was on the top storey of the old terrace house— it looked as though it had once been one great big room and was now partitioned into three. Luckily I had one of the front two with the dormer windows, and the possibility of climbing out onto the roof tiles on a nice day for a smoke and sunbake. Lizzie taught me this trick; she lived in the other dormer room and worked in a factory which had made ladies' clothing before the war and now made army uniforms. ('Dull as a post,' she complained.) She had a sewing machine in her room and let me borrow it sometimes, so I made a pair of shortie pyjamas out of an old dressing-gown and took up the hem on a second-hand dress.

In some ways Mrs Mulligan's was nicer than our house—the toilets were all indoors and there was a bathroom on the second floor with a huge clawfoot tub and a chip heater. As there were only nine women in the house, we could each bathe as often as three or four times a week if we liked, and there were few things as lovely as turning the lock on that door, lighting the chip heater, filling a steaming tub and lying down for twenty minutes, feeling the tension and grime soak out of me and dissipate with the steam.

My room had a single bed with a small table beside it, a shelf below a mirror which was crowded with all of my make-up and lotions, and a sink beside that. There was also a wardrobe that smelled so musty I scrubbed it out with white vinegar and warm water on my very first day, and a desk with a wobbly wooden chair beneath the dormer window. That was where I kept my gas ring for the kettle and tea. The floorboards creaked and the wallpaper was peeling, but as shabby as it was I loved it because it was my own.

CHAPTER 9

We're lying in our beds and the sky outside the window is dark. There is the rumble and occasional jolt of the engine far beneath us, a slight vibration I've grown used to. The reading lamp above my bed is still on, Grandma has just turned hers off.

It's weird hearing about Grandma's desire, but she has never minced words. She has always talked about bodies as though they aren't a big deal—because of her work, perhaps, because it is a part of everyday life. She talks about sex like she talks about shopping, with no filter. She was the one who told me how babies are made, while we watched a litter of kittens being born in her clinic, and she was the one who told me about menstruation and bought me my first packages of Kotex and Tampax. The boxes gathered dust in the bathroom cabinet for years. On the track and field team we bragged about not having our periods. It was a badge of honour. It meant we could be more like the boys. When my period finally came, when I was seventeen, Grandma didn't try to console me. She bought me a heating pad for the cramps. She told me not to lie around feeling sorry for myself too long. In any case, my periods never stuck around, and I was pleased when they disappeared again.

I can see, now, how it would have been for Grandma and Roy, and part of me longs for that clarity—that straightforward need. To desire someone without being caught up in what they think of me, of my body, not to always be on the outside looking in.

I'm so busy thinking about how others see me that I forget to see them. When Ash touches me I wonder what he thinks of what he's touching. Am I too flabby? Can he see the dimples on the backs of my thighs? I am so distracted by these questions I forget to touch him back. Only if I've had enough to drink or taken something else can I shut the thoughts down. Two glasses of wine or two Percocet and the inhibition disappears—only to return as regret later.

The last time Ash and I had sex sober was the morning I left, before we drove to San Diego to pick up Grandma. He came into the shower and I shivered beneath a stream of hot. I was going away; I couldn't say no. I focused on a spot of mould in the grout of the tiles. My ass spread, widened against the glass partition. I gritted my teeth, chin on his shoulder, hoping he would finish soon.

And it is strange, because in the half-fogged mirror I saw the parts of his body that I would never accept on myself. Little love handles on the sides. Softness where muscle or bone might be. Sometimes I wonder whether I would be turned on by a man who resembles what I want to look like. Someone with a BMI of less than seventeen per cent. On the forums I trawl through there are images of women who hover beneath eighty pounds. They are skeletons with skin draped over them: gaunt cheeks, hollow eyes. I gaze at their photos, but not with desire. With jealousy. If only I could possess their self-control.

If I could feel *that* empty.

Then, I think, I would be happy.

Yes.

I wait until I hear Grandma's soft snores, then I pull out the phone. I make my list. There was butter on my toast—it came buttered—so I only ate four bites. I can feel it, though, being absorbed as fat cells. I can see them springing from my thighs as I turn my phone to silent and put it beneath the pillow. I put my hand between my legs and try to think of Ash instead. Flying down a hill, all speed and grace. Playing the drums, eyes shut, his face glistening with sweat, tilted up, arms a blur. What does he see in me? How is it he can look at me with anything resembling love?

CHAPTER 10

Our first attempt was in my room at Mrs Mulligan's, on an itchy wool blanket spread on the floor because the frame of my single bed squeaked every time we moved. I was terrified that someone was going to hear us, or burst through the door, and I would be kicked out onto the street in my scanties.

'You're not enjoying this,' Roy said a few minutes in.

'I'm trying. I'm sorry.'

'It's not the right time, then. Here, just put your hand there for me, and move it like this—a little faster—not so tight. Yes. There.'

It was so strange I wanted to laugh. Lying on the floor, jerking my hand up and down this pink hot part of him, hearing Roy's breathing grow quick, seeing his eyes widen and clapping my hand over his mouth when he started to groan. Was this what people really did behind closed doors? Had my parents? Had Mrs Mulligan?

I think Roy decided it was the shame holding us back. His upbringing had been far more religious than mine; he was brought up Baptist, he told me, and his family went to church for three hours every single Sunday. His mother didn't believe women should work outside the home, so he'd told her about me but said we'd met at a dance rather than at work. He wanted me to take him to meet my parents, and I changed the subject when he asked until finally he took my hands and held them, saying, 'Are you ashamed of me?'

I shook my head. 'It's more them I'm ashamed of.'

'Come on, they can't be that bad. They made you.'

I had seen Mum and Dad, of course, since I moved out. Nearly every week I went for Sunday lunch. Afterwards we'd sit in the lounge room, making strained conversation like strangers, the one thing we never spoke of muffling everything else we said.

So, with just over a month until Roy left for New Guinea, I rang Mum from work while most of the other girls were on their lunch break. There was one telephone for an office of typists. I knew I had to be quick. I couldn't ring Mum directly, because she and Dad didn't have a phone: I had to ring Mrs Thompson and answer all of her questions about work and whether I was liking it and how my typing speed was going and then wait while she went and fetched Mum from next door. I felt guilty for my impatience when Mum came on the line, breathing heavily from her rush to get to me.

'Sarah, love, I've been hoping you'd ring. Your brother Fred sent a letter. He's been shot, but it's the leg, thank God. He'll be home soon, maybe next week. The knee, he says. Fractured his kneecap.'

'Oh, Mum.'

'I know, but he'll be safe here. Thank God it's just his leg.'

'Oh, Mum.' I was trying not to cry but the tears were coming already. 'I can't talk long, Mum, someone's waiting for the phone, but I'm glad he's going to be home.'

'You'll come to lunch next Sunday? He may be here.'

'That's what I was going to say. There's someone I'd like to bring—his name's Roy.'

'Yes, of course, bring him. Bring anyone you want.'

'He's American.'

I could hear her sigh, and a click on the line as one of the operators from the exchange picked up.

'See you on Sunday, Mum.'

'Bye, love.'

And I hung up, hurrying back to my typewriter and working through the rest of lunch, in case anyone had seen me making a personal call. I thought of Fred and his long legs, his skinny calves in school shorts, his knobbly knees. To think a bullet had entered his flesh, shattered the bone, to think of his uniform torn and bloody. I wanted to nurse him myself, to put a cool hand on his cheek and have him here, captive, safe from danger.

Dot dropped by later that afternoon. We went to the tea cart together and stood by the window in a quiet part of the corridor, blowing on our scalding tea so we could drink it quickly and get back to work. I told her about Fred being injured and Roy coming to lunch.

'What'll you say?'

'What do you mean?'

'If he asks you to marry him—what will you say?'

'Don't be daft. He's not going to ask.'

'He's shipping out, isn't he? I'm just trying to prepare you. Have you still got the dress on layby?'

I nodded. I'd kept up the payments. It was foolish to let some other girl take it, what with everything I'd already put in.

'Would you marry a Yank?' Dot asked.

'What's the difference?' I replied. 'Marriage is marriage, isn't it?'

Dot looked at me as though she couldn't believe she was friends with someone so dumb. Of course it was different, of course it meant something else, but here's the truth of it: I was so caught up in what it would mean for us to be together, really together, before he left for New Guinea that I shut my eyes to what might happen beyond it. I pushed down any thought of what might come after.

•

Roy picked me up from Mrs Mulligan's at half past eleven on Sunday morning, waiting downstairs in the lounge room as though he hadn't lain just last week half-naked on my bedroom floor. I could see the comb marks in his hair, the place where the razor had nicked his Adam's apple. He wore his uniform, neatly pressed, his shoes shining like the wet, black stones I used to gather from the creek at the farm. He bent down to kiss my cheek and smelled of vetiver and clove, and I grasped his forearm so hard I wouldn't have been surprised if my fingers left marks. We walked to the street and hailed a cab—Roy was always catching cabs—and he stopped to buy flowers for my mum. He showed me a shopping bag filled with boxes of chocolate and cigarettes.

'You shouldn't spoil them,' I said, and he rested his hand on my knee.

'Where I come from you never show up empty-handed.'

I had taken extra care with my dress that morning, choosing the cobalt-blue one with an embroidered yoke, fabric-covered buttons down the front and a tie belt. It looked demure enough for a Sunday, but the blue brought out the colour in my eyes, and I had left my hair in curlers until just before Roy was due to arrive, so it fell in soft curls to my shoulders. I hadn't gone out on Saturday night, instead staying in, lying in bed with a mask of cold cream and a head full of the hard metal curlers. I'd polished my tan leather kitten heels and chosen a bag to carry as though it actually mattered. It was as if I was meeting someone else's parents, not my own. I suppose I wanted Mum and Dad to see me as Roy did, as someone special, someone full of possibility. Someone with a life of her own, outside of theirs.

On the drive over to Forest Lodge I told Roy about Fred being sent home, about the injury to his knee, about how I imagined he would be upset, as being a soldier had meant so much to him.

'It's different, war, when you're in it. Different to how you imagine it being.'

'How?'

'Well . . . there's so much time spent waiting. Just sitting in the mud, not knowing—so many boys think it will be exciting, like it is in the movies. But they only show action. If you were to watch a movie about how war really was, it would be ten days long with ten minutes of fighting. It's the waiting that gets you.

The mindless, deadening wait. And then the fighting, when it comes, is over in the blink of an eye. Like a bad dream.'

He stared out the window then and I watched his jaw work. I wanted to ask what he was thinking about but I also didn't want to know. I didn't want to know if he'd killed anyone, or what a gun felt like when it went off in his hands. I didn't want him to tell me that he'd lost friends . . . I didn't want it to mar what we had. But you can't know a person without knowing the darkness in them too, so I blame myself for holding my tongue. I wasn't going to ask Roy to delve beneath that surface with me. I wasn't going to dive into the wrecked ship of his past, swimming through the dark, eerie cabins, light falling through cracks in sea-rotted planks. I wanted us to float sleepily in salt water beneath the sun. Eyes shut, the light making patterns inside our lids. I wanted to think I was all he needed.

Fred, Mum and Dad were all in the kitchen when we got there, Fred and Dad drinking beer from the bottle. They all stood, even Fred, and shook hands with Roy. I threw my arms around Fred, surprised by how much older he looked. He had a pair of crutches leaning up against the wall and a bandage around his knee but otherwise he didn't appear crook. He patted the top of my head and slapped Roy on the back—maybe a little too hard—and said something about how he'd warned me about those Yanks, hadn't he?

The place smelled the same—like it didn't get enough air— and I was glad it wasn't a hot day and we weren't all stuck sweating in there with the oven on and the cooker going full blast. Mum had combed her hair and put her lippie on, and though she wore her tatty apron, underneath it was her nicest Sunday dress.

Dad looked as though he'd had a few bottles already—despite its being only noon—and I hoped that the food would steady his keel. Fred led the men out to the lounge and I stayed to help Mum; she was making gravy, so I finished shelling the peas. Pulling the thread from the pod and then snapping it open to find those perfect, springy green pearls was a favourite job of mine since girlhood, and with the water nearly boiled and the peas beside an empty bowl I knew Mum had saved it for me.

'How is he?' I asked, once I was seated in the familiar old chair. I tilted my chin towards Fred's crutches, which he'd left in the kitchen, leaning instead on Dad as he walk-hopped to the lounge.

'Seems alright,' Mum said. 'Full of stories, of course. Been at the pub with Dad telling them yesterday.'

I hmm'd, having just popped three crunchy peas in my mouth.

'Save some for the pot, will you?' Mum said. She bent over to pull the lamb from the oven and the smell was so good it made my stomach ache with hunger, the dark roasted skin sizzling in the fat at the bottom of the pan.

'He wants to go back, but I hope they won't let him. The surgeon who pulled out the bullet said we'll have to wait and see how it heals.'

'And how's Dad?'

'See for yourself.' Mum poured the gravy from the pan into a jug and sat beside me, pulling the bowl of unshelled peas between us. She was twice as fast as me; as she stripped the peas her fingers flew, and the pale green orbs were scraped with a fingertip and the pod discarded while I was still finding a string. 'You'd think it was him who was over there, the way he tells the story.'

'And what about Jack?'

'On his way to fight the Japs. And from what I hear they'll have to fight hard. Where has your fella been?'

'He came over from the Philippines. But he's going to New Guinea in a month, Mum.'

'Do you wish he could stay, then? Taken a shine to him, I see.'

'Wait'll you see the chocolates he brought you—you'll take a shine to him too.'

Mum grinned into the bowl of peas. 'He's got nice manners and he dresses well,' she conceded. 'I just can't get used to someone calling me "ma'am". And I don't want him to take you away.'

'He's not taking me anywhere. What's he going to do, smuggle me in his gunny sack to New Guinea?'

She pinched my arm. 'You know what I'm talking about. But you're old enough now to make up your own mind about things. And you're not half as dumb as you look.'

Funny, but from her mouth the words were a compliment. I like to imagine what she was really saying was that she was sorry she'd asked me to spy on Dad, that she saw it was time for me to live my own life, and that she was proud of me too. She didn't know how to say such things, they were words that were never spoken to her, and in the same way I have trouble saying them to my own children. But I try—I do—and I like to think that I knew all the same.

The table was already set in the dining room and we carried in the dishes, Mum sending me to tell the men to come and eat. Fred was in the middle of a story and I could see it was meant to be funny from the way Roy was sitting back with an easy grin, the way Dad was already suppressing his guffaws, and I just wanted to grab Roy and kiss him on the mouth right there for putting up with my family. I waited for Fred to pause for breath before I interrupted.

'Don't go telling all your stories while I'm not here or you'll just have to repeat yourself. Besides, the food's on the table, getting cold. Come along.'

'I hope she doesn't boss you around like that,' Fred said to Roy, and Roy shrugged and smiled at me.

I stood aside while Dad and Fred went into the dining room, smelling of beer and cigarettes, and felt Roy's arm snake around my waist. I breathed in the freshness of his clean laundered shirt.

'You can boss me anytime,' he whispered, his lips near my ear making my breath catch, and he kissed me on the temple.

'I hope they're not being too intolerable . . .'

'They're fine. Your dad's not a big fan of MacArthur, but I can't blame him. So long as he doesn't hold me responsible for every decision the man has made. Your brother's great. But, man, they can put away some beer. I'm trying to keep up but this is the third bottle.' He held up the squat brown bottle in his hand and swayed a little, pretending to hiccup.

I didn't want lunch ending in a drunken spectacle. Mum must have had a word to Dad at the table, as they all slowed down and Dad even complimented Mum's roast, though mostly it was to agree with Fred when he said it was one of the things he'd missed most when he was away at war.

Fred kept us entertained with more stories about service life and then he started asking Roy questions and the two of them traded tales of different customs and places and battles I hadn't even heard of. They only told funny stories, I noticed, and they had plenty of those. Dad would interject occasionally with an opinion or a story of his own, while Mum just watched Fred, her eyes glistening. I wondered if I had that stupid sort of moony look in my eyes watching Roy and so I looked down at my plate and cut the meat into bite-sized pieces. Then I glanced around the room to see how it might look to Roy. The stained doilies and cobwebs in the corners. The upholstered chairs were faded, the table watermarked and splintering beneath the ironed cloth, and the paint on the windowsill was flaking, dead flies belly-up among paint chips.

The men talked casualties as casually as they complimented the meal, and I wanted to stand up and pound my fists like a child and tell them to call it what it was, death, final and permanent. There was my brother, his curly hair just growing over the top of his collar, his eyes squinting in a smile, his stubble coming in almost red on his cheeks, and there was Roy, his freckled nose, his straight sandy hair cut close to the scalp, his lovely white teeth and warm breath and hot skin against mine, and they were beautiful. Invincible. And yet—in a moment—they could be gone.

•

It wasn't until after lunch was finished and we were doing the dishes that I had a minute alone with Fred—he insisted that Mum stay sitting and Roy too.

'You're the guest, mate, stay right where you are.'

Dad didn't even offer to get up and help.

Fred filled the sink with hot, soapy water and tossed me a tea towel. 'I'll wash, you dry.'

He asked me about work and about people we both knew—whether I'd seen Ellis at all—and I said I had, though I didn't tell him that Ellis and Roy got in a fight. He wiped his hands, leaned back against the bench beside the sink and crossed his arms.

'Why a Yank, sis? Why'd you have to date one of them?'

'Stop calling him a Yank, Fred. His name's Roy, and he's a good fella.'

'He spends a lot of money on you.'

'No. It's not that. It's nice that he has money to spend, but I'd like him if he didn't have a penny. He's different. He's not here because I look pretty on his arm. He's smart and funny and he seems to think I am too—he doesn't just run off to the pub every time he wants to have a conversation.'

'Scared of talking to blokes, is he? A poofter.'

'Good grief, is that what I said? He just knows how to talk to women.'

Fred turned back to the sink and scrubbed the roast pan viciously.

'It's no good to come home to. We've been over there, getting paid nearly nothing, some of us dying to protect our country, and we come home to see our girls with these fast-talking, easy-living fellas. It drives me spare.'

I didn't have any reply to that, so I just watched him bent over the sink, his face and neck still sporting an angry rash from the tropical heat, a bandage on his leg and his shorts loose around his hips he'd lost so much weight. It wasn't fair, was it? I got that—I really did. I reached out and touched my brother on the arm.

He looked at me, still scowling.

'I'm glad you're here,' I said. 'I've missed you.' It wasn't enough, but he still cracked a little corner of a smile.

'You just going to stand there or are you going to dry this thing?' he said, thrusting the dripping roast pan towards me.

'You call this clean? Move aside. They might have taught you something in the army but they certainly haven't taught you how to wash up.'

•

Roy said we should catch another cab back to Surry Hills, but I suggested we walk a while first and see how far we got. I thought of my brother's words about money and wondered how much of being with Roy was that he could take me away from everything I wanted to escape. There was certainly plenty. We walked through the grounds of Sydney University, the sandstone buildings and wide green lawns, the fig trees with their knotted roots and low branches. It was still dark early and the sunset had turned the scattered clouds orange with the sky a purplish bruise. He took my hand and as we walked his thumb absentmindedly stroked the side of my thumb. Then I realised Roy had asked me a question but I hadn't heard it—he was looking at me, waiting for an answer.

'Sorry, I didn't catch that.'

'I asked what it is you want to be doing in ten years' time. Where do you see yourself?'

It was a funny question, because I'd never given it much thought. I considered the life I'd lived so far: losing the farm, moving to the city, Dad's drinking and his cheating and Mum's nerves. I seemed to live in reaction to my parents, and when I tried to picture what kind of life I wanted for myself the thought that came into my head was: away from them. A thought so clear I nearly spoke it.

We had reached Victoria Park by now, and I sat on a bench because there was a stone in my shoe. I unbuckled the strap, shook out the stone, and pulled my shoe back on over my stockinged foot. Stockings Roy had bought me. I felt his eyes on me the entire time.

'Well?'

'I want a family. Children—two or three? Not too many. A house with a big garden. A dog.'

'A farm?'

'Perhaps, but I also want to keep working. Maybe not typing; anyone can do that. Maybe I could go to university. I was good at school. I could have kept going.'

I felt surprised by my own words. I'd hardly thought them through before I said them, but they were true.

'You're smart enough, in my book. Smart enough to go with me.'

I tucked myself against him and took his hand into mine, threading my fingers through his. We started to kiss then but he pulled away after just a minute. A flock of lorikeets landed in the tree beside us and they made a ruckus as they settled in for the night.

His face was long, his jaw working again as if he were chewing gum.

'What's wrong?'

'I hate to think of going to New Guinea and coming back to find you with someone else.'

'Don't be silly. I'll wait for you.'

'It kills me though. It just kills me. And what if I get shot over there and we never—'

I clapped my hand over his mouth. 'We will, then. Before you go. We will.'

His breath was hot on my palm. He took my hand away and held it in his. 'I don't want us sneaking around though. Feeling like it's bad, somehow. Marry me, Sarah. Will you?'

Roy was looking at me now with his blue-grey eyes, and my heart was beating so hard I was certain he could hear it.

'I asked your dad and he said it was fine by him. Not sure how happy he was about it, though. I didn't want you to think—I didn't want you to think it wasn't something I've thought about—something I've planned for.'

I looked away across the park. Trees and benches were black silhouettes against dusky sky. I thought of him on the floor of my room, his body on a stretcher, the vulnerability of his freckled skin. I could not say no. Not to the chance to make him happy—for him to go over there with my photograph growing soft in his pocket and the hope of more life between us. And maybe I didn't trust myself either: I could (I knew this) fall for someone else. There were so many others. And they were all so eager, needy, desperate for love.

'Okay,' I said, running my finger along his cheek, as surprised by the word as he was.

'Really?' He kissed me, hard, and I could feel the way he'd been tempering himself, holding back.

'Yes. How soon?'

He groaned. 'Not soon enough. I'll have to get permission, and they need a ton of paperwork. Can you get a hold of your birth certificate? Can you get a dress together? And find a church? Holy smoke, we've got a lot to do.'

'I can,' I said, laughing, and leaned my body into his for another kiss, my skin tingling as he ran his fingers across my scalp, all of it alive with feeling.

CHAPTER 11

I roll over in my narrow bed and see the raindrops streaming
down the plexiglass of our window, the grey sky outside. When
Grandma got up to use the bathroom at dawn I woke as well,
and I haven't been able to go back to sleep.

'I'm going for a run before breakfast,' I say.

I sit up and dig through the drawers for my running shorts
and t-shirt.

'In the rain?'

'I never notice once I'm out there.'

'But the decks might be slippery.'

'I'll be careful.'

I need to be outside, away from our little cabin and the
smell of Grandma's perfume, her sighs and cracking joints.
I dreamed of Roy last night, of his freckled skin, the escape
he offered her. I fell asleep thinking of him instead of Ash.
Imagining myself as her. Wondering what I would have said.
I don't know the answer to that, but in the dream I said yes,

and we married in Vegas, in an Elvis chapel. Afterwards we gorged on lamb and boiled eggs, the lamb fat and eggshells sticking to our chins.

I know my way around the ship by now, and navigate the series of passageways and stairwells to the exercise track, a marked loop which on fine days is crowded with joggers and walkers trying to work off the onslaught of food. Today, I hope, it will be deserted, since most people seize on any excuse to avoid exercise. I've never had that problem. I can push past the unpleasantness of cold and rain, aching muscles, sore joints, hunger and thirst.

When I reach the track I start off slowly, warming up my legs. The surface does feel slick. The air smells like diesel fumes. I should just go to the gym and run on the treadmill, but there are bound to be others who've had the same idea. One of the best parts of running is being alone.

I look down at the watch I bought, against my mom's advice. 'You'll just be harder on your body,' she said. 'You need to take it easy. Avoid another stress fracture.' I turn it on and wait for the GPS signal to beep. The stress fracture in my heel was a few years back.

When Ash asked, I said exercise keeps me sane. I said I love cake too much not to exercise. I said all the things people say when they're trying to hide the truth about how they feel about their bodies. Trying to hide how much they care. I didn't say I want to see my stomach cave in rather than bulge out. I didn't say I like the lines of my own bones.

I have found that if people think of you as a runner, they are less likely to worry about you being skinny. After all, you need food to run, right? How can you exercise without fuel? It's true, but there is a fine line between how much you want and how much you need. I know how it feels to always keep myself a little hungry because it hurts less than being full. I know the acute sensitivity of my body when it is denied of food; how the light seems brighter, how hollow I feel. I have had years of practice. The first time I returned from treatment, when I discovered track and field I felt like I had found my religion. These were my people. I couldn't believe I was allowed among them.

I bounce off the forefoot, leaning into the stride. A ship might be the most boring place in the world to run. Around and around and around I go. Only my watch can tell the difference between one lap and the next. After a while even I lose count. By the time I started running, in high school, Dad had moved an hour away. He'd remarried, he'd even had another kid, but he still came to all my races. He'd played on the varsity football team at school; sport was something he knew how to talk about. Numbers, winners, losers, times. He was so thrilled when I went to the state championships. When I broke the girls' record at my high school for the mile. He made me a spreadsheet so I could keep track of my goals. Mom let it be his thing. She must have seen how much I needed his approval.

I slow for a corner then pick up the pace on the straight and nearly run smack into another person. I dodge out of the way, gasping out a 'sorry', grasping the rail to keep from slipping.

'Hey,' he says, 'watch where you're going.'

'Sorry,' I say again, still catching my breath.

'Okay. No problem. You alright?'

ELEANOR LIMPRECHT

'Yeah.' I look away to keep from staring. He might be the only person my age on board the ship, besides the waiters and rec staff. He's tall and has on the most ridiculously short running shorts; I can practically see his hip in the high slit. I wonder if he's Australian. I look out over the railing and try to push my smile down.

'You're up here a lot, running, aren't you?' he says.

I nod, glancing at him, and see he's squinting, rain clinging to his blond eyelashes. The accent is slightly off-kilter. Canadian?

I haven't noticed him before, but he must be up here a lot too.

'What's your distance?' he asks.

'Mostly halves, ten k's, five k's. What about you?'

'Marathons.'

Typical man. They always have to go for the toughest-sounding thing.

'Wanna race?' he says, and I feel like I'm back at elementary school.

I look at him again. He has long legs, ropy calves, a classic runner's build. But he's older, too, maybe ten years, and I know the shorter distances are my strength.

'How far?'

'One lap. Ending here. Loser buys dinner.'

I raise an eyebrow. 'Prepare to lose.'

'How 'bout you save your shit talking for when you've won. Ready, set, go!'

I'm slower to start since he caught me by surprise, but I make up for it at the end of the straight, letting my legs take over, keeping my breath shallow and steady, torso strong, arms low. There's less of me to carry. Around the corner I get the inside

94

edge and pass him, and though his legs are longer I can tell he is a typical endurance runner. He doesn't lean forwards and take advantage of his stride, which is more of a shuffle. The adrenaline of being in front takes over and when my arms start to feel heavy and burn I push through. I think of Ash on his skateboard, whooshing past. This guy's feet hammer behind me, thud, thud, thud, but not coming closer, not catching up, and my feet hardly make a sound. I put the last of what I have into my legs and collapse where we began, knees bent with my palms on my thighs, my heart in my ears, my lungs on fire.

'Damn,' he says, once he can speak. 'Do your feet even touch the ground?'

I grin. 'Looks like you owe me dinner, and that means not just the free buffet.'

'Do I look like that kind of guy?' His hair is plastered to his forehead from the rain, cheeks splotchy and pink. I know my own face is bright red, but I can feel my skin begin to cool, goosebumps rising.

'How about dinner with the captain, tonight at seven, on the bridge of the ship?'

I look to see if he's joking but his face is serious. 'Um, how does that happen?'

He holds out his hand. 'Alex Jackson. Second mate.'

We shake, our hands slippery with sweat and rain. I can't believe I just raced the second mate. It's hard to imagine feeling more embarrassed than I am right now. Keep cool, I think.

'Hannah Fray. I didn't think there were many passengers my age.'

'The demographic is more retired, isn't it?'

'That and families.'

'Overfed or nearly dead. So you'll come? I'll see you at seven? Dress is a little more formal than the regular dining room.'

'That means flip-flops? Sweatpants? College t-shirts?'

'Probably not.'

I rub the goosebumps on my arms with my palms. 'Okay. But one condition.'

'What's that?'

'I bring my grandma.'

He doesn't miss a beat: 'Grandmas are compulsory.'

'See you then.'

•

When I swipe the card to unlock our cabin door a few minutes later, my heart is still racing, though not from the run anymore. Grandma's not there—she must have gone to breakfast without me. I peel off my wet shirt, sports bra and shorts and turn the shower up as hot as it will go.

The scalding water is almost too painful to bear but it stops the shivering, and beneath the showerhead I stretch my calves, quads, neck and shoulders as well as I can in the tiny cubicle. Dinner with the ship's captain. I think of how glad Grandma will be, and worry about what to wear. I've already thought of a way to tell Ash without making it sound like what it was: a flirtation.

I wonder if hearing Grandma's stories has something to do with this thrill I feel. I want to feel what she felt then. When life was simply lived, not dissected into a thousand pieces. When it was grabbed tight and squeezed because tomorrow you might not be here. The water runs off me and swirls around the drain, taking strands of my hair with it. The steam is thick in the room, the mirror fogged. I turn off the shower and dry myself with the towel, squeeze the water from my hair. The room isn't cold but I'm shivering. With anticipation, I think. With something slippery, like possibility.

CHAPTER 12

A month isn't long to arrange a wedding, but it wasn't impossible, or even uncommon then. There were many fast marriages before soldiers—Australian and American—went overseas to fight. Mum asked if I was certain this was what I wanted.

'Yes.'

Dad asked if I was pregnant.

'No.'

'Well, you make your bed, you lie in it.'

'I said I'm not pregnant, Dad.'

'That's enough lip from you.'

Mum spoke to the pastor at her church and he agreed to squeeze us in between other weddings on the Saturday before Roy was due to leave. The paperwork was harder: we had to obtain permission from Roy's commanding officer, character references for both of us, my certificate of citizenship from the police and my birth certificate. Luckily Mum had the certificate from when she registered my birth—and she pulled it from a box I'd never seen before, with letters Dad had sent her when he was away at war and photographs of my brothers and me as babies. They were pasted into an old album which was falling apart at the binding. There we were on the farmhouse verandah, our clothes stained and worn, our faces wind-burned. I was only two or three in the photograph; Jack was a baby and I was holding him in my arms. Mum said I was like a little mother to Jack when he was born, always wanting to hold him and feed him, change his nappies. I felt a tear roll down my chin to my neck. I missed Jack so much it was an ache in my chest. I had never heard her talk about us as little babies, and until I heard it I didn't realise just how much I wanted to know.

'Do you miss the farm?' I asked, shutting the album and palming dust from the cover.

She sighed. 'It was so much work. I miss having everyone together, close, but I don't miss the work. Never a day's break. I was always so weary. You know the headaches I get?'

I nodded.

'It was almost a relief when I felt one coming on, as painful as it was. To be able to shut myself in a dark room for an afternoon. To lie down and not work.' She shook her head. 'To think a feeling like a shard of glass piercing me between the eyes was a welcome thing.'

•

The girls at work were excited to hear of the wedding, though Dot stuck out her tongue and said, 'Told you so.'

She and the girls from the typing pool gave me clothing coupons to use for gloves and shoes, and coupons to buy ingredients for the cake. Mum and Aunt Joy were going to make the other food, and Dot said she wanted to bake the cake for us, as a wedding present. She was going to be my bridesmaid, and Bob would be the groomsman. I told Roy about my dress on layby and he pretended to be upset that I had been saving for it so long before I met him.

'What, so I'm just the groom? I come second to the dress?'

He wanted to pay off the rest of it and I let him, so he came with me to Grace Bros to make the final payment and pick it up. I wouldn't let him see it, of course; it was in a garment bag for the ride home. It was strangely light, being cotton. Light considering the weight of all the hopes it carried, all the dreams I'd centred around it. Was it foolish? I wondered, as Roy dropped me off and held my wrist for a last kiss. Was a single garment worthy of so much hope? But at home I tried it on, and though it needed the hem taken up and the sleeves shortened, it looked as it did in my daydreams. It was just what I wanted it to be.

Roy and I hardly saw each other in those last weeks, we were both so busy with the arrangements, but he did sneak up to my room one night after work with the news that his CO had given him permission to marry. He showed me the letter, and we sat on the edge of my bed and toasted each other with a bottle of beer he'd brought shared out between two tin mugs.

He pulled a card out of his jacket pocket then and gave it to me. 'It's from my ma,' he said.

Dear Sarah,

We were awfully surprised to get the news that Roy is getting married. It wasn't what we expected, but sometimes life doesn't happen the way you think it will. I hope you two will be happy here in Roanoke. I'm sure that coming to America will be exciting for you. Roy sent a picture and we can sure see why he's fallen for you, do look after him. Send us a photograph from the wedding day.

Sincerely,

Mr & Mrs Ronald Jackson

I felt my ears grow hot as I read it. She wasn't one to mince words. And it talked about something we hadn't: that when Roy was back safe from New Guinea and the war was over, it was expected that I would join him in America. I would go where he went: it was just what you did.

'What's Roanoke like?' I asked, lying back with the letter in my hands, looking at the cardstock as if it were a map that could show me.

'Different,' he said, lying back beside me. 'It's real pretty. Mountains, and green as anything. But we don't have beaches, and it can get pretty damn cold in the winter. It's not got so much going on either, but there's good times. Picnics, walking parties, potlucks, church socials. I hope my ma doesn't put you off. She takes a while to warm to people.'

The way he said it made my stomach drop, but I told myself I was reading too much into it. I sat up and fanned myself with the card before sticking it in a drawer. I shooed Roy out with nothing more than a kiss.

'I've got a dress to take in, and you can't see it until you show up at the wedding,' I said, pushing him towards the door. And when the door was shut I sat down on the floor, arms around my knees, and let the tears come.

I guess I'd imagined Roy just taking me away, but I hadn't thought of where. Maybe the America of Hollywood. Family didn't come into my thoughts—at least not his—but now his would be mine. His family, his country, his life. A cold place with a woman who hated me before she'd even met me. A foreign place where I didn't know the rules. And now it was all in motion.

You make your bed, you lie in it.

The dress alone would walk me down the aisle. The others would hold me to it. I had given one of the last things that was mine to give.

My word.

•

The wedding was at the Abbey on Bridge Road, only a few blocks from us: a Presbyterian church where my mother had gone every Sunday for services since we moved to Forest Lodge, mostly on her own. The pastor said we were on at three o'clock and not to be late. There had been no time to send out invitations so we rang everyone we wanted to invite and hoped they could come at such short notice.

On Saturday morning I put my dress in the garment bag and packed my small overnight case. Dad picked me up in his delivery truck, honking his horn until Mrs Mulligan shouted and slammed her window shut. If it was loud enough to wake her, the Japs had probably heard it too.

We went to fetch Dot, and her mother helped her carry the wedding cake to the truck.

'I've been up half the night,' Dot said. 'What do you think?'

Tiny pink and green icing-sugar roses decorated the two-tiered cake.

'Oh, it's just beautiful. Where did you find the roses?'

'I made them.'

'Dad, isn't she brilliant?'

Dad just grunted and shifted the truck into gear.

At the house, Dot and I shut ourselves away in my old bedroom. Mum and Aunt Joy were busy cooking, and Mrs Thompson from next door had come over to help. The house was as clean as I had ever seen it. Mum had spent the last week beating rugs, mopping floors and scrubbing tiles. Everyone was coming over after church for the reception—a restaurant was too expensive. There wouldn't be a lot of room, but it'd be cosy. Fred and Dad were in the front yard cleaning the truck because they didn't know what else to do.

When Mum brought us sandwiches for lunch we had finished our hair and were both in our underslips. Dot had a bridesmaid's dress that her friend wore to her sister's wedding—green crepe with a satin bow—and we only had to make a few adjustments with Mum's sewing machine for it to fit perfectly.

'Are you alright, Sar?' Dot asked, when the machine was silent. 'You seem quiet. Not yourself.'

I told her about the card from Roy's mum, about wishing I'd never said yes in the first place.

'Oh, Sarah, it's only natural to feel that way. My mum told my sister every girl gets cold feet the day of her wedding. It's just all new, but at least—you and Roy, you've already . . . ?'

I shook my head.

She put her hand to her mouth. 'It'll be fine. I don't know why I thought—I suppose we don't all have your virtue!'

'We've nearly. But that's not what worries me, Dot. It's what comes after.'

She rubbed my back through the cotton slip, so it rustled against my skin. Her hands were warm and she smelled so familiar, as familiar as Roy. Why was it the friends we had to leave and the men we had to follow?

'You'll be right,' she said quietly, but she didn't look like she believed her own words.

We fastened our dresses and put on our powder and lipstick, and finally the two of us were ready. Mum came in and blinked fast at her tears.

'You look, Sar . . . that dress.'

Dot fixed Mum's hair into a fancy twist, then we walked to the church together—Mum, Dad, Fred, Dot and I. Everyone we passed turned to watch, cars honked; it was something, what a dress could do. Fred wore his uniform and was walking with only one crutch now. He was looking less gaunt since he had been home for a few weeks—I knew that Mum fed him at every opportunity. It was only Jack missing, and there had been no news of him in three weeks. It cast a shadow that we did our best that day to ignore.

The church was crowded, with people milling around in the gardens and paths out front, people from other weddings as well as ours. We had hardly arrived when Mum and Dot rushed me inside to the rectory to wait where Roy couldn't see me.

He was efficient, that pastor, though I suppose he had a lot of weddings to get through. So many young men in uniform getting married. So many brides in dresses borrowed or altered or scavenged. At exactly three o'clock I heard the organ start up the bridal march. Dad came in to escort me down the aisle. He had shaved off his moustache for the day and looked older, greyer, but clear in the eyes too. He was saving himself for the reception. He didn't look at me directly but he patted my arm as we began to walk.

'I hope you'll be happy, Sar.'

I wanted to ask him then what had made him unhappy in his marriage to Mum. Why he'd had to find someone else to make him feel alive. I wanted to ask what her name was, and where she came from, and what she said to make him laugh.

But I didn't and I never would. We were in the church by then, walking behind Dot, and there were twenty or thirty people gathered, enough to fill the front few pews but not the entire church, and as we walked past them they turned with us, their faces following our passage like flowers following the sun. I saw Roy then, standing beside the pastor in his black dress uniform with brass buttons, white gloves, his hair combed severely. He smiled—I could see he was nervous by the way he showed his teeth. Dad kissed me on the cheek, and I took Roy's arm. It was all so strange. I have no memory of what the pastor said to us; I only remember how fast he spoke and how my whole body felt light and not my own. Was it really me—Sarah—doing this? I longed suddenly to bury my face into the flank of a cow, to hear the sound of milk streaming into a bucket, to have Blackie's warm muzzle in my lap. These past three years I had become unfamiliar to myself. I let Roy kiss me and pretended my tears were not for what I'd lost but for what I'd gained, and all of us were crying—all the women, at least: Dot and Mum, Aunt Joy and even Mrs Thompson.

Afterwards we stood on the steps of the church for a photograph, squinting into the sun.

'That dress was worth every sixpence,' Roy whispered in my ear. 'You're the prettiest bride here.' I smiled. The flashbulb popped. My eyes watered.

We went back to the house for the reception and there was beer, rum, a table laden with roasts, rolls, salads and sausages; another with cake, biscuits, slices and boxes of chocolates from Roy and his friends. There were at least ten other Americans Roy worked with, most of them junior officers, and then all of the neighbours, Fred's friends, the girls from the typing pool. After the food was cleared away we put on the record player and even Mum and Dad danced, Mum's cheeks flushed red from her single glass of beer. In the window seat Fred was getting close with a girl I worked with, and Roy was laughing about something with Bob and we had one night until he left—a single night—and I'd had too much to drink and there was nothing I wanted more than to be out of there, for it to just be the two of us together on our own. That—after all—was why we'd gone through all this. I slid under his arm and he looked at me with a grin: 'What a party! What do you say, wife?'

Would I get used to him saying that? It sounded so queer. I stood on my toes to whisper in his ear. 'It's getting late. I might go change out of this dress. Will we leave soon?'

'Swell idea, sweetheart. These guys might catch a ride into town with us, if that's okay? Still early for them.'

I nodded, for I didn't want to look mean. I went into the front bedroom and shut the door, struggling to undo the wedding dress on my own. Ten minutes later I re-emerged in the two-piece navy suit with the pillbox hat, red lippie reapplied, carrying my overnight bag. Everyone rushed over to say goodbye—though it was silly, really, because it wasn't me leaving tomorrow, just Roy.

Mum hugged and kissed him, and Dad and Fred shook his hand, and finally we were out in the cool night air, stars peeking from behind light grey clouds. There were five of us, including the army boys, and they were drunk, their voices carrying in the quiet after the loud party. To tell the truth, I enjoyed being the only woman among these tall, smartly dressed, boisterous men. At Broadway we caught a cab into the city, and we dropped them off on George Street near the pubs and then continued on to our hotel, a tiny, tidy place in Woolloomooloo so Roy wouldn't have to go far to board his ship at noon the next day.

It was surreal writing our names in the reception book: Mr and Mrs Jackson. I felt like a fraud who was going to be found out. The receptionist showed us up to our room, which had an ensuite and a large four-poster bed. She drew the curtains and Roy gave her a tip, which didn't even surprise her; she must have been used to the Americans by now.

Once we were alone, Roy sat down and put his arms out. 'My Sarah, let's not leave this bed until it's time to go tomorrow.'

'Let's not leave it ever,' I said, and he undid my jacket, then the buttons of my blouse beneath. It was strange after all the waiting that the time was suddenly here—and I wanted now to stretch it out, to make it last. I stepped out of my skirt and sat down to unroll my stockings, and Roy removed his shoes and socks and pants. I had been given a silk nightie by Mrs Thompson—something she no longer fitted into—and, wearing just my slip, I went into the ensuite with my overnight bag. I brushed my teeth, washed off my make-up and undid my hair from the elaborate rolls Dot had fixed, brushing it so it fell softly to my shoulders. The ivory silk of the nightie felt like air on my skin. I came out and Roy was asleep, fast asleep, his mouth hanging open and a wet spot spreading on the pillow beneath him.

'Roy,' I whispered, sitting on the bed, running my hand along his shoulder. He stirred but didn't wake. It had been such an exhausting week that I couldn't be angry. I curled up beside him, feeling a queer mix of relief and disappointment. I lay there for hours, wondering at this turn my life had taken, before finally falling asleep.

In the morning we made love—and it is strange that I can't recall it better, what with all the anticipation leading up to it. I remember waking in a bright room feeling hungry, but forgetting the hunger as he touched me, and I remember the odd rubbery smell of the condom, which I had heard of but never seen before. I remember the dry feeling of friction. The pressure which was too much at first but which gradually eased and then, when I stopped worrying, felt good. If I moved it felt even better. He whispered in my ear as he rocked above me and it was the feeling of his breath on my ear that I wanted most, and as soon as he was done I missed him like part of me, as though he was already on board the ship and gone. We made love three times that morning—each time it was easier, though the last time it was also raw. And then he looked at his watch on the bedside table and cried, 'Shit—sorry—damn, we'd better go.'

The ship at the wharf was gunmetal grey with a huge, high hull. The deck was a smokestack, posts and ropes, guns at the bow and stern, and bunks below. It was a Liberty ship, and all I could think of was a conversation I'd overheard between Roy and his friends, talking of how the huge hulls were paper-thin and easily pierced by submarine missiles. How the ships travelled in a ring as it was less likely that the U-boats would penetrate a circle. How men slept with their clothes and shoes on in case they were hit, so they could get to the lifeboats as quickly as possible. On the decks were a mass of American army and navy uniforms. The dock was so crowded it looked as though it might sink, and we pushed through the crush, Roy holding tight to my hand, his bag slung over one shoulder. Finally we reached the gangway, and it was time for him to leave. He held my face in his hands and said, 'You'll write.'

'So will you. You'll be safe.'

'I will. I love you.'

'I love you too,' I replied, but my face was pressed into his jacket and to this day I don't know if he heard. We hadn't said it before and, though we'd write it, we wouldn't say it again. He walked aboard and disappeared into the swell of uniformed men and the shouts and calls. The women on the dock all screaming hysterical farewells, me just another with her handkerchief to her face, trying to stem the ridiculous flow of tears. I waited there until the ship blasted its deep, bone-rattling horn—three blasts as the tugs pulled it away from the dock—and watched until it disappeared over the horizon. And then I picked up my bag and walked through Woolloomooloo, through the Cross and Potts Point and Darlinghurst, all the way home to Surry Hills, stopping only to buy a meat pie and eat it in front of a shop window, watching my own reflection, wondering why it was I looked the same when everything had changed.

CHAPTER 13

That morning after breakfast, in the cabin, Grandma pulls out an old book, the cardboard cover a soft, mottled grey. The cover is tied closed with a fraying piece of string.

'What's inside?' I ask.

I sit beside her on the bed. There is a wedding photograph on the first page—taken in the church, perhaps. Her hair is up in rolls around an unsmiling face, and her narrow frame is swathed in this long dress with puffy sleeves. Her eyes are clear, serious, and her hands clasp those of the groom, who stands behind her, his arms wrapped around her. He wears his dress uniform and cap, and he's grinning over her shoulder, his eyes laughing.

'You look so young.'

'We were both nineteen.'

There's another photograph beneath it of the two of them leaving the church, in a shower of confetti, people all around them. He's looking at her, saying something, and she looks as though she can't decide whether to laugh or cry. Her eyes are liquid.

Grandma turns the page and letters spill out. They are untied, loose, some in their envelopes. We lay them out on the bed, finding pages that go together, deciphering dates, until we have achieved some semblance of order. I read them aloud.

Dear Roy,

It is only the morning after you left and already I have to write. Mrs Mulligan's seems horribly dull after our hotel by the docks, and last night was the loneliest of my life. I almost wish we hadn't married and spent a night (and morning!) in bed together, because if we hadn't I would never have realised what it is I am missing.

But then again I wouldn't give it up for the world, and as rushed as it was, I am so glad that I have the memory of it to sustain me while you are away. Today I am back at work—of course—and so I can't write for long. Soon I must dress and brush my hair and look respectable. Everyone will look at me differently now that I am married. What do the others in your platoon say to you? Tell your CO thank you for me—for letting us be together—and I promise to be the best sort of wife. Don't forget me now that you are on board a ship with the sea glittering like jewels around you. (Do they even let you out to look at the ocean?) Do stay safe.

Love,

Your Sarah

Dear Sarah,

We're on our way and I don't know when you'll get this or when I'll get your letters, but I promised I'd write. I can't think of anything but you, baby, and I wish I had another week in that hotel with you to show you how much you mean to me. Compared to you, everything is dull aboard—there's just poker, mess duty and giving the sailors a hard time until we hit shore. One guy in the next cabin over has filled a 32-gallon garbage can with mash and says it makes about a quart of alcohol a week. Everyone wants to be his friend, and I have to admit a little moonshine would help pass the time.

Last ship I was on, coming to Sydney, I cut out all these pin-ups from the magazines and stuck them above my bunk—Jane Russell, Jean Harlow—they were swell-looking girls. But now I have someone even more beautiful staring at me as I go to sleep. The boys make fun of me when I kiss you goodnight, but they don't know half of what I know. Please write me, write me as much as you can. Knowing I'll get your letters eventually is all that makes this bearable. They're calling us to the mess for scran (that's food) so I'd better go. Tell your mother that I'd kill for one of her roasts instead of the tasteless excuse for dinner they feed us here.

Love and more,

Roy

Dear Roy,

I'm sorry I haven't written for ages. The worst news has come. Jack is MIA, maybe captured by the Japs, and this has floored us all. Mum rang to say they had come by the house and told her. Mrs Thompson had to take the phone as Mum couldn't tell me without falling apart. She's been in bed all week, in a terrible way, and Dad's hardly left the pub. They say it was close combat, and our men were hugely outnumbered—trapped really. I have been staying here with them, to help Mum, and they've given me the week off work. Oh, Roy, I can't bear it, to think of him suffering over there, to think maybe you won't meet him, maybe I won't see him again. He and I are as close as a brother and sister can be, and there is something so gentle in him. I could tell he wasn't certain about joining up when he did, but Fred and Dad pressured him, and he probably felt as though he had no choice.

I have been going through his things all day: his shirts which I hid away, his jars of hair pomade, the books and form guides, his scrawled messy writing and his boots. Every pair of boots I see makes me want to cry. That was his job at the farm when he was little, cleaning the boots in the evenings, and he never whinged or carried on about it. He just did it, beautifully, with that sweet smile of his—and I can't bear to think that I might never see that smile again.

I can't stand this and I can't stand to think of losing anyone else. I don't want you there, Roy, I want you safe in my arms. I want you beside me.

Fred is in bad shape too, he wants to go back more than ever now, but the docs are saying his knee is no good. Mum can't bear him to leave, which I've been trying to tell him, but he just wants revenge. He wants to do something about Jack.

Please, Roy, tell me you're safe. Tell me you'll be with me soon. I need something to keep me going, some reason that life is still bearable.

Always yours,
Sarah

Dear Sarah,

Two letters—I was so glad to hear my name at mail call at camp—and both from you. But I was devastated when I read your most recent note. I am so sorry. I can handle my own pain but I can't handle yours. It just tears me up that you are there hurting and I am so far away, useless to you. I know it's not much, but there's a chance he's alive, and you need to hold onto that hope. I remember how your eyes always lit up when you spoke about Jack, and I just know I'll get to meet him one day. He is just a kid, I feel like we're all just kids, and it's some of what makes me so angry now. I don't want to be here anymore, baby, I don't want to risk this chance of happiness that we have together, but I don't know any way out either. I just have to finish this deployment and see if I can get a discharge. I know we haven't talked about it much, but I had a lot of time to think on the ship over here and I'd like to picture us on a farm together—you and me—with kids, raising cattle and pigs and growing—I don't know—pumpkins. Does that sound like something you'd like to do?

The mail's not going to be so regular here with everything going on but still write as much as you can. I'm not meant to give any details in my letters, which is why they sound a little vague, but I am not in danger and things are going well for us. It is hot—hotter than anywhere I've ever been—and our uniforms are just crazy in this heat. Next time you see me I'll be black as a native, at least until you take off my shirt.

Just writing those words has sent me into delirious daydreams, sweetheart, but I won't tell you everything. I'll show you next time I see you.

Sending you all my love and wishing you didn't have to go through this. Tell your family how sorry I am. Tell Fred that your mom and dad need him there.

Yours and yours only,

Roy

Dear R,

Your letter has been the only bright spot in these last weeks—the only time I smiled was thinking of you taking off your shirt. There is no sense to this world which tries to keep us apart. I can't make heads or tails of it.

I'm back at the office. All the girls have been very kind to me, and seem to understand when I burst into tears when someone walks past in the Australian army uniform or when the phone rings or the door slams. But sometimes I just want to scream. I'm a mess, but there's nothing to do but get through it, and if I could be half as brave as you are that would be enough.

The farm sounds perfect. I laughed about the pumpkins but funnily enough I can see you doing it. I think
you probably do have a green thumb. Mine's pretty black,
sorry to say—I accidentally killed those violets you gave me
before you left. (Overwatering? Underwatering? No idea.)
But yes to kids and we also need dogs, and lamb roasts on
Sunday. Do people even eat lamb in America? See how far
you go, darling, towards cheering me up?

Mum got out of bed this week and sat up to eat her
meals with Dad and me—Dad told her he'll starve if I keep
cooking—and he didn't go to the pub at all on Sunday. I'm
still paying for my room at Mrs Mulligan's and I hope that
when Mum is feeling better I can get back there, but for
now I know she needs us all close. And I feel like if we're
here together hoping for him, the chance of Jack surviving
is better.

Look after yourself, my love, for you are what's keeping
me going. Keep your shirt on, please, and your heart safe.

Love,

S

Dearest S,

My heart is safe, my shirt is on, but my mind is going crazy
thinking about you. I can't even tell you all the daydreams
I've had because I know the censors read all of our letters,
and I don't want them getting their kicks thinking
about you. Safe to say you occupy pretty much all of my
thoughts, babe, pretty much all of the time.

There's a guy here who also married an Aussie gal and she's signed up for one of those ships going back to the US. He told me there's this thing called the War Brides Act— have you heard of it? Pretty much it means you don't need a visa or to go through immigration to move to the US, and Uncle Sam will transport you over there free of charge. Wow—was I excited when I heard about this! Because if I do finish up after this deployment, they send me straight back to the US. And this way we wouldn't have to pay to get us both over there. He said you've only got to get on the list over at the US consulate, taking the letters we got and the marriage certificate and things. What do you think, sweetheart? I know that you don't want to leave your family now, but you wouldn't have to. It takes them a long time to find all the wives space on the boats. They told this guy's wife it might be a year or more before she gets a ship over.

I know it sounds sort of far-fetched, but it's given me so much hope to think of both of us being done with this mess and together.

Love & lots more,

R

Dear R,

Funny, I'd read about The War Brides Act in the news-paper but I hadn't realised what it meant for us. I have to tell you the truth, darling, I was upset to read that you wouldn't be coming back here to get me—in my daydreams you're stepping off that boat into my arms on Australian soil, not the other way around. But I'll do whatever it takes to be with you, so I've already gone down to the consulate and filled out their forms and put my name on the list. I haven't told Mum and Dad yet, but I will.

You were right, the lady said it could take ages because the ships are mostly being used for wartime purposes, so I'm glad my name is down. She was very nice, she also told me about the Wives and Fiancées of US Servicemen's Club—so I'll go along to their next meeting and maybe get a little more information from other girls who are in the same position. Or maybe they'll just be friends to have when I'm over there. I can't quite imagine what life there will be like, but that's not to say I'm not excited. I know it will be just fine as long as I have you.

Yours,

S

Dear S,

I'm sorry, babe, I feel like an oaf for not thinking about what it would mean for you to come to America on your own. I was just thinking about how much I want you in my arms. It isn't easy to leave your home behind, especially with Jack missing and your family needing you. I understand you being a little upset, and I am too, to think of you having to say goodbye to them to be with me. And if we can do it another way, sweetheart, we will. If you want me to stay in the army longer I might get another Sydney shore leave, and you just might be able to meet me at the docks again at Woolloomooloo. Maybe we could go back to that little hotel again too—I'll stop here before I get too carried away . . .

Tell me what it is you want, baby, what you're thinking. I hate trying to have a conversation this way and waiting for your reply, not knowing whether I'm making things better or making you sad. I just want us to cuddle up together and tell each other everything we're thinking, not to have to write it all down and then wait for a week or two before we know whether or not we've been understood.

Know this, Sarah: I'll do whatever it takes for us to be together. That's all for now.

Love,

R

Dear R,

No, now I've thought it through and I'm sure this is the right way. I'll get on one of the ships and we'll meet up over there. Of course it will be hard to tell Mum and Dad, especially Mum, but it's been hard living with them again these past weeks too, and I'm reminded of all of the reasons why I moved out in the first place. And while that hotel in Woolloomooloo gives me all kinds of delicious memories, we can make more memories wherever we end up, as long as we're together. I know the lady said it would be a while but I'm starting to hope they call me up soon.

I've been over to the club I told you about on Castlereagh Street and met some nice girls, and talking to them has eased my nerves a little about the journey to come.

Yours with love,

S

It's so strange to read their private words out loud, the words that Grandma wrote all those years ago. She doesn't even blush, but sometimes the corners of her mouth twitch into a smile. I can see how the letters let them get to know each other better. How they gave them a place to talk about things that were difficult to say face to face.

Maybe I should write a letter to Ash.

Or to Mom. And Grandma. When there are so many lies, though, where do you begin?

I've never gotten better. I've just gotten better at hiding the truth. Grandma and Mom always do their best to support my choices—track and field, pre-law, nursing school—but they wouldn't have if I had been honest with them.

And Ash . . . Ash, who has told me I'm too thin, who has said he's worried I don't eat enough—I have told him so many lies. I'm just like this, I say: I have a quick metabolism. And I ate such a huge breakfast. Or a late lunch after my lecture. He drops it quickly, like it scalds his tongue. Men are so careful when speaking to women about their weight. Even doctors and therapists, male ones. They realise how much is tied up in their gaze.

In the hospital stays, at my lowest points, it was never the doctors or the therapists whose approval I wanted; it was the nurses. They took one look at me and brought extra blankets, the ones which are starched, and bleached as white as Miss America's teeth. They didn't ask stupid questions. They were straightforward and strong; solid with steady hands. They put in IVs and watched me go to the bathroom after meals, they watched me swallow my meds and held my wrist to count my pulse. They knew the business of bodies better than anyone. Better than the doctors, who fumbled over charts and tests and long-term plans. Better than therapists, who asked questions and sat through interminable silences. Nurses counted pills and pounds and heartbeats; they seemed to know when to speak and when to stay silent.

They weren't all like this, of course; there were the ones who sighed at a bedpan, who flinched when they saw the outline of your bones, who asked things like, 'Don't you want to have babies one day?'

But the good ones were really good. Some even looked at you with something like admiration. A nurse is a person who admires self-control. Who doesn't take shit from anyone, but feels sympathy for everyone, because don't we all suffer? Isn't it part of being alive?

In nursing school we learned this: how physical pain takes over, how we forget things quicker in pain and how our brains can be tricked by it. It's why you can distract yourself from something which really hurts with just a pinch.

A nurse is a person with the power to cause pain and relieve it. Adderall, Clozapine, Ambien. Lactulose and Ativan, diuretics and Demerol. Hydrocodone, OxyContin, Percocet and Fentanyl. Of course it is controlled, of course they are meant to keep track of every pill, every patch, but there are always tricks. Sometimes a patient misses their dose. Sometimes a patient dies before the meds stop coming. It is those who count who know how to mask the truth.

The thing about the truth, though, is that if you decide to tell it you have to tell it all. You can't hide some things and tell others. Because they're all connected, the lies, like the scaffolding of a skyscraper. I imagine myself as the building inside, my structure rotten, only the lies holding me up. I'm not strong enough without them. I'd certainly tumble to the ground.

CHAPTER 14

I wanted to hide from Roy how difficult things had been since Jack went MIA, because he was over there fighting himself, but I couldn't keep some of my frustration from seeping into my letters.

I had come home to help Mum, but all the unresolved issues from the year before began to haunt me. I was hiding the truth from her, and it meant that I could never be completely myself. I was always on guard now, in case I let something slip. Sometimes I thought perhaps it would be easier just to tell her. She would forgive me. But would she forgive Dad? And was now the time, when she was so fragile, to destroy her idea of him? No matter what I did, I felt as though being in that house was living in a lie.

Mum let her grief pull her soft, worn out body into bed, her eyes distant and rubbed raw. While she floundered, Dad pretended that nothing had happened, that life just went on as it ever did, and when Mum started to talk about Jack he'd pound the table and shout, 'Enough, woman! Let it rest.'

He drank as much as ever but it didn't seem to give him the relief it once did. He treated going to the pub like a job: if he didn't do it the world might stop, he might have to face his life in some unfamiliar way, and he was not prepared for that.

As for Fred, he was growing more like our father every day. Between the two of them they kept the delivery business going, but only just; they spent more time quenching their never-ending thirst. While Mum was broken by Jack being missing, and Dad blundered on as though nothing had happened, Fred became angry. He was angry at the Japs, angry at the Yanks, angry at the women who turned him down and the kids who mimicked his limp on the street. He was angry at me for looking after Mum—saying she didn't need to be coddled—and angry at the doctors who told him he couldn't go back and fight because of his knee. He was most angry at himself, at his body, at how it no longer worked in the way it should. At the pain that came unexpectedly, keeping him awake some nights.

Meanwhile, I tried to lose myself in the past. I fossicked through Jack's trunk, slept with his old shirts, smelled his jars of hair pomade. But then I realised the past wasn't going to bring him home. It was down to luck, to hope, and I would be better off following my own path—where not every lanky man with light hair, dark eyes and a sweet smile caused my heart to skip and then sink.

I dreaded telling them all that I had signed up to go on the list for America. I dreaded Dad's silence and Fred's anger, but most of all I dreaded Mum's sorrow.

I finally told them at dinner one night. Mum was cooking again most nights—because no one could bear my attempts—and afterwards I would clean up while she returned to bed. This night it was a rabbit stew with dumplings and we ate as we usually did, in silence, just the sound of chewing, cutlery clinking, the legs of Dad's chair creaking as he shifted in his seat.

'I got a letter from Roy,' I said, staring down at my plate.

'He's safe then?' Mum said. 'Thank God.'

'Don't worry, the Yanks are good at saving their own skins,' Fred said sourly.

'That's not fair,' I protested. 'Plenty of them have died as well.'

Mum's face had begun to crumple and Dad gave me and Fred a hard look.

I continued, 'It looks like after he finishes this tour, they'll be sending him straight back to America, so he reckons it's a good idea for me to get on one of the bride ships—you know, the ones which will take all the wives and fiancées over.'

'Huh,' Dad grunted, still chewing his mouthful of food. He swallowed and took a sip of beer. 'How do you get on one of them ships, then?'

'Well, you put your name on a list at the American consulate, and they call you up when they have a place for you. It doesn't cost anything. They pay for your passage and meals and all. So I'm going to do it, because otherwise Roy will have to pay my way over, and it costs a fair bit.'

I glanced over at Mum. Her lips were pursed, her hands in her lap. She looked up and our eyes met over the table, which was enough to make me cry.

'Oh, come, come, Sarah,' she said, and I went and hugged her, kneeling beside her chair. 'I don't want you to go, but I can't hold you back either. He's a good man. He'll look after you.'

Dad and Fred looked away as Mum stroked the back of my head. She smelled of talcum powder and stew, and her body was soft but I could feel her bones. She had grown thinner these past weeks.

Dad coughed and took another sip of his beer. 'He's not a bad bloke, is he?' He looked at Fred as though for confirmation.

Fred got up and limped towards the door. 'See you at the pub, Dad,' he called, letting the flyscreen shudder behind him.

'It's hard for him to be the one who's left behind,' Mum said.

She blew her nose in her handkerchief, and I stood and went back to my chair. The three of us finished our meal in silence. So much now had gone unspoken that nothing could safely be said.

•

Peace was declared on 15 August 1945. All of Sydney celebrated, but at our house it was just a reminder that Jack was still missing. I had moved back into Mrs Mulligan's, and met up with Dot and some other friends and went into the city. People in the street were blowing whistles, banging drums, linking arms and dancing. The pubs overflowed into the streets and men in uniform were kissed by girls for just walking past. I had a few drinks with the others, rolling over that word, 'peace', in my head, watching Dot dance with a sailor, his hat tipped sideways on her head. I tried not to worry about Roy. I hadn't heard from him in a few months.

After the war ended Dad decided it was time for the family to go back down south near Milton/Ulladulla. He had a friend who was going to sell him land cheap and he'd have another go at farming. He'd saved money from the delivery business—God knows how—and could buy enough equipment, now, to run a proper dairy. Mum didn't say much about it, but I could see it would be good for Fred. I wondered whether Dad had broken things off with the woman I saw at the races. Whether it was just farming he was giving another go, or his marriage as well. I wished I could be there with them, in the valley, leaning my head on a cow's flank at dawn. I had to stay in Sydney, though, and wait for my boat.

In October I finally had a letter from Roy.

Dear Sarah,

Well, things have been rough but I'm alive and that's what matters. Just before the war ended we got caught in an ambush, hand-to-hand combat, and nearly half my unit didn't make it through. I had a hit to the hip and woke in a pool of blood. They must have thought I was dead. Turns out I wasn't, and the doctors have done a good job stitching me up, but there are things I'm having trouble with, like walking's pretty stiff, and there've been some other problems too. Lucky I had your letters in the pocket of my coat, not my hip pocket. Your photograph as well, though it's looking mighty worn. We're on a hospital ship headed home now. There's plenty of boys worse off than me and some of my best pals are dead. Ma and Pa wrote and said I should write to you and tell you all this, in case you change your mind and don't want to come. I know it sounds bad but it's okay. Like Ma said, you'll have to make up your own mind about it.

Love,

Roy

Dear Roy,

Oh, love, what awful news, but I am also so glad you are alive. It breaks my heart that I can't be there on that ship with you, nursing you myself. Of course I still want to come, I am coming, and the only reason I won't is if you tell me you don't want me anymore.

You do still want me, don't you?

Did the doctors say whether or not you could still have children? Because if you can't we'll be fine. It isn't the end of the world. I wondered if that was what you meant, though, reading between the lines. No matter what's happened I still want us to be together. I have heard that now the war's over they'll start bringing more of us over on the bride ships, so it can't be too long. I won't have my job much longer, as the Americans are all headed home. Mum, Dad and Fred have moved down south, but I want to be here in case there's a ship. Write again and tell me how things are. Wishing I was there to hold you.

Always yours,

S

Dear S,

Of course I still want you to come! I was just preparing myself for the idea that maybe you wouldn't want to. I'm home, finally, in Roanoke. It's all the same, which is strange, since I'm different. Not just different because of the war, but different because of us. They can't tell yet about children. If I can't, babe, I want you to think about this a little harder. I don't want you to give up your dreams because of me.

Love,

R

On 12 December I got the telegram: in two weeks I would sail for America on the SS *Mariposa*. After landing in San Francisco I would be put on a train to Virginia, to Roy. I rang Dot and wrote a letter to Mum and Dad with the news. I telegrammed Roy and tried to push down my fear. There was even an article in the newspaper about the ship.

Sydney Morning Herald, 12 December 1945

Fitted out as a floating nursery, the liner and troopship *Mariposa* sailed from New York bound for Australia to pick up 1,200 wives and 400 children of American servicemen.

The surgery and medical wards have been converted into nurseries with special baby equipment, including 500 toys, 18,000 safety pins, and 20,000 paper diapers. It has playpens, bassinets and baby bathrobes. The brides and babies will be looked after by the Army until they are delivered right to their husbands.

The Army has created an organisation to handle every detail of transport of dependants of Americans from overseas—estimated to total 50,000 wives and 20,000 children. The first big batch of Australians is expected in San Francisco in early January. The

Army will take charge of the girls on arrival, getting their baggage through Customs, then putting them on special trains under train commanders, with Red Cross girls and medical enlisted men to help. Telegrams at Government expense will be sent to the waiting husbands advising the date and time of wives' arrival. All the husbands have to do will be to meet the train and take delivery of his wife after signing for her.

Mum rang to ask if I could still come down for Christmas.

'Of course,' I said. 'I'll just have to tell the US Navy where I am, and I'll have to leave again on Boxing Day.'

I gave notice at Mrs Mulligan's and at work—I had started a new job at a law office when the Quartermaster Corps left Sydney—and then tried madly to organise everything, packing my trunk and deciding what to bring and what to leave behind. and Dot came around to help me finish the tablecloth I was embroidering as a gift for Roy's mother. We were going to stay at his parents' house at first and then we would find a nice place together. I knew it might take a while because there were housing shortages everywhere.

Mum had been posting clippings and recipes to me since she moved down south. There were housekeeping hints, recipes she had written out on notecards and a few cuttings from advice columns in the women's pages of the paper. One read: *Married couples must go on making love as they did in their courting days. Romance must not be forgotten. Once lovemaking has been relegated to a fixed time and place, the glamour has gone, and marriage rapidly begins to fade into boredom.*

I wondered whether she had thought of herself and Dad when she read it, when their marriage had begun to fade, or whether the 'glamour' ever truly existed for them at all. I had told Mum about Roy's injuries but hadn't said what they might mean for him, that our lovemaking might already be a thing of the past.

The ship was due to leave on 28 December, and on Christmas Eve I took the train to Nowra, where Mum and Dad were to meet me at the station and drive me to their place. I wanted to eat Mum's Christmas dinner one last time, watch Dad and Fred drink all the brandy besides that in the pudding, and give them each the presents I'd chosen out of the things I wasn't taking with me. For Mum, my sewing shears, which were brass-handled and sharper than hers. For Dad, the carved bone comb I had won at school in a spelling competition. And for Fred, my hot-water bottle, since the cold made his leg ache.

I'd received permission from the military police to go, and didn't think anything of it when I saw the MPs' car pull along-side the train in Kiama as we followed the Princes Highway along the coast. At the station in Kiama two uniformed MPs boarded and walked through my car. 'We're looking for a Mrs Sarah Jackson. Is there a Mrs Sarah Jackson on board?'

I stood, my voice shaky. 'That's me.'

'We've got orders to bring you back to Sydney. Ship's leaving early.'

They helped me with my bags and I followed the two men off the train. There would be no Christmas after all, no gifts or goodbyes. My chest felt hollow at the thought I might never see my family again. Throat tight, I said, 'Can I at least call ahead to Nowra? Mum and Dad are at the station there. I need to tell them—so I can say goodbye.'

One of the men looked at his watch but the other nodded. They drove me to a hotel in Kiama where I could place a call. The operator connected me to Nowra, where I asked the station agent to find Mum and Dad. Mum's voice came on the phone all crackly, and my voice broke.

'They've brought me back, Mum, the ship's leaving early. I don't get to have Christmas. Or say goodbye.'

'Oh, love, if only we'd known. We'd have come to you.'

'I know, Mum.' I was sobbing now; I didn't want to go anymore. 'I'll cancel the whole trip.'

'No, Sarah, you've got to go. He's your husband. You belong with Roy.'

'I don't want to. I don't want to leave. It's awful, saying goodbye like this.' The MPs were watching me from the bar and the whole place had gone quiet, listening to my end of the conversation.

'Now, Sarah, don't be foolish. This is it, your big opportunity. It's more than I ever had.' I could hear Mum's voice break a little, even with the poor connection. 'You'll enjoy this voyage. At night, look at the moon on the water for me. I've always wanted to be on board a ship at night, to sit up on the deck and watch the moon reflected on the water.'

'Really?' I had never heard Mum speak like this. I even wondered, for a moment, if it was really her.

'Well, yes, I would have loved to travel. But Dad didn't want to when he was home from the war. And now we're too old. But think of all you'll see, Sarah. Try to be brave.'

'I love you, Mum.'

'I love you. I'll give the phone to Dad now. He'll say goodbye.'

I heard Dad clear his throat; I could almost smell his cigarettes and beer from the night before.

'Goodbye, Sar. Don't go and start talking like one of 'em, now.'

'I won't, Dad.'

'If he gives you any problems, you just let us know. We'll figure out a way to get you back.'

'Alright. You look after Mum, okay? And say goodbye to Fred for me.'

'Bye now.' And he hung up before I could tell him I loved him too, in spite of everything.

•

The *Mariposa* sailed from Pyrmont on 26 December 1945. She was a cruise ship that had been refitted as a troop carrier during the war and refitted again to carry war brides and their children now that the war was over. She dwarfed everything else at the dock, as big as Roy's Liberty ship, with nine decks and two funnels, and still painted that gunmetal grey. There were American sailors milling about on the decks, and on the pier were the Australian brides, some carrying babies or holding small children by the hand.

'I hope you don't get a cabin with one of those,' Dot said, and lifted her chin towards the babies. 'Imagine being trapped at sea in a tiny cabin with screaming babies. I'd rather be torpedoed by an enemy sub.'

She hadn't let go of my arm since we'd arrived at the pier. Her brother had brought my trunk. I had spent Christmas Day with them, after being brought back to Sydney by the MPs, and despite the efforts of her whole family it had been the loneliest Christmas I had ever experienced. We spoke of what Christmases would be like in America: snow, real fir trees, sledding.

'Like some kind of storybook,' Dot said. 'Excuse me if I turn green with jealousy.'

I knew she was trying to make me feel better, but she was having a hard time too. She'd fallen for Bob but he'd disappeared a few months ago. No 'I'm being called up,' no 'I want to end things'—he'd just vanished without a trace. He didn't leave a forwarding address. Even Roy said he had no idea where he'd gone to when I wrote and asked. Dot even called Bob's CO but no one could—or would—tell her anything.

Dot's brother passed my trunk to two of the sailors who were loading the ship. I'd labelled it clearly with my name and Roy's parents' address in Roanoke. It would be stowed in the cargo hold for the trip.

Dot pulled out her hanky and blew her nose, then she grabbed me and held me tight.

I was trying my hardest not to cry by then, and I whispered, 'Don't go having too much fun without me.'

'I'll miss you,' Dot said, her voice quavering.

'Stop, now—you'll make me want to stay.'

The truth was I already did want to stay. It took all my will to leave.

I handed the officers my paperwork then boarded the ship, fighting the urge to turn and run. At the top of the gangplank was a nurse, who gave me an injection—a smallpox vaccination, she said—and then a lady from the Red Cross said she would show me to a cabin. She must've seen the look in my eyes, and she talked non-stop to distract me. I would have five room-mates, and she said I was lucky because there was a porthole and it was on one of the upper decks. 'Some of them haven't got a window,' she said.

As we climbed the flights of steep metal staircases, she explained that the bow was the front, the stern the rear, port was on my left and starboard on my right. Every wall had a railing you could grab on to if you needed to steady yourself.

She paused in front of a narrow doorway. 'Now, just put your bags inside then come up on the deck when you're ready—we're departing soon.'

I stepped over a ledge and into the cabin.

It was tiny, with three double bunks. Two of the lower bunks were already taken and one upper, but not the one closest to the porthole. I placed my suitcase on that upper bunk. I sat on the edge of the lower bunk, buried my face in my arms and began to cry, relieved to be alone now, with no need to worry about what others thought. It wouldn't do, though, not to wave goodbye. Dot and her brother would be watching for me from the dock. I stood up. There were two sinks in the room, each with a little mirror above it. I was splashing water on my puffy, swollen face when the cabin door opened, and there was the lady from the Red Cross, showing in a tall brunette in a smart red dress. Her name was Brynn, she told me as I helped her to lift her case onto the other top bunk. I asked her if she wanted to come up to the deck with me to wave goodbye.

'Oh, yes, please,' she said. 'And if I try to jump off the ship will you stop me?'

'Only if you do the same for me.'

'Deal. Is your family here?'

I shook my head.

'I had to leave mine in Melbourne,' she said. 'It was the worst day of my life.'

Together we made our way to the deck, and then climbed one staircase and then another to go higher and higher. The ship was a maze of steel stairwells and decks—I couldn't see how I would ever find my way around. We found a good vantage point from where we could see the pier, and stood at the railing. Finally I saw Dot and her brother and shouted, waving, standing on the lower rail so they might see me.

'Don't go falling in now,' Brynn said with a laugh, holding me by the belt.

There were streamers stretched between the boat and the dock, and on the pier a band played 'Waltzing Matilda' and 'Now is the Hour'. All around us other girls were waving too, many of them in tears. I held out one arm to Dot and with the other blew her a kiss. The sun was beginning to set over the city when, after three deep blasts of the ship's horn, two sturdy small tugs began to pull us out to sea. Dockworkers in boats around us untied the mooring lines and I heard a few of them calling out, 'You'll be sorry!' Brynn leaned over the railing and shouted, 'No I won't!' to the applause of the other brides and hoots from American sailors. The last I saw of Dot was her skinny arm waving, her silhouette merging with thousands of others, a black mass of everything we were leaving behind.

•

We managed to find our way back to our cabin, where we met the others. There was Min from Perth, Barbara from Sydney and Jane who had come down from Brisbane. Barbara was pregnant, and she already looked a little green. They all seemed friendly enough, though I noticed Min liked to mention that she was an officer's wife several times in every conversation. We had one empty bunk in the cabin on which we piled our cases.

As the boat sailed out of Sydney and through the heads, the churning made us fall silent. I lay in my bunk, holding my stomach, the porthole opened as wide as it would go. Beneath me Barbara lowed like a cow calling her calf. To move without throwing up felt impossible.

'It will be calm once we're through the heads,' Min said. 'Have a light dinner tonight, or nothing at all.'

At eight o'clock an announcement came saying it was time for dinner in the main dining room. The voice seemed to come from the sky itself, and when I jerked up in shock, nearly banging my head, Min pointed to the circle with tiny holes in the centre of the ceiling.

'There are loudspeakers in every room that connect to the radio room, so they can make announcements and such.'

It seemed Min knew everything we didn't. Just then there was a knock at our door and a young redheaded sailor entered. He introduced himself as Clarence, and told us he was going to be our steward and he wanted to make sure we knew where the dining room was.

I groaned. 'I'll stay in bed.'

'Go on, get up,' Clarence urged. 'You'll feel better with some fresh air. You don't have to eat.'

THE PASSENGERS

Barbara said she was staying put, but asked us to bring her back something bland. We made graceless progress towards the mess, the four of us clutching our stomachs and swaying from side to side. Another announcement came over the loud-speakers as we walked.

'This is an American ship. All personnel will keep to the right using gangways and ladders.'

We quickly moved to the right of the gangway and just then encountered a group of sailors, who had been laughing but quieted as we passed.

'Evening, ladies,' one of them said. 'Enjoy your dinner.'

'Good evening,' I replied, and once we were clear of them the others giggled.

'They're cute,' Jane said, once they were out of earshot, and Brynn replied, 'You've got a husband!'

Clarence was blushing so much his face was brighter than his hair.

'You've got a husband!' became a popular refrain among us, since Jane thought every man in uniform divine, and I wondered if I should feel sorry for the husband who was meeting her in San Francisco.

I'd had no idea what to expect of the food on the journey. I assumed it would be simple and bland, probably not fresh. But I was in for a shock, and I certainly wasn't the only one who gasped when we saw the buffet table in the main dining room. There were platters of roast turkey, dishes of corn on the cob, loaves of bread and an entire cart dedicated to ice-cream. Too bad I didn't feel up to eating a bite of it. I took a dry bread roll and followed the others to a circular table set with cutlery and china. Min complained about the lack of tea, but I was still in awe at the sheer quantity of food. I had never seen so much in one place, ever.

After nibbling my bread roll I thought I would try to find my way back to the cabin on my own. I had several packets of salted crackers for Barbara—Min had called them saltines— and a banana.

I walked slowly, taking a detour outside to the deck to stand by the railing and breathe in some fresh air. There were only a few exterior lights on the ship and it took my eyes a moment to adjust to the dark. There was the deep engine sound, the slap of waves against the hull and shreds of voices carried by the wind. The water was so far down, and if I leaned over I could see the lights from portholes, all the cabins below. A cluster of sailors stood at one end of the deck, and along the railing were several small groups of women. I could pick out the glowing ends of cigarettes and longed for a smoke; it would certainly help the nausea. I decided to buy a pack at the commissary the next day.

The sky was clear, and when I looked up it was like being at the farm again, all the stars, and my eyes pricked at the memory of a place that I'd certainly never return to now. I hadn't seen so many stars since coming to the city, and there was a half-moon, reflecting on the dark ocean below, and I thought of Mum, who had always wanted to see this. I decided I would be brave for her sake.

It was hard to pull myself away from the sky. I could have slept out there beneath the moon and stars better than in our small close cabin with the others breathing, snoring, groaning in their sleep.

That night I dreamed of Thomas Ryan, the boy who'd sat in front of me at the Yatte Yattah school all those years ago. I dreamed I looked down from the ship and saw him floating face down in the ocean, his small pale neck, hand still grasping the nub of a pencil.

•

Dear Mum,

Well, we are away, and while I haven't quite got my sea legs yet, I haven't been as sick as many of the girls. It's like we're constantly rocking in a giant cradle: the side-to-side motion never stops. I will get used to the sway eventually, I suppose. The boat is very nice. I'd heard some horror stories about the Liberty ships but this is all first class, and the Red Cross ladies have organised so much for us to do. There are movies every night, games on the sports deck, lectures on things like fashion and make-up, and even a talent show. I certainly won't have time to brood. The other girls in my cabin are friendly—well, actually, three are friendly and the fourth seems to think herself better than us, but I will pay her no mind.

Right now I am sitting in one of the low timber deck-chairs (the writing room was full), so excuse my messy writing. Around me there are girls playing shuffleboard, and others crowded around a wireless listening to music as loud as it will go. Later I will go to lunch. Our cabin is in the early sitting, and after being seasick yesterday I've got more of an appetite today. The food is plentiful, so you needn't worry about me starving—more whether

I'll be twice my size by the time Roy sees me! When we dock I'll send a telegram before I get on the train to Virginia. We don't spend any time in San Francisco, as previous brides have had such a good time there they didn't want to travel to their husbands! Mind you, they seem to give us lots of these warnings.

Mostly they are terribly nice though. The Red Cross ladies not only organise everything but give us writing paper, pencils, soap and all the other necessities when we need them. Cosmetics, leg paint, cigarettes and chocolate are sold in the commissary.

It was so hard not being able to say a real goodbye to you and Dad and Fred. I was looking forward so much to a last Christmas together. I worry that I'll never see you again. I tell myself to be glad that I'm on the ship, but I feel as though part of me is at the farm with you all, and part of me is over with Roy, and as the ship moves I'm stretched thinner and thinner between.

Have you had any news of Jack?

Your loving daughter,

Sarah

•

We soon grew accustomed to shipboard life. The loudspeakers in the cabins and passageways were the source of all information, and Clarence was there if we needed help finding something. He brought us fresh fruit if we desired it and ginger ale for Barbara's nausea. We were woken by the loudspeaker at six-thirty, and the five of us took turns with the shower and toilet.

At seven-thirty we went to breakfast; lunch was at eleven-thirty and dinner at five. After dinner we were allowed to mill about, but passageways were cleared at ten-thirty, when everyone had to be in their cabins with the lights out. I spent the first few days figuring out where things were, there were so many spaces to be explored. A few times a sailor would stop me to say, 'Passengers aren't meant to be down here, ma'am,' but most of the ship was open. Except for the sailors' quarters, of course. We weren't meant to fraternise with the sailors; in fact, they could get in a lot of trouble for even being seen with us.

The ship's previous life as a cruise liner was barely evident anymore—when it became a troop carrier all of the luxury items were stripped out—but luckily they'd kept the library intact, and I spent many hours there. There was also a chapel, a radio room, and what felt like acres of deck.

There was an infirmary ward staffed by nurses (we often took Barbara there, as she was still feeling unwell) and several large rooms that had been converted into nurseries. I liked to visit the babies; most of them seemed to be handling the voyage well. In their nursery, rows of high chairs stood beside racks of baby bottles and thousands of jars of strained fruit. I would imagine myself a mother, if it were still possible, my own neat nursery and the baby food I would keep in my pantry: strained peaches, pureed sweet potato, rice pudding, pureed pear. The bigger children had dolls and dollhouses, toy trucks and many sturdy little wooden ships.

Now that my seasickness had passed, I attacked the buffet table with gusto, imagining that one day I would be cooking this sort of food for Roy. (Of course, this was a fantasy, since I could barely cook the simple food I had grown up with.) One night, after cleaning my plate, I decided to choose something from the ice-cream cart.

A young man with a crew cut was scooping the different flavours from giant metal canisters into glass bowls.

'What would you like?' he asked, grinning. His shirtsleeves were rolled up to show an anchor tattoo on one bicep. The other bicep had a girl's name—Marie.

'What are the flavours?'

'Vanilla, chocolate, butter pecan and Neapolitan,' he said, pointing to the different canisters as he spoke. I'd never heard of Neapolitan, but it looked as though it had ribbons of chocolate, strawberry and vanilla, each distinct from the other, and you got all three flavours together in a single scoop. I stood there for a moment, unable to cope with all the possibilities.

He coughed politely into his arm.

'What's your favourite?' I asked.

'I'm partial to the butter pecan. But if you can't decide, you might want the Neapolitan. Or you could choose two or three.'

'I'll try butter pecan. I'll save the others for another night.'

He scooped the ice-cream into a bowl and handed it to me with a wink, saying, 'Good idea, there's plenty of choices aboard this ship.'

I hurried back to my seat, making a mental note not to flirt with the ice-cream boy again.

CHAPTER 15

Grandma is more excited than me that we are dining with the captain, and she insists we visit the hairdresser that afternoon. Her hair is set in curls and mine is blown straight. She paints my nails afterwards and I do hers—none of the elaborate designs we used to do in treatment, just a single colour, mauve for me and coral for her. Our cabin steward brings an ironing board and I iron Grandma's blue satin dress on the lowest setting, and then the summery white linen dress which I bought on sale at Anthropologie in the Grove. At seven we walk up, arm in arm. There is an elevator but Grandma insists she will be fine on the stairs.

'We'll take the elevator later,' she says. 'After we've had a few drinks.'

She looks so elegant in her long dress, her white hair a froth around her head, her lips painted and her eyes as bright as they ever were. Her cheeks are rosy from the trick she taught me the first time she showed me how to apply lipstick, in the hospital, when I was thirteen. She used a tissue to blot my lips, and then rubbed the tissue into what she called the apples of my cheeks: the part that sticks out when you smile.

I can imagine her, at twenty-two, leaning over the railing as the ship pulled away from the shore, waving to Dot as the band played and the streamers snapped. But I cannot fathom what it must have meant to leave everything she had, to venture into the unknown without plans to return. Everything we do now is so safe. Even the short trips I've been on—to Mexico, England, France—have been planned months beforehand. I have email, I have my phone, I have my return tickets and travel insurance and a spare credit card and photocopies of my passport in case it is lost or damaged. I have an itinerary that says where I will stay every night and the numbers people can reach me on if my phone isn't working. I know what the hotel will look like from websites and travel reviews. I know what to expect from everything. Maybe the not-knowing was part of what made it so thrilling. Maybe it's why we seek danger in other ways now.

Alex is waiting for us on the bridge, looking sharp in his white short-sleeved uniform shirt with epaulets and gold braid. He has on white pants and a naval-looking cap, which he removes to greet Grandma, a gesture that makes her cheeks turn even pinker than the blotted lipstick has made them. I can see that she likes him, and after he compliments us and leans in to kiss my cheek, he guides us with a hand on each back and leads us into the small oak-panelled dining room. There are twelve or so people already there, and their names leave me as quickly as I hear them, except for the captain, whose first name is Sam, and who has a silver-flecked black beard that shakes like a bush of birds when he laughs. I am seated next to Alex; Grandma is on his other side, next to the captain, who immediately begins talking to her about Australia and the places they have both been. Alex and I sit in awkward silence as a steward pours my wine.

'I forgot to ask,' Alex says, 'is there anything you don't eat?'

'No,' I lie, 'I eat everything.' My stomach has already tightened to a fist in dread of this meal.

'Good to hear.'

On my other side is the cruise director, who asks what activities Grandma and I have done on board the ship.

'We've mostly been talking,' I say, 'so not much.'

'Oh, that's a shame. Did you know we have at least ten activities happening every hour between six am and ten pm? Swing dancing, Pilates, poker club, tea parties, bingo, history lectures, music appreciation, mosaic-making, stretch and tone . . .' She ticks them off on her fingers. 'There's so much happening— you've got to be in it to win it.'

'Win it?' Alex repeats. 'What exactly do you win in an exercise class?'

She ignores him. 'Does your grandmother play bridge? Bingo? Does she like to scrapbook?'

I shrug as the woman tells us about a bridge competition taking place at this very moment.

'What does the winner get?' Alex asks, as bowls of creamy soup are placed in front of us. 'A trophy?'

'A keychain,' she answers. 'With a picture of the ship.'

I try to suppress my grin and take a tiny mouthful of soup, burning the tissue-thin skin inside my mouth.

'You okay?' Alex asks, and I realise I must have flinched. My eyes are watering. I can feel a flap of skin on the roof of my mouth that has peeled away. I nod and glance at Grandma. She is still deep in conversation with the captain.

'Sorry about the seating,' Alex whispers, his breath warm against my ear. 'I didn't know she was coming, and, well . . .'

'Don't worry,' I whisper back. 'Just keep talking, please.'

CHAPTER 16

They are whispering, their heads together, and there is colour in Hannah's cheeks, probably from the wine. It bothers me that she does not recognise her own loveliness, that she does not know that she will look back in twenty, thirty, forty years and wish she had enjoyed her beauty while it was so vivid. I am glad to see her flirting with Alex. I would have done the same at her age; he has that quality of looking you straight in the eyes when you speak, as though he is listening closely, considering what you say. And of course he is handsome. Part of me wants to tell her to beware of handsome men, or those who know that they are, but I have to remind myself that things are different now. There is less at stake. I envy the freedom she has to spend a decade sleeping with different men, deciding which one is right for her. Practising living together, playing at keeping house.

The captain is telling me about his children, who are Hannah's age—in their twenties—and he sees me watching my granddaughter and Alex. He smiles, and I can tell he understands but does not want to say anything in case they overhear and are embarrassed.

'When I was Hannah's age I travelled from Sydney to San Francisco on a ship full of war brides and their children,' I tell him.

•

Up on deck one day I saw a woman with a little girl tied to her: the mother had one end of the rope around her wrist and the other end was tied around the little girl's waist. The mum kept dozing off, and so the rope was her way of minding the child, who was too young to be trusted on her own. Every time the girl came to the end of the rope it would jerk her, and tug on the mother, and the girl would wail and the mother get cross. I thought about how much I missed Mum; it felt like there was a rope tying us together as well.

I went over and offered to mind the child for a bit. The woman—Shirley was her name—said that she and the girl, Iris, had been having a rough journey.

'There's twelve of us, mothers and babies, in our cabin, and we're low in the ship with no portholes, so the room is stuffy and damp all of the time, and each time one of the babies gets sick we all do. We've all spent the trip with diarrhoea, vomiting and everything else you can imagine.'

I said I would take Iris for a little stroll if Shirley wanted to nap on one of the deckchairs, and she took me up on it. As I held the girl's chubby little hand and walked from one end of the deck to the other, I wondered what things would be like now if Roy and I hadn't been careful, if I had fallen pregnant on our wedding night and was bringing our child with me. What if it had been our only chance? Why is it only when opportunities are lost that we start to wish for them so keenly? I wanted a tangible piece of him, but I also knew that the journey would be much more difficult with a baby. Now I only had to be responsible for myself, and though I felt trepidation at what lay ahead, and sorrow for what I had left behind, it was also an adventure.

I kneeled down to Iris's height by the railing and pointed out the seagulls diving into the water. 'Birds!' she called.

'If you're lucky, you might see a dolphin. I saw a school out of them here yesterday.'

I looked up and one of the naval officers stood above us in his white uniform with dark blue epaulets. I stood up as well. He had binoculars in his hand and passed them to me, and I held them low for Iris to look through.

'How old is your little girl?'

'Oh, she's not mine. I'm just watching her. But I think she's about two.'

The officer nodded and smiled. It was a smart uniform, certainly, and I thought of Min and the innumerable times she'd already mentioned her naval officer husband.

'Do you have children?' I asked.

He shook his head. 'One day I'd like to. I'll wait until I leave the navy though. I'd hate to miss out on seeing 'em grow.'

'That sounds smart. Have you got a wife?'

As soon as the words were out of my mouth I wanted to grab them and shove them back in. He shook his head and looked away. For a moment all was quiet except for the screaming gulls.

'Would you like to take her up to see the wheelhouse? Have you been up there yet?'

'I haven't. Are we allowed?'

'Not normally, but I can take you.'

'Let me just go tell her mum.'

'I'll wait here.'

When I got to Shirley's deckchair she was fast asleep, so I decided not to wake her. We returned and the officer held out his hand.

'I'm Jim, by the way.'

'Sarah.' I hadn't shaken many hands in my life and it made me worry I was doing it all wrong. Were you meant to squeeze? I was glad when he let go. I lifted Iris and she shook his hand with her chubby little one.

'Iris,' she said quite seriously in her squeaky voice, and Jim and I grinned.

'Hello, young lady. Nice to make your acquaintance.'

We followed Jim up sets of narrow stairs to the bridge. As we walked he pointed to various doors. 'Chief engineer's room, staff captain's room, captain's dayroom, captain's room, chart room, my room . . .' He paused.

'You're up here then? What's your role?'

'Ensign.' Jim's face flushed. I could see he was both proud of his position and embarrassed by his pride.

We stood at the door of the wheel room and Jim pointed out a binnacle, a steering telegraph, an engine telegraph. He showed us the radio room, where the wireless operator, wearing headphones, was turning the dials on a large black machine, writing something down. Beside it was the telegraph room, which held a telegraph machine and a switchboard.

'Are we allowed to go and see the engine room?' I asked.

Jim looked at his watch. 'Can I show you another time? I'm meant to be on duty in five minutes, and it will take us twice that to get there.'

'Of course. Another time.'

Jim carried Iris down the steep staircase to the main deck for me, then he hurried off to report for duty. Shirley ran up, looking flushed and frantic.

'There you are! Oh, thank God—Iris.' She took her daughter and clutched her tight. Iris began to whinge and squirm.

'I'm sorry, Shirley, an officer offered to show us the bridge, and I came to tell you but you were asleep . . .'

'I got such a fright. I forgot that you had her when I woke, I was in such a daze, and I thought I'd fallen asleep looking after her and that she must have fallen overboard and drowned. It was the most awful feeling.'

Shirley was crying now, and Iris patted her mother's arm. 'Dere, dere,' she said, and we both laughed, Shirley laughing and crying at once. She never asked me to watch Iris again, and for many years I didn't understand it. I didn't understand the sheer terror that comes with having children, the possibility of losing something much more important than yourself. The love so deep it defies logic, knowledge or reason.

•

When Jim showed us the radio and telegraph room he'd explained how only the most important messages could be conveyed this way, because they competed with maritime signals and other communications between ships. We were officially a US naval ship, and though the war was over, navy protocol remained.

In the week we'd been on board I'd only twice heard of brides receiving radio or telegraph messages. One was from a girl's mother back in Sydney—her father had died. I saw the woman, slight and splotchy, weeping in the dining room. She was given the option of disembarking when we stopped in Suva, in Fiji, and taking the next ship home, but she decided to continue her journey to America.

Brynn said, 'She's scared if she goes back to Australia now she'll never leave,' and I understood completely.

The second message was for a woman who was not yet married—her fiancé was from New York. He sent a telegram saying that he no longer wanted her to come. She wasn't the weeping kind. She lay unmoving on a deckchair, refusing to speak, until she left the boat in Suva.

Suva was all we had spoken of for days by the time we docked there; it was our sole chance to leave the boat during the journey, and we would only be allowed one day to walk around. None of us in our cabin had ever been outside Australia, so the chance to see a different country was a thrill I felt physically, a prickle on my skin. Min didn't seem to understand why we were so excited.

'It's not as though it's civilised,' she said. 'I don't think I'll even bother getting off. You never know what to expect from natives.'

Brynn rolled her eyes and I tried to suppress my snort. It was hard to say what you really thought of a person's opinions when you shared a tiny cabin for three weeks. Certain words could not be retracted.

As it turned out, the Fijians were gathered on the wharf to meet our ship, and they welcomed us with singing. I tried not to stare but I had never seen such dark skin swathed in such bright fabric, the contrast of colour. Some wore their hair loose and others in intricate braids, and there were some men with their hair shorn, dressed in similar clothes to those you would see on the streets of Sydney.

How good it felt to step onto solid land. There were palm trees in a little park beyond the wharf, and just to lean against the trunk of one and feel bark against my skin, the scratchiness of it, to feel something which was not man-made, was delicious. The cabin had become stifling with everyone's bodies and breath, the damp and the salt air. Brynn had a little Brownie camera and we took turns photographing one another leaning against the palms, beneath a sky unsullied by clouds. We walked up Usher Street to the markets and spent some of our carefully folded US dollars on souvenirs for our new families in America. I bought a little wooden mask and some necklaces made of shells and beads. And then we saw the wide white arches of a hotel, the Metropole.

'Surely it's time for a drink,' Brynn said.

Once our eyes adjusted to the dim lighting we saw a long, polished bar crowded with men, and then small tables served by waiters dressed in white uniforms. Ceiling fans spun lazily overhead. We sat at a table and ordered rum cocktails and leaned back against the cushions of the cane chairs. Some of the sailors from the *Mariposa* were at the table beside ours, and they tried to buy us drinks, but we refused.

'We want to make it back on board the ship on time,' Brynn said sweetly, so as not to hurt their feelings.

I hadn't noticed Jim when we entered, but he must've seen us and made his way over.

'These are married women,' he said to the sailors, gesturing with his own fruit-garnished drink. 'Watch yourselves.'

'Thank you, but we are perfectly capable of looking after ourselves,' I said to him. My tone must have come out sharper than I intended, as the sailors beside us snickered and Jim gave a neat little bow and retreated to the bar without another word.

Brynn pinched my thigh.

'What?'

'He's the one who showed you the bridge, isn't he?'

'Yes, and?'

'You ought to be nicer to him, the way he looks at you.'

'He doesn't look at me in any way.'

Brynn sighed and drained the last of her cocktail. The paper straws wilted as quickly as the ice melted. 'Does too. Now let's go. If I have another drink I'll stay in Suva forever.'

•

As the ship drew away from the wharf I stood on deck alone, feeling the breeze press my skirt around my knees, and the strange pang of homesickness for a place I had only known for a day, wishing we could have stayed longer. I had never been terrified and amazed by so much, and I tried to figure out whether it was fear of arrival that made me want to slow the journey, or the journey itself. Before this, the furthest I had been was the distance between the South Coast and Sydney—some six or seven hours.

For the first time our arrival in America became something real. And then I would have to get to know Roy all over again. We had become so tender in our letters to one another, but I couldn't forget my hesitation before we married, the fear that I'd rushed into something I'd regret. So yes, there were days when I just wanted to stop time, and I would lie on a deck-chair in the sun, watching the gulls overhead, listening to the rumble of the engine from far below.

A day after leaving Suva the main Red Cross representative, Miss Farr, knocked on our door.

'The captain wants to see you,' she said to me.

Startled, I replied that I would be right out. Brynn and Jane were sprawled on their bunks and Barbara was in the bath-room, probably vomiting into the toilet beneath the showerhead. I quickly pinned back the loose strands of my hair and reapplied lipstick in front of the little mirror above the sink.

'What's happened?' Brynn asked, tossing her magazine to the floor.

'No idea. The captain wants to see me.' My hand was shaking and I had to wipe the lipstick off and start again. I wondered if something had happened at home.

'It's probably nothing. Do you want me to come?' Brynn stood and brushed biscuit crumbs from her skirt.

'I'll be fine. Can I borrow your cardigan though? The pale blue one?'

Brynn fetched it for me, and I slipped it on.

Miss Farr was waiting when I shut the cabin door behind me.

'This way.' She spoke as though she were snipping the words with scissors.

Her dress billowed behind her and her neat, white tri-cornered cap bobbed ahead of me up the steps. Miss Farr was older than all of us, probably in her late forties, and there were deep lines beside her mouth that looked as though they were etched by disappointment. I hadn't once seen her smile. She normally dealt with the girls who were particularly homesick or had what we called 'women's problems'—those girls whose monthlies had stopped or who had something else going on down below.

The weather had grown rough after breakfast, and the waves were spilling over A Deck. We held on to the rails as we climbed, and I felt the familiar nausea swirling at the pit of my belly. The air was dense with an approaching tropical storm.

Miss Farr knocked at the teak door of the captain's dayroom and all the dread and nausea churned inside me. I had only ever seen the captain from afar.

'Come in,' he called.

I followed Miss Farr inside. There on a floral upholstered couch sat the captain. He had cropped grey hair and sharp features. Jim stood beside him, a stiff expression on his face.

'Good day, ma'am,' the captain said, standing. 'You are Mrs Sarah Jackson, from Sydney?'

I cleared my throat. 'Yes.' My voice squeaked like an old hinge. Was this about how I'd spoken to Jim in Suva? I felt furious at him for dragging me in front of the captain, for not speaking to me himself if I had angered him.

'Please, sit down.' He sat and gestured to Miss Farr to sit as well. 'This is Ensign Jim Rice; I believe you've met?'

I nodded. I felt sweat bead on my forehead, roll down my neck, pool between my breasts and at the waistband of my skirt.

'Mrs Jackson, we received a radio message from your mother yesterday.'

'What's happened?' I looked from the captain to Jim, who was studying his shoes intently, refusing to meet my eyes.

'I'm afraid they've received confirmation that your brother Jack died in a Japanese POW camp. I'm so sorry to give you this news.'

The sweat felt as though it were melted ice. 'No. They must be mistaken.'

Miss Farr put her hand on my arm. 'Now, dear . . .'

I moaned, a sound that I didn't even recognise as my own, and felt the hope I'd held on to ripped away.

'Mrs Jackson . . . Sarah.' Jim had pulled over a chair to sit beside me, his stiffness gone. 'I'm so sorry. If you like, you can return home to be with your parents, but your mother said to tell you not to come home, that you were to continue your journey.'

The captain nodded, looking down at his hands rather than at me.

'You'll not make yourself sick, Mrs Jackson, with sorrow,' Miss Farr said sternly, patting my hand as if I were some sort of imbecile.

I was breathing fast and shallow, my face wet and my voice trapped in my nose. I wanted to jump over the side and be swallowed by the sea. I wanted grief to sink me like stones in my pockets.

Miss Farr looked at me with her tight mouth. 'There, there, dear. There, there.'

I couldn't bear the pity in their eyes. I stood up abruptly and rushed from the room.

Outside the rain had begun to fall and the bridge was slippery with it, sheets of water blown by the wind, sailors on the decks below clearing the chairs and battening down for a storm. I ran across the deck and as close to the bow as I could get, leaning into the metal rail, letting the rain drench me completely, the spray from the waves soak me. It was so thick I could not even see the sea beneath us but I knew it was there. How quickly it would hide me in this weather. It was my leaving which made this happen. If I had only stayed, if the family were still together, if our hope was unbroken, he would still be alive. He would have made it home. I put my foot on the middle rail, so the top pressed into my thighs. It was vertiginous, a dizzy feeling which kept my head quiet for a moment—two. Somewhere beneath the rain and crashing waves was the thrum of the ship's engine, a sound so deep I felt it in my bones.

Then hands grabbed my waist and pulled me down, wrapped a coat around me. I was pressed against something smelling of wet wool and diesel fuel.

'I promise it's not the end of the world.'

I tried to twist away from him but pictured his kind face in the captain's office, how he had pulled up a chair to sit beside me.

'Let's go inside. I'll make you a cup of cocoa and fetch your friend. It's an awful thing, war, but it will do your parents no good to lose you as well.'

I could not even speak to reply. Brynn's cardigan was sopping wet, probably ruined from the rain.

•

'It doesn't matter,' she said, half an hour later, as I passed it to her in a heavy bundle, along with the wet clothes which I had changed out of. My teeth chattered. It wasn't even cold, but Jim said it was probably the shock of it all. We sat in the captain's mess—empty, thankfully, apart from us—and as promised Jim had brought me towels, cocoa and Brynn. He'd also found a dressing-gown—only he called it a bathrobe—which surely must have been his own, as it brushed the tops of my feet.

Brynn held my hand and stroked it. 'Your mum said not to come back, didn't she?'

'She's just being brave,' I said. 'She'll be lost.'

'But what about you?' Jim said, drinking from a glass of whiskey that the steward had brought with the cocoa.

'What do you mean?'

'If you go back, it would mean postponing the rest of your life. I think your mum was telling the truth: she'd probably rather think of you happy, starting anew.'

•

I lay in my bunk for the next four days, curled as tight as a cat, pressing my face into the blankets, wishing myself home. None of the others knew what to do with me. I heard Min whispering, 'Oh, how awful, can you imagine?' and Barbara shushing her. Brynn approached with offers of toast and mugs of cocoa. I lay looking out the porthole and watched the ocean and sky, a line that moved up and down and only changed marginally in hue—the water nearly always darker, always the thing beneath. I knew that he would have died an awful death. Beaten and starved, sick until he could work no more. I found small ways to hurt myself, which stopped the thoughts for moments. Pulling out my hair, strand by strand. Digging my fingernails into my skin so hard they left angry red crescents.

The rain kept coming for days, a flood of water. I dreamed of Blackie's warm muzzle, her cold death. I dreamed I left her in a valley where she drowned, unable to swim, still tied to her chain.

On the fourth day Jim came. 'There's another message,' he said.

I sat bolt upright and banged my head on the ceiling.

'Careful.' He winced.

The others left the cabin, but I could sense Min behind the door, her ear to the metal. I hoped Brynn would drag her away.

'It's from your mum,' he said, and my skin was sharp with goosebumps.

I hadn't eaten or bathed in days, hadn't brushed my hair, and I imagined briefly what I must look like to Jim. He didn't seem to care.

He took the slip of paper out of his pocket and cleared his throat. He suddenly thought of something and went pale. 'Do you want me to get Miss Farr?'

'God, no. Just read the bloody thing.'

I could see him force down a smile at my language. I nearly smiled myself then, remembering the phrase my father used to use: 'foul enough to make a sailor blush'.

Dad would be proud.

The message was only a few words copied onto a slip of paper. Had Jim written them down or the radio operator? There were so many strangers who must be speaking about me in hushed voices.

Jim was holding up the paper for me but I couldn't see the words. My eyes were swimming with tears.

'Just go. I want to read it alone.'

I lay back down on my pillow and heard him place the slip of paper on my sheets. He shut the door quietly behind him, and there was a murmur of voices in the corridor outside. I rolled over onto my side and looked at the paper, as thin as my skin. I could feel the bones of my knees pressing together, the hollowness inside me. I curled my fingers and toes and shut my eyes. Sometimes it is worse to know than not know. I didn't want to know what my mum had to say. If they had buried Jack. If his remains were never found. The ship pitched to starboard—the weather was worsening—and the movement caused the paper to fall. I forced myself to climb down from the bunk to snatch it. I knew I had to look.

JACK'S SERVICE HELD TODAY AT MILTON PRESBYTERIAN. KEEP GOING TO ROY. NOTHING NEEDED HERE. LOVE, MUM, DAD AND FRED.

They had said goodbye without me.

I must have cried out, because Brynn rushed in.

'Are you okay, Sarah? What happened?'

I shook my head, holding the paper out to her. 'They've had the funeral. I've got to keep going.'

She sat beside me and gathered me in her arms, so that my head was in her lap.

163

'Oh, Sarah. I'm so sorry.' Her fingers in my hair were like leaves, and I slept beneath a eucalypt in the paddock, dreaming back what I'd left and lost.

•

Brynn helped me shower and change. I hadn't washed my clothes all week so she lent me a top and a pair of trousers. We were close in size, but she was a little taller, so they were baggy around my ankles. I had never had a pair of trousers. I rolled them up and she brushed my hair after it was dry. The other girls had returned to the cabin and Brynn told them the news for me. I was glad not to have to speak, merely nodding at their murmured condolences. As we walked down the corridor to the dining room, I felt like I had been split open and glued back together again, but not quite in the right places. I didn't know what to say or how to move my face anymore. It all felt somehow wrong.

The dining room was nearly empty as mealtime was almost over. Brynn went to the counter to ask if there was any broth I could have; she said she would tell them I had been ill. As she walked off I saw some women who were getting up from a nearby table look at me intently. They left, talking in low voices. I wanted to shrink into my seat.

Jim appeared from behind me and sat in the chair beside mine. 'Is there anything you'd like me to do?'

I shook my head.

'Brynn said you're going to keep on. I think you're doing the right thing.'

Brynn returned with a tray then.

'Hi.' She nodded at Jim and they exchanged a look that showed they'd talked about me at length. She patted my shoulder. 'They'll have some soup for you in five minutes. I've brought you a roll and some vanilla pudding.'

'Thanks,' I said, and turned to Jim. 'I know you're trying to be kind but I don't want anyone's sympathy. I'll be fine. I just want to be left alone.'

'Alright then.' He scraped his chair back and stood. 'Good evening, ladies.' He marched away, replacing the white cap he must have taken off when he sat beside me.

'Thank you,' Brynn called after him. She faced me with her lips pressed together.

'What?'

'You could have been nicer. Oh, never mind. Just eat your soup.'

And just as she said the words a sailor set it in front of me: a bowl of yellow broth funnelling steam, flakes of dried parsley floating on the surface.

I can still taste that soup; it was chicken broth, with soft grains of rice sunk to the bottom and small cubes of carrot, celery and translucent slippery onion. Globules of fat shimmered on the surface, and while my hand shook bringing the spoon to my lips, each mouthful was like a sip of warmth which spread into my face and my chest. This was not the end.

'How is it?' Brynn asked, slicing her thin grey steak and piercing it with her fork.

'Good,' I said, and made myself smile, feeling the effort it took to rearrange my face.

CHAPTER 17

At four in the morning I gather my clothes from the floor. I dress by the moonlight coming in through the window. Alex's room is stark—a small bed against one wall, a desk against the other, an open-doored closet where half a dozen identical shirts hang like empty torsos. The night before is fuzzy—I feel that sinking sense that I've embarrassed myself but I can't recall how. Why do I do this? I won't drink for the rest of the trip. The rest of my life. Regret makes my whole body hurt.

Alex is asleep in the single bed—I can't believe the two of us fitted in there—and his mouth is slightly open, triangular, slack against the pillow. There is his bare chest with the sheet at his hip, loosely tucked to hide his soft penis in its nest of curls, testicles hanging in their sac of loose skin. Last night comes back to me in brief scenes.

My glass refilled again and again by the steward and all of the voices rising; shouting and laughter filling the room as the night went on.

Grandma talking about her brother Jack, who died as a prisoner of war. The radio message she'd received while on the ship, and how she'd wanted to return home.

The captain telling a story about an outbreak of gastro that caused the evacuation of an entire cruise ship of passengers on a small Pacific island. How the local hospital couldn't cope.

Alex's leg pressed against mine beneath the table.

Grandma tipping her head back to laugh, the silver flash of her fillings, the quiver in the hand that held her glass. An image of her hurting herself, pulling out her own hair, but I don't know where it came from. A story she told? Does she know how physical pain can save you—can make the real pain disappear?

I remember the textures of the crème brûlée—the crunch of the toffee, the smooth sweet butteriness inside. I must have eaten the entire thing.

Walking Grandma to our room. The three of us huddled together with laughter. Alex waiting outside while I helped her find her nightgown. Her toothbrush. While I kissed her goodnight.

'I'm going to stay up a little later with Alex,' I must have said, and Grandma smiled, her eyes already closed.

'Have fun,' she murmured. 'Stay out as late as you like.'

Walking the length of the ship on the promenade deck, the sky clear, the challenge of another race. Holding the dress at my waist, him beating me, blaming the dress.

The stumble of a kiss, my balance uneven from wine, his breath sharp-tasting and the skin of his back soft beneath my fingers, covering ribs and muscle and the knobs of his spine.

The different smell of him: chemical smells I don't recognise and, beneath, the earthy smell of his sweat, sweet-musky, like when you strip the bark from a tree.

His room somehow—I can't remember how we ended up there—and our bodies without clothes, the bones of them bumping together, the skin rubbing and stickiness and latex smell. I remember the feeling of sex, that wonderful drunk sense of being obliterated by it. There but also gone. Also elsewhere, and the caught gasp of it. The fucking beauty. Ridiculous.

Now it is just four-in-the-morning slide and sorrow. How could you let him, Hannah? Why would you do this to someone you love? How could you do this to Ash? How could you let him see your ugly body? How could you lose control like that? Berating myself all the way back to the cabin—so stupid; how could you be so stupid—and then pressing the handle quietly, pushing open the heavy fireproof door. Slipping off my shoes, dress, underpants and bra. Beneath the pillow my PJs. Not even brushing my teeth. The bump of my elbow against the nightstand, muttering, 'Fuck,' and Grandma turning, waking or half asleep still but hearing.

'Hannah,' she murmurs, and I say, 'Sorry, Grandma. It's late. Go back to sleep.'

'Okay, love,' she says, and turns on her side, facing the wall, away from me, so her voice is muffled but I still hear what she says.

'I'm glad you had fun.'

I lie in bed thinking of Ash. When I sleep at his apartment he brings me a cup of coffee in bed in the morning. He always uses the mug he knows I like best, the speckled blue one. The morning we left to pick up Grandma he brought me my coffee and sat on the edge of the bed, making up a song about Hannah and bananas from Alabama, grinning in that guileless way of his when I hit him with a pillow and told him to shut up. There is something wrong with me that I could do this to him—to us.

•

Sometimes I feel as though my life can be measured in setbacks. Steps backwards rather than forwards. Ground lost instead of gained. The freedom of moving away from home to go to college my freshman year, the scholarship I had to study at the University of Virginia, the grades and SAT scores which had gotten me there were all usurped by the after. The residence hall of other young women, the dining hall where we studied each other's trays: how much was there, how much was left uneaten. My roommate who shared her caffeine pills and ipecac. I could stay up longer, eat less, drink more, and never had I felt so unencumbered. Those were months of being mere bone and brain. It felt good.

I was light and exceedingly free.

But I was also blacking out at parties and waking up in strange beds, strange couches, on unfamiliar floors, with boys I didn't know—or maybe I did and couldn't remember? I had bruises from linoleum, from closet doors, from I didn't know what. Rug burns on my elbows, the small of my back. I was sore but I could not remember why. Still I sought obliteration. There was nothing, it seemed, my body couldn't sustain.

Mom took one look at me when I came home for the mid-year break and said I couldn't return.

'I thought you were better,' she said.

'Oh, Hannah,' Grandma said.

'What happened?' Dad asked. He actually cried on the phone. He said he wished that he could help.

I told him not to worry. I told him, all of them, I was sorry for letting them down.

CHAPTER 18

I re-entered shipboard life slowly. The level of giddiness on board increased the closer we got to San Francisco. Outfits were hastily mended, washing pegged from the ropes and railings of the boat, where it flapped in the breeze. The little commissary sold out of leg paint, lipstick and hairpins. I existed outside this level of thrill; all I wished for now was to finish the voyage quickly, to get there. I noticed more and more women ducking around corners, behind lifeboats with sailors. Of course there were whispers. Jane had a sailor who would call by the room sometimes and they went 'walking'.

Min would start up as soon as the door shut behind them. 'I have half a mind to tell her husband myself if he's waiting for her in San Francisco.'

Brynn would respond: 'Tell him what? Let her walk, Min. She's not doing any harm.'

Min would snort then head off to practise piano in the lounge. She was playing Beethoven's Moonlight Sonata for the talent show that had been organised to make the last days pass more quickly. Brynn was juggling—a trick her older brothers had taught her—and Jane was dancing with a group of girls she often sat with at mealtimes. Their table had the most raucous laughter, and I sometimes wished I could sit with them, though I knew I wouldn't fit in. It felt like years since I had laughed. I had seen them practising and knew the dance would be a hit with the sailors—they wore shorts and brassiere tops, swaying their hips to Glenn Miller's 'In the Mood'. Barbara and I were not doing anything. She said nobody wanted to see her looking like she'd swallowed a watermelon. Crying was my only talent lately, and no one wanted to see that either.

It's a strange phenomenon I've observed throughout my life that once your negative thoughts about yourself begin, they can easily spiral out of control. Mum not wanting me to come home for the funeral became no one ever wanting me, and I began a list in my head of foolish things I had said and done to make people not love me. I forgot the ambivalence I had felt about Roy at first and only remembered how I had dragged him away from the reception and made a sour face when he wanted to share a taxi with his friends, how he had fallen asleep on our wedding night. The truth was we'd had so little time together that it was easy to overthink each of our encounters and attempt to pinpoint a time when his love for me had begun to diminish.

'You're being crazy,' Brynn said when I told her my worries as we walked the deck one windy morning, the day before the talent show and three days before we were due to dock in San

Francisco. 'You need to stop thinking those thoughts. Do you know how foolish they are?'

We stood looking out to the grey ocean, the waves white at the tips as they crashed into the hull of the ship, tiny drops of spray landing on the skin of my face, the salt water making it feel stretched and tight as it dried in the wind. Brynn turned to face me, pulling a stiff clump of hair from my mouth. The wind in my eyes meant she couldn't tell I was crying.

Brynn decided that I needed to be kept busy, and since she couldn't get me to perform in the talent show she insisted that I help with the set design and decoration. The committee of women who had organised the thing were like every committee I came across later in life. People inflated with a sense of self-importance; nitpicking and power trips over things as inconsequential as chair configuration and bunting colours. I kept my mouth shut and worked diligently, twirling and sticky-taping lengths of streamers, typing programs to mimeograph and painting backdrops on bedsheets stretched and tacked into place. There were more artistic girls than me on board, but I could do a swathe of sky and lose myself in the purpose of filling every white space with blue.

The day of the show I woke up early to help hang the backdrops. The show was to be held in the ballroom and sailors were in there helping to move furniture and set out chairs. Up on the stage talking to the committee were the ship's captain and Jim. I carried a great long roll of painted bedsheet to the back of the stage, a box of tacks in the pocket of my skirt.

Jim glanced over at me and I smiled. I'd thought often of

how rude I'd been to him and had been hoping for the chance to say sorry. Perhaps this would be it.

But he just blinked and looked away.

I hurried to tack the sheets into place and did a shoddy job, hardly able to see for the haze of tears in front of my eyes. I didn't want to even see this show. Why was I even there? Brynn was wrong to think it would keep my mind off things. It just made me more aware of what I'd lost.

Thanks to my half-hearted effort, the bedsheet with the painted sky and sea, the palm trees swaying on tiny islands, the distant silhouettes of seagulls dotting the sky, fluttered to the ground in the middle of Min's piano performance that afternoon. The choked-back laughter made her hands stumble over the notes and I felt sorry for her as she stood and curtsied at the end. She was the sort of person who would always be disappointed. Others would never measure up to the exacting standards she held herself to.

The show went on for hours, and the ballroom grew stuffy. Most of the sailors who could be excused from their duties came, and their whistles and clapping were particularly loud for Jane and her friends, who shimmied and shook across every inch of the stage, not exactly in time but with enthusiasm to spare. Their costumes showed more skin than they covered, but that skin was all golden tan and unblemished. I stood up and applauded at the end of their performance, and for Brynn's—not just because they were my friends, but because I could see that they were the genuine article. Brynn didn't sit around and brood about what others would think of her juggling; she didn't worry that people would whisper or laugh or think her not ladylike enough. She got out there with her broad shoulders and long legs, her infectious smile, and made it all look so effortless.

Even at that moment I knew exactly where in the room Jim was, towards the front on the starboard side, his hat in his lap, appearing relaxed and laughing with the other officers. Not once did he turn and look back at the audience, though I was certain he felt my eyes on the back of his neck, the hair bristling where it had been shorn by the ship's barber. When he got up to leave during the intermission, he walked straight past me without so much as a glance. Barbara and I stood to leave not long after.

'I'm starving,' she said as we stepped out into the cool air of the early evening. 'Will you come to the dining room with me?'

We walked in silence along the narrow passageways of the ship. I thought of how we were landing in two days, and how the last three weeks of my life had been the strangest yet. Learning of Jack's death in one part of the world while I was steaming towards another, both of us as far as imaginable from our shared childhood. Yet that was where I thought of him now: not in a prison camp, but running down the bracken-spackled hill as fast as his short legs would carry him, me giving chase, Blackie bounding ahead. I could hear his baby laugh still, that high cackle of joy.

We pushed through the swinging doors into the large empty dining room and headed over to the buffet, which was still being set up: big metal trays of steaks, mashed potatoes, salad, green beans, dinner rolls, creamed corn, dishes of butter and gravy, mustard and dressing. Barbara filled her plate and I took some salad and potato, a soft white roll. As plentiful and appetising as the food was, I missed the familiarity of the bread at home, the denser texture, the absence of that airy sweetness. And I preferred the flavour of lamb to this bland dry beef we always ate.

We sat and Barbara talked of the nursery she would set up for her child, the clothes she had been sewing, how her husband's mother had been asking whether she would baptise the baby once it was born. Barbara was Protestant but had married a Catholic from a large Italian family in Boston.

'I wonder what it will be like, having all these relatives all of a sudden, all these strangers in my life?' She chewed thoughtfully, her face rounded and flushed, looking more like a girl at that moment than a woman.

I shrugged and we both ate in silence, lost in our thoughts about a future that was unknowable, despite our furious imagining.

•

How I would have survived those last days without Brynn I'll never know, for the despair of travelling to the future while longing for the past is as bad as any I have felt. She and I lay side by side in deckchairs on our final day on board the *Mariposa*, wrapped in our coats as the weather had turned cold. She read to me from a pamphlet the Red Cross ladies had been handing out: 'A Bride's Guide to the USA'. It was compiled by *Good Housekeeping* in Britain for brides moving to America from England, but the Red Cross had told us that the advice ought to apply to us as well.

'*Keep your accent while you can,*' Brynn read in her haughtiest voice. '*Most English accents, especially when spoken by a girl, are regarded in America as charming.*'

'Where are you from, little lady?' I replied in a deep Southern drawl.

Brynn swatted me with the pamphlet. 'Pay attention. You'll never succeed in bride school if you don't pay attention.'

'Pardon me. Continue.'

'*Remember that, except in the smallest towns, lipstick is expected.*'

'Even on men?'

'Especially on men.'

'So wear lipstick and speak with a Pommy accent?'

'Wait, there's more.' Brynn flipped some pages. '*Work.*' She read: '*Your main job will be running the house. Since your husband's prospects of promotion may be improved by an attractive home, you may add more to the family budget by homemaking than by working for pay, unless you can get a really good job at a good salary.*'

'Promotion to what? Head tobacco farmer?'

'And what, pray tell, is a good salary?'

'Give me some hopeful news, please!'

Brynn flipped more pages, frowning and pursing her lips.

'Quick!'

'Shut up . . . Oh, here we go. This is the best news I've heard all day. *No one will think you are a lazy housewife when you use tinned food, if it is good.*'

'Really?'

Brynn nodded.

'That's the best news you can find?'

'Tinned peas. Hallelujah.'

I snatched the pamphlet from her hands. The cover had a photograph of a happy-looking couple dressed in civilian clothes, standing in front of the Statue of Liberty. She was leaning into him, and he stood strong, his two American feet firmly planted on his home soil. I leaped out of the deckchair and ran to the railing.

'What're you doing? Sarah!' Brynn followed me, reaching out to grab my arm, but I evaded her grasp.

I tossed the booklet as far out to sea as I could. A few brides watching us gasped, and Brynn put her arm around my waist, both of us watching as the sodden speck of white grew more distant. A seagull swooped in and bobbed beside it for a moment before flying off, beak empty.

'See?' I said. 'Even he recognises how useless it is.'

Brynn rubbed my back, sighing, looking at the distant horizon where we had been told America lay.

'You'll be fine,' she said, her voice thick with the tears I had swallowed. 'I know you will.'

•

When I recall the day we pulled into the harbour at San Francisco I think of the low fog, the deep, eerie horns which broke through my sleep that morning like fish breaking the surface of water. I dressed quickly, skipped breakfast and stood against the rail of the ship, the brides around me straining to see, patting their hairdos, pulling out compacts and reapplying lipstick. The engine strained as it turned and shifted, the red steel of the Golden Gate Bridge loomed, only appearing when it was just before us, magically revealed from beneath a layer of fog. I hadn't expected the low mountains on all sides of the harbour; their brown earth and scrub reminded me a little bit of home. But the sky was so different, so moody, as was the way light cut in rays through the patches of fog. There were fishing boats, tugs, ferries, sailboats and tinnies weaving and dodging through the chop. The wind whipped our hair into our mouths, across our eyes, lifting hems of skirts and dresses. The sailors were all business now, every one of them occupied.

A ferry pulled alongside us and many of the women began shrieking; there were husbands of some of the girls on board. They had a loudspeaker and called out to us, the men's voices crackling with static.

A US Army band played on the pier as we neared our berth. Brynn held my hand and danced with me. She had spotted her husband on the ferry, and they had waved and blown kisses.

'He looks strange,' she said, twirling me around. 'He's grown a moustache—he looks like someone's father.' We laughed and I wondered what Roy would look like. Few of the men were in uniform. The war was over.

The Red Cross ladies were frantically checking lists, and even after we docked it was ages before we were allowed off the boat. I suppose the logistics of organising six hundred and nine brides and two hundred and seventy-four children were quite complicated. They called us off alphabetically by surname, and Min was among the first to leave. She descended the gangway, two sailors following with her trunks.

'Goodbye, girls, and good luck. Do write.' She waved a

handkerchief at us, her face splotched with excitement. 'I hope it all turns out for the best.'

We strained for a glimpse of Min's husband. He was a portly white-haired man with spectacles and fleshy lips, which he immediately pressed against her, while she recoiled, nearly falling backwards into the harbour. We clutched each other, giggling.

Barbara, Jane and I were taking trains, and Brynn was among the next group called. She hugged me for a good minute, rubbing her gloved hands along my spine.

'You'll be fine, you'll be strong, whatever happens. It's an adventure. Think of the day when we'll tell these stories.'

I held her face and gave her a kiss on the cheek. 'How would I have made it this far without you?'

I watched as Brynn walked down the gangplank and her husband ran to greet her. He wrapped her in an embrace then bent to kiss her. I saw her soften, her shoulders drop and ease into their sockets. When they drew apart she looked back at the ship, eyes scanning the crowd still on board until she found me. She blew me a kiss and waved. I shut my eyes tight and wished they would be happy.

CHAPTER 19

'What happened to Brynn?' I ask. 'Did you stay in touch?'

We're sitting on the beach in Tonga, where the ship has stopped for the day. Most passengers are on cultural tours or shopping tours or have just gone off sightseeing on their own. Grandma asked what I would like to do and I said I just wanted to wander around the old town, sit on the beach, be away from crowds for a while. Away from Alex, I thought, but didn't say. One thing about a cruise is that you're always one of a horde. I know our visit is probably good for the economy of Nuku'alofa, but I can also sense the island cringing as the ship disgorges its cargo, white American tourists in leisure wear with fanny packs, comfortable shoes, sun visors and camera bags.

'We did write some letters,' Grandma says, running her fingers through the sand. 'It wasn't long before she had twins. They lived in San Diego, and we talked about visiting each other again one day, but it didn't happen, and our letters sort of faded away. We started up again when life became less busy, but not long after she was diagnosed with lung cancer, and she died less than a year after we got back in touch.'

I touch her arm. 'I'm sorry.' The poignancy isn't lost on me. Now Grandma lives in San Diego. She moved to California a few years after Grandpa died, buying a little apartment in a retirement community, saying their big old house and the East Coast winters were too much for her. She'd had enough of shovelling snow and cleaning rooms she no longer needed. I wonder if she thinks about Brynn much, about the missed chance to be close to her friend again.

'I'm sorry too,' she says. 'I wish I'd been better at staying in touch with her. I never told her how glad I was for her friendship.'

'I bet she knew.'

'I have met her girls, though. They're lovely. They come visit now and then. I think I remind them of her. They say we talk the same.'

Grandma's accent has softened but she's kept the pronunciations she grew up with. I used to mimic them, not to tease her but wistfully, until Mom would tell me to stop, it was rude. Grandma puts her arms out and I jump up to help her to her feet.

'I'm thirsty,' she says. 'Will we find somewhere to have a drink?'

We make our way slowly back up the beach, brushing sand off our clothes, to the paved street nearby lined with cafes and restaurants. Posted beside the doors are laminated menus printed in English.

We choose a place with umbrellas for shade and order sodas that come in thick glass bottles, the painted labels worn away by washing. Grandma has a Coke and I have a Sprite, and the cold bubbly sweetness tastes so good, which is more than I deserve.

It has been two days since I left Alex's room. Since then we've had a single, awkward conversation after bumping into each other on the rec deck, in which neither of us acknowledged what we'd done. When Grandma asked if I'd had a nice evening, I said yes, but I was lying. Inside I am disintegrating, but outside I keep my face smooth, my expression unchanged. Every moment since that night I have been filled with self-loathing, with guilt. Why do I do this? Why do I act without thinking? Since when do I let my body decide? I think of Grandma curled in her bunk, mourning her brother. The red marks of fingernails on skin. Pulling her hair out, strand by strand. The strength it took to continue. How do you choose between giving up and going on? Or is it not a choice you make consciously?

I feel the pull of old habits. This Sprite will be the only thing I have today, I tell myself. As soon as I decide this I feel better, less muddle-headed, in control once more.

I drink the rest of my soda slowly, savouring it, making it last. Imagining I feel every bubble of carbonation pop on my tongue. Hunger will pull me away from the desire that made me fuck things up. Hunger will hone me again, like a sharp blade of steel.

I wait for my ice cubes to melt, sticking my straw between them.

That old feeling of deprivation soothes me. Soon there will be only one thing on my mind.

CHAPTER 20

A few brides and fiancées who were meant to be met at the harbour were not, and the Red Cross ladies bustled them to a hotel, where they would spend the night making frantic phone calls and sorting out their situations. Had their husbands forgotten? Changed their minds? So many whispers. I tried not to take part.

Those of us continuing on took a tram to the railway station, stopping first at a telegraph office to let our families back in Australia and our husbands in the east know we'd arrived. I sent two messages. Same wording, two destinations: Conjola, New South Wales, Australia and Roanoke, Virginia, USA.

ARRIVED IN FRISCO, ALL WELL, TRAIN TONIGHT.
LOVE, S

Barbara was off to Texas and Jane to New York, and at the station we were directed to different platforms before we had a chance to say goodbye. I knew their smells by then, I could tell you every detail of their clothing, their make-up, when they brushed their teeth and the type of talcum they used. And just like that, they were gone. We all promised we would write. Those of us going to Virginia, Maryland and Washington DC were put into a carriage together. The porters loaded our trunks into the luggage car and I carried my suitcase on board, stowing it in a rack above an empty seat. I sat beside a window with a latch in the hope that it would open. There was grime on the outside but inside it was clean, and I rested my forehead against the glass for a moment, just to close my eyes. It had been such a long day.

When I woke it was dim in the carriage and there was a woman asleep beside me. Outside it was black, so I only saw my reflection—crumpled hair, frock, face—in the window. There was the travel-weary wail of a baby, a mother humming under her breath, and the *thump thump* of the rails beneath us, the carriage rocking from side to side almost imperceptibly. The long, low whistle as we passed another train, the whoosh of air between us.

I stood up and went in search of the toilets. The carriage was full of brides, most of them asleep, some clutching babies or small children. Two of the Red Cross ladies dozed in the last seats. They would see us through to our final destinations.

There was a blast of wind and track noise as the door at the end of the carriage slid open and the conductor walked in, grey-uniformed with a ticket machine slung around his waist. 'Excuse me, ma'am,' he said, and I turned sideways to let him pass. 'You going to Virginia, Maryland, or DC?' he asked.

'Virginia,' I replied.

He tilted his head. 'Huh?' He hadn't understood me.

I said it again, trying to pronounce it as he had, *VurGINyuh*.

'Oh, Virginia.' He nodded and started to walk away.

'Pardon me, where is the ladies' room?'

He turned back around and pointed in the direction from which I had come. 'Two carriages down. If you get to the dining car you've gone too far.'

I struggled with the door for a moment before sliding it open. The air I stepped into made me gasp. My eyes watered, cheeks tingled and my breath made clouds of vapour. San Francisco had been chilly but this was real cold. I had on only a thin cotton dress, a woollen jacket and a pair of nylon stockings, and the cold made me feel small inside my clothes. I looked out over the railing between the two cars and blinked for a moment. On either side of me mountains and rocks stretched towards the sky, which was only visible as a crisp ribbon dotted with stars. There was something light, almost glowing, on the ground and the stones, and I gasped when I realised what it was. My first glimpse of snow. It was white-blue in the moonlight, sparkling on the rocky landscape, making the ground glitter as the stars did. My teeth chattered and I grasped the next door and slid it open, the warm air of the carriage meeting me like a strange embrace. I might as well have been on the moon, it was all so different. I hurried through the second carriage, steeling myself for the icy air beyond, for the blast of night and cold. I wasn't going to pause this time, but perhaps the engineer saw some wildlife on the tracks, deer or even a bear. The train let off its high, piercing whistle again and the sound carried on, lingering and mournful, echoing through the valley and bouncing off cliff walls. It was the eeriest sound I'd ever heard, that whistle, on its own in a valley of mountainside and granite, ice and snow. I wanted to gather it and place it against my chest, to warm it. But it belonged in this narrow, hollow place.

I pulled back the door to the next carriage and ducked in. Inside there were restrooms, washbasins and a lounge area. The air was smoky. A few men were playing cards, bottles of whiskey on the tables between them. They looked up and away as I entered, and I hurried into the ladies'. Inside there were three small cubicles with toilets. The lids were down and when I opened one I saw why: beneath was cold black air, which rushed up to meet me. I sat on the seat and let the stream of urine go; I could smell the steam from it and, though I was probably imagining it, I thought I could hear it hit the ground beneath. At the speed we were going it would be long gone. I don't know what got into me but the thought of it made me laugh out loud. Those men would think I was strange if they heard me. And I was strange: I was foreign, I spoke funny and looked different and didn't really know where on earth I was, in this train, speeding towards a destination where I might not be welcome. And yet I felt inexplicably happy— as though the past and all its burdens were gone, down the toilet, already miles behind us. And here I was: light as air, cheeks flushed, and cold to my very teeth. Strange and empty. Hollow and free.

•

Sleep didn't come until dawn, and then I slept half the morning and missed breakfast. When I woke again, the woman beside me introduced herself—her name was Mary—and told me when they would be serving lunch in the dining car. We spoke a little about where we were each going and our husbands, but I'd had enough of that chatter. It seemed very old to me now; it made me want to sleep for the rest of the journey.

'I'm ravenous,' I said. 'I'll go wait for the dining car to open.'

'Do you want me to come along?'

'That's alright, I know the way.'

It felt rude, but I wanted nothing more than to be left alone with my thoughts. Where had the grief gone? What had changed?

Pausing between carriages I saw we were travelling through a different landscape now: flat, with grass which undulated in the wind, grass which glowed gold against the sky, stretching on endlessly, with barely a hill or tussock in sight.

'Wheat,' said a voice beside me. 'We're in Colorado now—wheat country as far as the eye can see.'

I turned, but I already knew it was him.

Jim was leaning on the railing of the little platform, legs wide to steady himself. He was still in his officer's uniform. I wondered if he wore it even when off duty just to make himself feel important.

'Are you following me?' I said, but I smiled as well, squinting up at him.

'Hate to disappoint you but I'm not. I live in Virginia when I'm not at sea. My folks are on the Chesapeake. What we call the Northern Neck, little town called Kilmarnock.'

THE PASSENGERS

'Northern Neck,' I said, mimicking the way he'd said it. 'VurGINyuh.'

'Are you making fun of me?'

'No—I'm just trying to say it right, so people can understand me.'

Jim grinned, scratching his cheek beneath the ear. I could see that he hadn't had a chance to shave since he boarded the train and there were little flecks of black stubble on his skin. It would feel like rough sandpaper, like a cat's tongue.

I shook the thought out of my head and stared back out at the wheatfields. 'I've never seen such flatness.'

'You ought to keep your accent,' he said, ignoring my last comment. 'It's nicer than ours. We're all hard r's and swallowed g's. It sounds like music when you talk.'

'What else is in Virginia?' I didn't bother saying it their way this time. It was easier to speak when I didn't have to think about every word.

'Geographically speaking? Mountains and rivers, farms, cities and such?'

'No, for you. Are you staying in the navy or have you got another job?'

Jim looked at me now; he'd been staring out at the fields too. His eyes were soft, velvety around the pupil, flecked with strands of gold. 'How about I tell you over lunch? The dining car's about to open and it's first in, first served. Being back on solid ground makes me hungry.'

I suppose I felt fine sitting to eat with Jim because he was the only person I knew from the *Mariposa*; all the others were strangers. Jim knew about Jack, I didn't have to explain myself to him. I could just sit and listen to him talk about his family and his home town and his boats and his high school girlfriend who'd married someone else while he was off at war. I cleaned my bowl of soup and ate a sandwich that looked unappetising but tasted divine, layered with crisp bacon and tomato, lettuce and mayonnaise.

'What's this sandwich called? It's the best thing I've tasted in weeks.'

'You mean you've never had a BLT?'

'A what?'

'Bacon, lettuce and tomato. You Aussies are strange. I couldn't stand your bacon, all soggy and pink. We never eat bacon if it isn't crisp. And this is the best way to eat it, right here. Soft bread, juicy tomato, crunchy lettuce and mayonnaise.'

'You're on to something. The combination is delicious.'

We both sat back in our chairs. We were beside a window and there was the blur of yellow and blue—wheat and sky—outside. The sun was coming in at an angle, falling across our table, warming my bare arms and making the butter in the dish liquefy.

The dining car was very neat with its paper-covered tables. A waiter moved along the aisle carrying a pot of coffee and a jug of water to refill empty mugs and glasses. There was the steady *thunk thunk* of the tracks beneath us and above that the light clink of silverware jostled by the movement. The car smelled of bacon frying, black coffee and the powdery sweet smell of someone wearing too much perfume.

Jim smirked when he saw me glance back at the woman behind me, crinkling my nose.

'Smells like a Chinese whorehouse,' he whispered.

I tried to turn my smile into a disapproving look.

'That's what one of the sailors used to say whenever he smelled too much perfume. I'll bet he knew from experience— but don't worry, I've never been in such an establishment.'

'I wouldn't care if you had.'

He began to fold his napkin into smaller and smaller squares, and I didn't want to leave this small rectangle of light, the company of someone who tethered me to my previous world.

'Tell me more about Virginia,' I said. 'Tell me what's different about Americans. Brynn had this silly pamphlet that was full of advice like "always wear lipstick". Tell me what I really need to know.'

Jim took the little square of napkin he'd folded and wiped his mouth. The light was behind me, in his eyes a little, and he squinted. 'Lipstick's crucial. People've been shot for not wearing lipstick.'

I rolled my eyes.

'No, just be yourself. Don't try too hard. If they don't like you for who you are, they're fools.'

'Yes, but what do they expect?'

'You know as well as I do there's a million answers to that question. Depends on the family. His are probably traditional, Southern. What sort of farm did you say they have?'

'Tobacco.'

'Well, wasn't so long ago their crop was farmed by slaves. So that's one thing: they'll believe people are worthy or not worthy depending on the colour of their skin.'

'And you don't?'

'Do you?'

'No! But you're from the South too, aren't you?'

'That doesn't mean anything. Hell, I think segregation is terrible. I think negroes should have the same rights we have. But it's not something you can talk about anywhere, you know? It's one of those . . . sensitive things. What does Roy think about it?'

I realised then that I didn't actually know. There was so much I didn't know about him. If he were a library, I would have only read a handful of the books.

'You don't know, do you?'

I shook my head, ashamed.

The waiter had come and taken away our plates, and now he brought a little slip of paper on a saucer. Jim reached into his pocket for his wallet. I had my purse, and I pulled it out as well, but he put his hand out.

'Let me get this. I've just been paid. Burning a hole in my pocket.' He grinned, counting out the bills, and it was a boy's grin, absent of irony.

'But the Red Cross has given me money for my meals. I have enough. I should know, shouldn't I?'

'What?'

'What Roy thinks of things. Only it was so short. It all happened so fast. I hardly remember how he looks anymore. I don't even know if I'll recognise him when I see him.'

The waiter came and took the bills away and Jim looked at me. He had thick dark lashes.

'It was like that, the war, wasn't it?' he said. 'It made us do strange things.'

'What did you do that was out of character?'

'Let's save that for our next meal. Will we meet for dinner at seven?'

'Only if you let me pay for my own meal. I need to get used to the money here, what the bills and coins mean. Maybe you could explain it to me?'

Jim put out his hand. 'Deal.'

I shook it, and it was warm and dry, and solid, and still, despite the unceasing movement of the train.

CHAPTER 21

It's so funny listening to Grandma speak, because I know this story is not about the food she ate on the train, but for me, right now, it is. The crisp bacon: I can feel it snap between my teeth. The juicy tomato. The creamy mayonnaise.

I lie in the bed across from hers, feeling the ship rock from side to side—the first bad weather of the voyage. It's been very convenient: all day I've said that I'm too seasick to even consider eating. Even standing up feels like too much of an effort; I'm too tired, and my head starts to spin. Grandma goes back and forth to the dining room looking worried, and I wonder again why she doesn't just get angry with me. See through me. I've forgotten the strength of my own willpower. I've stayed in bed all day, sleeping intermittently, not eating a single thing. All I had yesterday was breakfast and the Sprite. I have not stopped thinking of food for a moment, though. I know tonight I will dream of the BLT. But I feel myself shrinking, too, disappearing, and the smaller I become, the smaller my self-loathing. I close my eyes. Grandma keeps talking.

CHAPTER 22

We met for meals after that—all the meals which were served in the three days it took to cross the country. When we weren't eating I was in my seat, staring out the window at the ever-changing landscape, or out on the observation deck, my face to the wind. We passed some cities and small towns, but the landscape was mostly rural: trees, grass, rivers and fields, the greens greener than anything I had seen back home. I thought of the grey-green mottle of a eucalypt, the smell of tea tree beside the creek and the flap and screech of sulphur-crested cockatoos. I thought of the dairy farm, remembering the feel of an udder in my fists, the flank against my cheek, I thought of Roy in the hotel—his flushed face, the way he gazed at me, wet-eyed, from above. I'd had no word from him since I'd left Sydney, no guarantee that he would be waiting for me at the station, no idea what world I would enter. But there was no use worrying; barrelling blindly forwards was the only way.

It helped to have Jim to sit with at meals, to speak with. We talked about the war, about farming, about relationships. He told me how his father had died before the war, and how much his mother relied on him, how hard it was to leave her. He told me about a woman he'd fallen for in Brisbane, how on their third date she had told him about her husband, who was over fighting in France. I told him how my parents had lost their farm before the war and that was how we ended up in Sydney, but how they'd gone back to give living off the land another try.

He gave me his copy of *The Grapes of Wrath* to read, and it was like no book I had read before. I hadn't read a novel in years, filling my head with vacuous magazines instead. I fell into a real world of hunger and poverty, where the small lives of the characters showed the unfairness of it, the wealthy taking so much from the poor. Men with sunburnt skin and sun-whipped eyes. When I read, 'The sun was setting when the truck came back, and the earth was bloody in its setting light,' I thought about Dad driving us away to Sydney in his truck and how we weren't so different from the Joads, just a little less poor. We'd always had just enough to survive.

The next time we sat together Jim and I talked about the Okies and the Joads and how it was that big farms threw away food rather than feed people who were starving. How it was that people could do a day's work and still not be able to afford to feed their children. I'd never read a book which made me think so hard. Jim said he wasn't red himself but he agreed with some of the ideas of socialism. I felt stupid having to ask what those ideas were. He had a way of explaining it, though, that didn't make me feel dumb for asking.

At other times he asked me to explain things to him. He wanted to know how the political system worked in Australia and why it was we were still part of England. He wanted to know whether I thought he should look to move out when he got home or go on living with his mother. If it was cruel to his mother to turn down her efforts to fix him up with her best friend's daughter, a girl who was pretty, according to Jim, but only interested in talking about hairstyles and which girls were better- or worse-looking than her.

'I'd been on a few dates with her before this tour. I mean, she looks good in a sweater but I grew tired of having to re-assure her of that fact.'

'Imagine being married to her,' I said, staring out the window. 'It's not as though she's going to change. People only seem to grow into their worst selves.'

Jim rubbed the back of his neck. He had been to the train's barber that morning for a haircut and shave. There was the red speckle of a rash beneath his chin and I could see the contour of his scalp. 'That's a positive view of marriage you got there, Sarah.'

'Well, if your parents were happy, good for you.'

'I'm guessing yours aren't?'

'You're guessing correct.'

It surprised me when I began telling him about Dad and Mum, about the other woman. Seeing her with Dad at the dogs, the way she looked on his arm, tall and glamorous, nothing like Mum. I'd never even told Roy. Jim just sat there and listened, sipping his coffee, eyes on the passing landscape.

'That's a lot for your mother to ask of you,' he said when I paused. His hands cradled the mug of coffee. 'To spy on your dad like that. I'm surprised she'd do that. She put you in the middle of things. It's not a place for a child to be.'

'I'm not a child. I wasn't then either. I was nineteen.' My words came out sharper than I meant them to be and Jim looked at me, his eyebrows drawn together.

'I didn't mean you were a child then—I mean it's a lot to ask of your own children. Your offspring, your daughter or son. It's a selfish thing to ask.'

'What was she meant to do? She was only trying to find out the truth any way she could. I was the selfish one for not telling her. My mum is anything but selfish. She only ever thinks of other people.'

I felt my throat tighten and my chin quiver and I stood, pushing in my chair. 'I'm going back to my seat.'

Jim leaned back in his chair. 'Go on. You've gotten this far running away from the truth. Why stop and examine it now?'

I strode back to my carriage, pushing a fist beneath my ribcage. I couldn't bear his smugness, his certainty that he was right. I slid past Mary into my seat and rested my head against the window, the vibration juddering my thoughts.

Mary turned to me. 'You alright?' She was knitting a baby's jumper, yellow as a daffodil, with sleeves so narrow they seemed suited for a doll.

'Just tired of this train. When do we bloody arrive?'

'Tomorrow, haven't you been listening? I think we'll be in Roanoke before lunch. You're lucky; I've got to wait until dinnertime before we get into Washington DC. I can't wait to see my Owen.'

'Is the jumper for your baby?' I had been so busy wandering around the train, eating with Jim at every meal, that I hadn't even noticed whether or not Mary was pregnant. She must have thought me impolite.

'Yes, but I'm not expecting yet. Though it won't be long, I hope.' She smiled and tucked in her chin, looking down at the yellow yarn. 'It's cold, isn't it? I thought if I do fall pregnant soon, it would be good to have a few little warm things laid by for the baby. My mum won't be there to make them for me.'

'You're clever,' I said. 'I wish I was half as clever as you.'

'Oh, you're smart enough. You've always got your nose in a book, or else you're talking to that tall officer fella—I've seen you in the dining car.'

'That's just Jim. We met on the ship.'

'You don't need to explain yourself to me.'

I picked up my book then, feeling exposed, for Mary had been watching me, along with who knew how many others. I stared at the pages of print, but the words swam before me, the things Jim had said making my head ache. I didn't want to talk anymore about babies or woollen jumpers, about husbands waiting and mums who we'd left. I wanted to read about the Joads in the government camp and Winfield passing out picking peaches because he hadn't had enough to eat. I wanted to read about the Joads breaking strike and not making enough money to eat anything but cornmeal mush. Pushing away my world, I buried myself in theirs.

CHAPTER 23

Hannah is asleep. I know she has hardly heard a thing I've said today, but I haven't stopped talking when I've been in the room. The words are filling the space of what I should be saying. *I'm worried about you. It's time to call Caroline.*

I watch her sleeping as I shuffle around finding my things. She is beautiful with her face relaxed, though too thin, and the shoulder poking above the sheet is mostly bone. I remember noticing it for the first time when she was thirteen—she had gone through one of those chubby phases that adolescent girls have but rapidly grew, and with the height came a leanness which surprised me. It wasn't just that she was thin but that her knees and elbows seemed too big because her limbs were too skinny. I watched her push the food around on her plate when she visited for a weekend, saw her read the nutrition information on the cereal and yoghurt before she took a few bites of breakfast. She was all hair and metallic braces, all skin and bony hips swallowed by too-big pyjamas.

'I'm worried,' I said to Caroline when she came to pick her up one Sunday. I'd asked her to come out to the garden, ostensibly to look at my camellias, but really to talk about Hannah. 'Is she eating at home?'

'Of course she's eating. What do you mean?'

'I'm not criticising you. I've just noticed how thin she's become. And this weekend I've been watching her. She doesn't so much eat as move the food around.'

Caroline's face fell and she wiped her nose on her sleeve. 'I've been bugging her about it all year, but she's just getting worse,' she said, 'not better.'

Work had been so busy, Caroline explained, and Hannah no longer went to her dad's as often since he'd remarried and moved further away. When she saw the bags of candy in the trash she thought at first that Hannah was having friends over after school. It was only when one bag fell out while she was emptying the trash that she realised the candies had been unwrapped, chewed, and spat back into their wrappers. Then she found lists, she said, where Hannah wrote down every item of food she ate in the day and the number of calories. The lists were getting smaller. I still remember one Caroline described. It had four teaspoons of cottage cheese, half a glass of Crystal Light and three slices of apple.

I told her we had to make some sort of plan, to talk to the doctor, and maybe it would take something more serious. 'Whatever it costs, Caroline, I can help pay for it.'

She tightened her jaw and shook her head. 'I've already talked to the doctor. He said it's normal for girls her age, and not to be worried. He said I just need to make sure she eats—as if it's that simple.'

I still wish I'd insisted we got a second opinion, visited a specialist. The next time I saw Hannah she was in the eating disorders clinic at the Children's National Hospital, along with a bunch of other girls (and a single waifish boy) who competed in their desire to disappear. Who cried at mealtimes and took an hour to eat half a sandwich and seven green beans.

I found a locum for the vet clinic and stayed with Caroline for a month—she'd already used up all her leave. I rode the metro to the hospital every day, taking playing cards, books, magazines.

When Caroline and Andy had grown up I had thought I was done with that awful vulnerability of parenthood, but it was even worse with Hannah, for I felt not only my pain but Caroline's too—the anguish was doubled. At night Caroline and I would sit with frozen burritos we had microwaved and speculate on what might have brought it all on, looking for a moment when we could have prevented it.

Caroline blamed herself. She remembered how after the divorce her own body image had plummeted and she had wondered aloud to Hannah if she would ever again be attractive to a man.

'It's not your fault,' I said. 'It's not like you put her on a diet.'

'But if I just hadn't said half that shit I said. I remember telling her to chew slowly, to drink water to make herself feel more full, partly because I was reminding myself. I wish I could go back in time.'

What else would you change? I wanted to ask, but didn't.

What would I change? There were so many mistakes, but they also led there, to her, to Hannah. Who made it all worthwhile.

'The doctor said she might always have this disorder, it will just be a matter of how well she can manage it,' Caroline told me, and so we figured out ways to live with it. We didn't ask her to clear her plate. We let her eat at her own pace. We let her exercise, once we knew her heart would be okay. After returning from the first hospital stay she started running, and because it required her to be strong Caroline and I were happy with the choice. I would go to her races when I could get away from the clinic and watch her fly around the track. Her dad was always there too. I wondered how much of this could be blamed on him. The determination in her narrow face. The desire to control the world which otherwise seemed beyond her control.

She was better for so long that we were surprised when Hannah came home from her first semester of college. She had gone into pre-law. She had pledged the law sorority. She came home twenty pounds lighter than when she left, with dark half-moons beneath her eyes and an addiction to laxatives and ipecac to purge what little she did eat in the dining halls. Her new friends didn't think this unusual. They weren't concerned; they were envious of her self-control. Her professors only saw her grades, which were always high.

Caroline checked her in to another facility, this time a private residential clinic in Alexandria, and Hannah didn't return to pre-law. She bounced in and out of treatment, costing us tens of thousands of dollars. There was simply no choice.

Having found my phone, I move out to the corridor, steadying myself against the wall in case the ship pitches suddenly. Hannah has shown me how to log on to wi-fi and make a call over the internet.

Caroline picks up on the fourth ring.

'Mum?' Her voice is sleep-heavy. The connection is surprisingly clear.

'Sorry, love, did I wake you?'

'It's three in the morning! What time is it there?'

'Not sure. Around eight or nine.'

'Is everything okay?'

'I'm worried about Hannah. She hasn't eaten all day, and I'm not sure she ate yesterday either. She's been saying she's seasick, and I brought her crackers and Sprite, but I found the crackers in the bin later. And the sink was sticky; I think she poured the soda out.'

Caroline's quiet for a moment. I hear her shuffling around, probably getting out of bed.

'Shit. Is she there now?'

'She's asleep. Let's not get angry with her. That won't help, will it?'

'I know, Mum, it's just . . .' She sighs. 'It's not fair for you to have to look after her. She's meant to be helping you.'

'She has been. This has only just happened. We've been having a lovely time up to now. She's always so full of questions, and I've been telling her about my trip over—you know, on the bride ship. About being a girl on the farm before that. About Sydney during the war.'

'I'm glad. I am. But what now? Is there a doctor on board?'

'There must be a dozen.'

'Can you get one to check her over? Tell them her history. And she needs to call me, too. I won't yell, but she needs to call. I'll be sick with worry.'

'Okay, doctor tomorrow. I don't want you to worry.'

'You know I can't help it, Mum. But thanks for the heads-up.'

'Get some sleep, love. Sorry I woke you.'

I hang up and push open the door to our cabin. Hannah's still asleep and I can see the network of blue veins beneath the surface of her skin. The skin itself looks dry, flaky; even in the dim lamplight I can tell the colour isn't right. I wish I could go into her brain and fix that strange compulsion she has to hurt herself. I wish there was something useful I could do.

●

I hardly slept that night on the train. It was black outside and everyone else was asleep around me when I finally reached the last page. The dam they built against the floodwaters breaking, Rose of Sharon losing her baby, the family torn apart. Rose of Sharon feeding the starving man with her dead baby's milk, from her own breast. The strange image stayed with me. I was left with that hollowness at the end, that feeling of wanting to stay in the lives of these people but not being allowed. The window rattled against my head and I saw my own reflection, yellow from the reading light, wan and worn.

I fell asleep with the book on my lap, the pages soft from use. I dreamed of picking grapes, squeezing them in my fists so they popped, and rolling their slippery skin between my fingers. I dreamed of Roy on a wagon, riding away from me, clouds of dust like a sheer curtain between us.

I woke thirsty, my mouth dry, and stumbled to the ladies' room. I drank straight from the tap and splashed water on my face. Rather than go back to my seat I wandered through the train, walking towards the front. It was the middle of the night, the last night of the journey, and I was terrified of it ending. It wasn't until I saw him that I knew what I'd been looking for. He was awake, staring straight ahead into the darkened car. I tapped his shoulder. He jerked, started to speak, but I put a finger over my lips, walking back the way I'd come, motioning for him to follow.

The viewing platform was the last car, and he stood beside me, the entire train snaking forwards at our backs.

'I finished,' I shouted over the noise.

He leaned in. 'What?'

'The book. I finished it.'

'What'd you think?'

'So many things. I've never had a book make me feel so much.' I felt protected by the dark and the movement of the train. I could say whatever I wanted. 'And I'm sorry. I shouldn't have been angry, you were right. I feel so bad that I never told my mother what I saw, so I can't blame her for asking me to find out.'

Jim looked at me through half-closed eyes. I could see that he was looking for words, and I didn't want to hear them. I didn't want to think about the past or the future anymore, and I understood Dad then more clearly than I had ever understood him. I saw him in his hummingbird-wing hat, his chest out, the woman on his arm, the dogs sleek on the track before him, the draw of the here and now. I was more him than anyone. It was a terrible thought, a wonderful thought, one that was both joy and sorrow at once.

I let go of the sorrow and leaned into Jim's chest. His stubbled chin was on my forehead, his hand on my waist. He lifted my chin with his finger and he kissed me, our mouths the only warm things, the train pulsing forwards. I slid my hands between his shirt and jacket. He pulled away.

'We should stop,' he said. I saw the censure in his eyes and felt the sorrow rear up with such force it nearly knocked me backwards. He followed me to my seat, but I couldn't speak to him. I had said all there was to say. He left, the shadow of his body like a bruise against the door of the car, the noise as it opened of outside rushing in.

·

When I woke it was to the long, low whistle of another train and a jerking movement. Mary was shaking me, her slender fingers on my arm.

'We're almost there. Don't you want to wash up? Be pretty for your husband?'

I scrabbled in my suitcase for a clean set of clothes and a comb, rushed to the ladies' and had to stand in a queue of other girls. None of them were getting off in Roanoke, though, and so they let me go ahead of them, no doubt seeing what a state I was in and how badly my hair needed fixing.

In the cubicle I changed as quickly as I could, splashed water on my face and hair and ran a comb through the worst of the tangles. Had I really kissed Jim? What was I thinking? Shame made my eyes ache. I hurried out, my dirty clothes crushed in my hand, and back at the seat I used a compact to finish tidying my hair and apply lipstick with a shaking hand.

'Here,' Mary said, taking the tube from me, passing me a tissue. 'Wipe it off and we'll start again.' She pushed the tube against the contour of my lips, her hand steady, her breath smelling of coffee and pastry. I could see the blonde hairs on her upper lip, the raised mole beside her ear.

'Hold still!'

She finished and leaned back to appraise me. 'He'll think you look gorgeous. What's his name?'

'Roy.'

Saying it brought tears to my eyes.

'Don't you dare,' Mary scolded. 'You'll mess it all up!'

'Sorry,' I said. 'It's just . . . I don't know what I'm doing. I'm so homesick and I'm not even there yet. I hardly know him.'

'Oh dear. We all feel the same. But we're here now, we've got to make the best of it.'

We were pulling into the station, and I could see the platform, a low building of red brick, a clock reading ten past ten, a few scattered clusters of people.

'Brave face. Chin up. That's a girl. And don't forget your book.'

Jim's book! I'd forgotten to give it back to him. It was too late now. He would think me crazy for throwing myself at him on the viewing platform. At least I would never see him again. At least I could pretend it never happened. I put *The Grapes of Wrath* in my overnight bag. I'd post it to him, without a note, once I was settled in.

The Red Cross ladies came to fetch me from my seat. I was

the only war bride getting off at Roanoke, though I could see from my window other passengers disembarking.

'Goodbye, Mary, thank you.'

'Good luck,' she said, looking up from her knitting. I couldn't meet her eyes.

I had my overnight bag and my coat, and as we stepped down onto the platform I saw a porter carrying my trunk off the luggage car. 'That's mine,' I said, and we went to fetch it. The Red Cross lady looked at her wristwatch. 'Do you see your husband? Is he coming to the station?'

'He's meant to be.'

It wasn't a busy place, nothing like a city train station, and the clusters of people were already beginning to disperse. Beyond the station was a great big hill, and on the horizon were the outlines of mountains, so soft they seemed to float there. My breath came in puffs of vapour, and I could smell wood smoke and coal. I was glad for my coat but it wasn't lined, and I wished I had a warm hat and gloves as well.

'What should I do with this, ma'am?' the porter said, gesturing to my trunk.

'Just put it beside that bench there and Sarah can wait with it. I'm not meant to leave you, dear, but the train is going to depart in five minutes. Have you got a telephone number?'

I shook my head.

'I'll take you to the station agent.'

She bustled me to a small hot office where a fat man sat drowsily eating eggs and bacon from a white plate with blue edges.

She explained my predicament and the station agent nodded, wiping greasy fingers on a handkerchief and pushing the plate away. The sight of the eggs, even congealed, made my stomach ache with hunger. I had slept through breakfast again. He put on his spectacles. 'Roy Jackson, didja say? The Jacksons are from over Boone's Mill way. I've got a telephone number for him here. You go on and I'll look after this, don't worry. We'll get this girl to her husband in no time.' He grinned, showing teeth stained brown from tobacco. 'You're free to sit in here if you like. Outta the cold.'

'I'll sit with my trunk, thank you. I'll be just there.' I pointed to the bench outside.

'Suit yourself.'

We hurried out and the Red Cross lady frowned at the train, which let off a whistle. 'I hate to leave you here,' she said. 'All on your own.'

'They'll be here. You heard the station agent. I'll be fine.'

If she'd known me, that lady, she might've heard the strain in my voice. Recognised that I would not be fine. But she was a stranger to me, and I to her. She boarded the train, and then there was the slow rumble and chug of it starting, of the forward movement, of it leaving without me.

CHAPTER 24

I wake up and the cabin is empty. I don't know where I am, there is just the dull ache in my head and the sharp pang in my stomach. Then I remember.

Grandma's stories come rolling back in with my own memories, as though they are part of my life now too. I can't believe she kissed Jim on the train. I can, too. I feel her barrelling forwards towards Virginia, towards Roy, trying to grab on to something, anything which might slow her down. I know what it is to screw up on purpose.

In therapy they have tried to get me to pinpoint a time when it started. I tell them how after Dad left I watched Mom looking backwards over one shoulder to see herself in the mirror from behind, the back of her thigh rippled with cellulite. The sheer size of her ass, how when she sat it squashed against the armrests of a chair. I looked at my own little ass that night, standing on the toilet seat so I could see it in the bathroom mirror. It was small and bony, like the rest of me. My mother's softness was her weakness. I would never have that excess flesh, breasts spilling over the top of the bra. The belly in folds, sagging. The arms jiggling when she stirred the soup, mixed the pancake batter. I would stay small forever. I could fit in the gap between the fridge and the wall. I could hide in the cupboard beneath the TV. Disappear behind the living room curtains. If I stayed this size I could always slip away.

I tell them about playing Barbie with my neighbour, Jessica, because she always let me be Skipper. I didn't want to be anyone else. Skipper didn't have those ugly lumps and bumps. Skipper's clothes were easy to take on and off, she was straight and narrow. Jessica liked to be Shopper Barbie or Glitter Beach Barbie and go off in the convertible to lie down in the back seat with Glitter Beach or Shaving Fun Ken. They moaned and clacked their hard plastic limbs together in the back seat of the Fun for Four convertible, while I gave Skipper tiny braids or a change of wardrobe for when they finally emerged.

'Your hair's a mess!' Skipper would say to Glitter Beach when she was upright again. 'And your boobs are showing!'

Jessica would pull the shirt down over the hard tan breasts and slip the tiny pink stilettos back on. 'Don't be so boring!' She'd wave the little plastic hand with painted fingernails at Ken, who was driving towards the laundry basket at a breakneck speed. 'Bye, Ken!' Then she'd turn to her skinny, prepubescent sister. 'Hey, Skipper, let's go to the mall.'

I tell them that when puberty started I noticed rolls around my belly when I sat on the toilet and even my fingers began to look fat. My flesh reminded me of the raw cookie dough I would eat from the fridge after school, soft and easy to squash. The worst thing would be to turn into my mother.

I don't tell them about how in my English and history class there was a boy, Jake, with a flop of hair over his eyes. When he smiled there was a single dimple in his right cheek. His binder had stickers of band names I'd never heard of. The boys at school all knew when we started to wear bras; there were a few who ran around in the lunchroom feeling for straps on our backs, giving them a sharp snap. Jake wasn't one of those boys.

In eighth grade we went on a field trip to Colonial Williamsburg, to see a Revolutionary War re-enactment. The buses left early and came home late—it was a two-hour drive each way. Mom dropped me off early, so I was one of the first people on the bus. When Jake paused beside me, my heart stuttered.

'Is this seat taken?'

I had been saving it for my friend Amy, but she'd understand. I shook my head, whispering no. He threw himself down. I breathed on the glass and drew a picture with my finger of a tree, mountains behind it. He didn't say anything. I spent the first hour trying to think of something to say.

'Have you ever been to Williamsburg?'

'Did you pack a lunch?'

'What are you doing your report on?'

Everything I thought of sounded stupid, so I stayed silent. My face was hot. Every once in a while I saw Amy peer over the top of her seat at us. She'd want to know what happened as soon as we got there. It was too hard. He'd pulled his headphones over his ears and I could hear a muffled beat sometimes, indecipherable, the sound of his fingers tapping the vinyl seat. I decided I'd pretend to sleep instead. I put my jacket over my lap, my backpack against the window as a pillow. I shut my eyes.

I'd nearly fallen asleep when his fingers crept beneath my jacket. Like insect legs along my thigh. I froze. He must have felt my muscle tighten. The hand slid up along the side, where the seam of my jeans sat. Then the hill of my leg, the top of the thigh. What was I meant to do? His fingers were on the inside now, almost tickling. Higher. And again. I wanted to push him away. I didn't. I'd forgotten how to move.

He touched me and ignored me at the same time. I know because I opened my eyes, and saw that he was still staring straight ahead, nodding to the beat of his silent music. I closed my eyes again. I wanted to melt into the window, like my breath did. I wanted to disappear.

When the bus came to a shuddering halt in the vast parking lot of Colonial Williamsburg he got up, grabbed his bag and shrugged it over his shoulder before joining the line to get off. He didn't even look at me. Amy was waiting when I climbed down the metal steps.

'Well, what happened? I am so jealous! He's the cutest.'

I shrugged. 'Nothing much.'

'You had to talk about something—it was two hours!'

'Yeah, he's nice, I guess.'

I couldn't say what I'd let him do. How he'd touched me there and I froze. I spent the entire excursion watching black-smiths, butter churners, musket makers and grownups playing dress-ups in a weird fog. It was my body's fault for changing. Because it even felt good, a little, and that was half the shame. Not eating lunch helped. Denying myself the yellow cornbread muffins which steamed when you broke them open, the pats of fresh-churned butter melting into the coarse crumbs.

But on the way home—here's the thing—I let it happen again. I don't know why. And I didn't know why again and again that year when he cornered me in the stairwell between classes, beneath the bleachers during PE—when he touched my body as if it were just a thing. He never looked at me. We hardly spoke. I'd always been agreeable to everyone; it was part of being perfect.

It takes work to become invisible. It doesn't happen all at once. I wore more and more clothes. Sweaters with necks that swallowed my face. Sleeves that hid my hands. I had to roll the waistbands on my pants because I was losing so much weight. I started to keep lists. There was so much else I wanted to write in my diary, but this seemed safe. What I ate. Every. Single. Thing. In one of the clinics, later, there was a therapist who said: 'When you let deprivation feel good, you let in the possibility of disorder.' Did the deprivation feel good? It felt better than the alternative.

I skipped field trips and changed the way I moved through the halls. I hid in the girls' bathroom so often I memorised the graffiti in the stalls. *Samantha loves Jason 4Eva. Eric has a big dick. For good times call 843-2353. Chastity is a Cunt.* I sat on the other side of the classroom, as far away from Jake as I could. I sat with Amy and our other friends in the cafeteria, picking at the salad or the sandwich on my tray. I didn't look up when groups of guys walked past.

One day he was on my school bus home. I was sitting beside Phuong, who was in my PE class, but she got off at the stop before mine. When she left he shifted and sat beside me. His headphones cradled his neck.

'What're you doing?'

'Going home.'

'Can I come over?'

Later on I thought of all the things I could have said. *My mom doesn't let me have friends over. I have too much homework. I have gymnastics practice.* None of it was true. But I could have lied. I was getting good at lying. Why could I not find that word? No.

I did say no, later, when we were lying on my bed and he pulled my jeans down to my ankles. But I said it softly, so maybe he didn't hear me. And it wasn't exactly no. 'I don't want to,' I said. 'I don't want this.'

It hurt because he didn't even touch me first, like he had on the bus. All my muscles were tense. It wasn't going to fit, but he kept trying, pushing, and I was crying, and finally he stood, zipped up his pants, grabbed his backpack.

'Gotta go,' he said. 'Basketball practice. See you round.'

When he'd left I pulled up my jeans, ran downstairs and locked the door. I looked in the mirror and saw where I had bitten my lip on the inside until it bled. I filled the bathtub and sat in it. I was still there when my mom came home. She opened the bathroom door, after calling and calling and me not responding, and I was lying there, the heat lamp on, prone in the cold tub, shivering. I saw her cringe at the sight of my naked body, as she took in the bones and the gaps.

'Oh, honey, what's wrong?' she said, grabbing the towel from the rack and holding it out to me.

'I'm so fat,' I said. 'I'm so fat I want to die.'

CHAPTER 25

Dear Mum,

I am here now in Boone's Mill with Roy and his family and I wanted to write and tell you I am safe and all is well. It is a big farm, 200 acres planted with tobacco and hay. They have pigs and chickens, two horses, and I haven't counted but somewhere around 20 cats and kittens. They live in a large house of red bricks with white columns, and in the evenings—except on the coldest nights—everyone sits out on the front porch (what we call a verandah) on the porch swing or rocking chairs, watching the sun set over the mountains. The mountains here are like nothing we've seen. They're not big craggy mountains but soft-looking, middle-sized ones which sort of fade and change colours into the horizon, so that every night the sunset is all of these pinks, oranges and blurring shades of blue. I wish that I could paint, it is the sort of thing which a watercolour could show, but as you know I haven't got an artistic bone in my body.

Everyone wakes at dawn here—just as you are again, I imagine—and before breakfast Mr Jackson (his name is Ron, but I still call him Mr Jackson) is out feeding the pigs, and I help Mrs Jackson (Martha) in the kitchen. There is so much to be done, for they preserve all of the fruits and vegetables from their garden and cure their tobacco and pork and make everything from scratch, each meal feeding not only the four of us and Roy and me but also the four farmhands, silent men whose names I can't remember yet but who call me ma'am and take off their hats and scrub their dirty hands in the kitchen sink with soap that smells of lye. The food is so different. Every morning for breakfast there are fresh biscuits (which are more like our scones) and homemade berry jam and fried eggs and slabs of pork and brewed coffee. Mrs Jackson says she will teach me to make biscuits soon, but she is always running from one place to the next with flour in her hair and an apron tied on crooked.

Her husband is tall with white hair, big ears and a beard, skinny as a flagpole and just as hard too. I haven't seen him smile once since I've come and he's always bossing the farmhands and complaining that they don't work quick enough planting or fertilising or whatever it is they're doing. I shouldn't be too judgmental though. I know farming is not an easy life.

Roanoke is a small city less than an hour by car from the farm, we go once a week to buy supplies. There is a closer town, Rocky Mount, but there's not much there— just a school, a bank, a feed store and a grocer. Roanoke is a pretty, orderly place, and people seem nice enough, though they find it difficult to understand me. When I tell them I am from Australia some are surprised that I have white skin, that I speak a version of English. It seems that they do not know a great deal about the world beyond their own. They're keen to tell me how things are done here, for they seem to think it's the only way, and that this is the very best place on earth to end up. Everyone goes to church on Sundays, including us, for hours of singing and sermon. Some in the congregation have sons who have been away at war, and some of those sons haven't come back, but that war was so far away it seems like it hasn't changed them. They didn't even have rationing coupons or blackouts.

Something else different is the cold. It's so cold that you feel you'll never get warm. The second night after I arrived it snowed, and in the morning when I woke up the world had changed completely. Everything was covered with a blanket of white. I thought it was beautiful but Mrs Jackson said it only meant more work at the end of the day. It *was* beautiful, though, Mum. I wish you were here to see it. It makes the cold worthwhile. And the house is warm, at least: there are fireplaces and oil furnaces in every bedroom.

So really it is as cosy as anyone could wish for. I'm glad that Dad's hip is better and that the new herd of cattle are settling in. I'm glad you've got help with the milking so it doesn't all fall to you and Dad and Fred. Give my love to everyone and be sure to write soon. I can't tell you how happy it made me to get your last letter.

Love from your daughter,

Sarah

•

As I posted that letter in Roanoke I thought of everything I hadn't told Mum. I didn't tell her how Roy was late to the train station to pick me up, or how he limped in with his mother and father on either side. How strange he looked in his pressed pants and snap-button shirt, belt buckle high on his waist, his hair grown long over his ears, the grimace which was his new smile. He grabbed me in a tight embrace and said, 'You are a sight for sore eyes, Sarah. Thank God you're here.'

I buried my face in his chest. He still smelled of clove and vetiver, and I breathed it in. It had been so long; I had thought so often of this moment. Only I hadn't considered that his parents would be watching.

They watched as he asked me about the train, the ship, as he put his hand on my waist and looked into my eyes. I felt certain he could see the truth there, the ways in which I had been unfaithful.

'I can't believe you're real,' he said. 'I kept thinking that I'd dreamed you.'

'Same,' I murmured, standing on my toes to kiss him again, feeling his mother's eyes on me the whole time. I thought of our first kiss, outside the house in Forest Lodge, of our kisses on the streets of Sydney, and I felt his belt buckle again through the fabric of my cotton dress.

As we walked to the truck Roy tried to draw us all into conversation.

'Ma's cooked a real delicious supper for us, Sarah, I hope you're hungry. That's why we're late—she had to wait to get the pies out of the oven.'

'Sounds wonderful,' I said. 'I missed breakfast this morning so I haven't had a thing to eat.'

His mother looked at me with tight lips and muttered something about hemlines being longer round here.

Roy squeezed my hand. 'Give her time to get settled, Ma.'

'How are you?' I asked, looking down at his stiff leg.

'Oh, it's okay. Lucky to still have two legs, I guess. Shouldn't complain. But I'm not much good at catching hogs these days.'

At that his dad snorted. I thought he was mimicking a pig at first, but it turned out that was as close as the man came to laughing. Truly. I could see that they were not going to make for easy company.

That night after washing up, Mrs Jackson passed me an article she'd cut out of the newspaper. 'I saved this for you,' she said.

WHEN YOUR MAN COMES HOME

Don't ask questions. If he wants to tell you anything of his experiences, he will in his own time. Be a good listener. Don't let him feel that you think he has changed. And don't expect too many compliments on your appearance. Don't urge him to do things. Let him do what he wants in his own time. Remember that he has been shoved around and ordered about for quite a long time.

Don't expect him to meet people. See that his civilian clothes are ready for him and that his ties etc. are in the place where he remembers them. Let your sympathy mainly be unspoken.

Well, at least I was good at keeping silent, I thought. And I'd be lying if I said things didn't feel safer that way.

Roy and I slept in his childhood bedroom, with his high school diploma and a framed picture of Jesus hanging on a cross on the wall. There was a low shelf of books beside the bed and on top of it were trophies from when he had played baseball and models of aeroplanes he must have spent hours gluing and painting. They still smelled faintly acrid. He wore blue-and-grey-striped pyjamas which his mother ironed, the creases falling down the bones of his legs. In the mornings after breakfast I saw his mother go into our room to make the bed, changing our sheets on Saturdays, and I wondered if Roy had ever done that on his own. I told her to let me do that small thing, and she tightened her lips but agreed with a curt nod. It was as though she would fight me for every inch of her son. Surely she could smell our bodies in that bed.

Our first night together he sat on the edge of the bed, looking tense and uncertain.

I shifted to sit beside him. For a few minutes there was nothing but the sound of each of us breathing. I could have told him then, about Jim, about the kiss, about the madness that came over me. He might have forgiven me. I listened for the house to creak, for the sound of his parents getting into their bed.

I put my hand on his knee. It was hard beneath the cotton fabric, a dent in the flat part of the kneecap and ringed by bone. My hand travelled slowly upwards. His muscle twitched, flinched.

'Did the doctors say you could?'

He nodded. I was surprised by my own desire.

Very slowly I moved my hand up his thigh, keeping a steady pressure, making a sound between my teeth as though calming a distressed animal. The muscle in his thigh was soft now.

'They said I probably can't have children though. It's okay if that changes things for you. It's not too late for you to find someone else.'

I shook my head. I didn't know how to take what he was offering then. I pushed down the sadness that reared its head. Instead I kneeled at his feet. 'Let me take off your slippers.'

I took off his knitted slippers and rubbed his calloused feet. Feet which were unfamiliar to me. The ways I knew him were fewer than the ways I did. There were blond hairs sprouting beneath the knuckles of his toes, the toenails were thick and yellowish. I lifted his feet onto the bed and he obediently lay back, letting me shift his legs and hips. My hands shook.

I squeezed in beside him and tugged the quilt over us, nuzzling into his side.

I ran my hand up over the cotton of his pyjama top, feeling the hardness of the buttons, the stiff piping at the seams. I put my hand beneath it to feel his skin, thinking of the flank of a cow, the calming touch. His stomach was soft and vulnerable. Somehow these months home, this injury, had made him a child again, a boy in a man's body. I brushed my hand down over his pants and felt his arousal there. The waistband of his pyjama bottoms was tightly knotted. I fumbled for a moment, then released the cord, slipping my hand down. Near the side of his hip, beside the curved bone, I felt the raised shiny ridge of his scar, the place where the bullet had entered and been cut out of him, where the bone had splintered and sort of healed.

'It's disgusting,' he said.

'Not at all. Feel how smooth this new skin is.'

I took his hand in mine and put it there, where the skin had grown back shiny. I moved my hand towards the centre of him, hearing his breathing grow harsh. This was what could bring us together again. He lifted his knees to tug his pants down to his ankles. I lay on top of him, feeling the twitch of him pressing into me through the fabric of my nightdress. He made a sound, a kind of low cry, and I put my mouth on his, kissing him, thinking of the rush of air when you step out onto the platform between the cars of a moving train.

'Remember,' I whispered, 'in Sydney, before you left.'

He swallowed hard and his throat constricted. In the lamplight I saw the hollow in his cheek as he clenched his jaw. It came so quickly then, for he shoved me against the wall and was on top of me before I knew what had happened, his one hand pulling up my nightdress, the other between my legs, then him pushing inside me.

He jerked and heaved, thumping my head against the headboard, his elbows pressing down either side of me, his face with a pained look. It hurt, for it had been a long time, and I had meant for us to take it slowly.

'I missed you,' he rasped, as he collapsed on top of me.

'I missed you too,' I said, but my words were smothered by him.

•

What we had was different there. I woke each morning to the smell of ham frying, high brown biscuits, coffee starting to boil in the pot. Wishing for the familiar creak and call of a currawong. The trees were winter-bare, the fields bleak and brown, and nobody spoke to me but to tell me what chores needed doing. Roy slept or toiled in the fields. At dinner one night his father told me: 'It takes thirteen months a year to grow good tobacco.'

They grew seventeen hundred plants per acre of bright-leaf tobacco, which had to be tended from seed to crop through to curing and market. Besides the hogs there was fescue grass for hay. So Roy was bone tired, and at night his terrors caused him to shout and thrash. The whole house seemed to hum with his nightmares. In the evening he and his father drank jars of moonshine, which was not offered to his mother or me. It made his limp and his terrors worse.

Everyone smoked; it was tobacco country. I grew used to smoking after meals, enjoying the enforced pause, the few minutes of staring into space. We rolled our own cigarettes from tobacco from the fields, and Roy and his father chewed tobacco as well, spitting streaks of brown sickly-sweet-smelling juice in the dirt or into old teacups they kept inside for the purpose. In spite of her fear of disorder, Mrs Jackson didn't seem to mind that the men of her house were spitting indoors. Somehow the fact that they were doing it in chipped cups made it okay.

The yellowed lace curtains quivered in the mornings when I opened them, the floorboards creaked as I swept them and kittens sprang in and out of my lap in the square curing barn, their claws poking through my stockings like tiny thorns, the sharpness a glad reminder of pain outside my homesick heart. I tried to talk to Mrs Jackson. Passing her dishes from the sink to dry I would ask questions about their neighbours, but her one-word answers were an admonishment for asking. I wondered if her silence was a measure of blame. If Roy had not married me perhaps he would never have been in that battle in New Guinea. Perhaps he would not have been injured. Because he had left in one piece, married me and come back broken, she blamed me rather than the war for his injury.

When visitors did come—the preacher, the women from her quilting circle, her gardening club—she shut the sitting room door behind them. The rise and fall of voices was steady then, and though I knew they spoke of me, I wanted more than anything just to feel that buzz of talk. To hear chatter surround me rather than the swallowing echo of my own loneliness.

•

One Sunday morning while we dressed for church Roy asked me what was wrong.

'You seem quiet,' he said. 'Different than before.'

I'd been so busy thinking of how he had not lived up to my expectations that I hadn't considered that I wasn't meeting his.

'I'm alright,' I said, turning my back to him so he could fasten the top buttons of the pale blue dress with the hem that fell below my knees. I had let down the hems on most of my dresses just for the sake of his mother. Roy hadn't seemed to notice. 'Just homesick. It's so different here. And with Jack . . .'

Roy put his hands on my shoulders, solid, only they gripped a little harder than was comfortable.

'We all lost something in that war, you know.' His voice cracked at the end. It was as close as he came to talking about his injury.

'I know.' I turned and put my arms around him, hearing his heartbeat against my ear before he stepped away. I thought of Jim on the train, the rattle of the china between us.

'You have to try too,' he said. 'You can't expect things to be the same here as they were at home.'

'I know. I'm sorry. I am trying. What else can I do?'

'Try smiling every once in a while, to start with. Not looking so glum.'

I clenched my cheeks, raised the corners of my mouth.

'That's better,' he said, kissing the top of my head.

He left the room and I heard his unsteady gait on the stairs, pictured his sideways descent, favouring the left hip.

I looked at myself in the mirror, keeping the false smile. He was easily placated. If only I were too.

CHAPTER 26

I wake in a strange room. The walls are pale green and I am in a low bed with metal rails. There is the long narrow tube of an IV, the cloth tape holding the cannula in place in the crook of my arm. An ECG monitor beeps. A furry feeling in my mouth and the dull persistent ache of my temples. I touch my nose. At least there isn't a tube. Thank God there's not a tube. I touch my torso, my empty belly, my jutting bones and feel relief. A doctor walks into the room. Grandma slips in behind him.

'Are we still on the ship?'

He looks at Grandma, an expression I can't read, and nods. 'What do you remember?'

'Being seasick. Having to lie in bed for a day, maybe two.'

'You passed out. Your grandmother tried to get you to stand up, to help you to the bathroom, and you fainted. When is the last time you ate something?'

'Not sure,' I lie.

He shakes his head, writing something on the chart.

'Your grandmother tells me you have a medical history of anorexia.'

I nod.

'Sometimes changed circumstances—different diets, different situations—can exacerbate these conditions. Do you think that's happened to you, Hannah?'

My immediate instinct is to deny, but I see Grandma watching me with her liquid blue eyes. She sees right through me.

I would cry if I had the strength. I swallow the lump in my throat. 'Maybe.'

He makes some more notes on his clipboard, the sound of the pen scratching amplified by the sparsely furnished room, by our silence.

'You're severely dehydrated, and there are signs of malnourishment as well. I'm not really equipped to treat this kind of long-term condition here—we deal with emergencies and tummy bugs. I'm going to recommend you disembark at the next stop—New Zealand—for hospitalisation.'

'I can't.'

'Why?'

'It's my grandma's trip, her trip home.' My nose begins to run. He passes me a tissue. I haven't thought about how this might affect Grandma. How it could ruin her trip.

'Please,' I say. 'What can I do?'

Grandma comes over and puts her hand on mine. 'Don't worry, love. It's more important to get you better than to finish the cruise. We can do it another time.'

The doctor looks at her and I can see he's thinking what

I am. How many years does she have left? How much longer will travel be possible?

He runs his hand over his shining bald scalp. There is a rim of black hair around it and a short-trimmed beard which covers the lower half of his face. 'I suppose . . .' he says.

I hold my breath.

'I suppose if you agree to a nasogastric tube for two or three days I could consider letting you continue to Sydney. But I'd need to run a few tests first: kidney, heart, liver function. White blood cell count, thyroid function. The last thing we want is an ambulance or, worse, the coroner coming to meet us at the next port.'

Grandma's face crumples. She hides behind her hands.

'Sorry,' the doctor says, 'but we do need to take all of this into consideration.'

'No, don't you be sorry.' Grandma's voice is muffled. 'I'm cross with myself. I let it get this bad. I should have seen it earlier.'

'It's not your fault,' he says, placing the clipboard on the metal table, putting his cold fingers on the inside of my wrist and looking at his watch. He counts my pulse. His lips move silently. I know what he isn't saying.

Whose fault it really is.

•

When she found me in the tub, Mom called the eating disorders clinic at the Children's National Hospital. I agreed to go because it meant I could get away from Jake. I had thought, in the tub, about a razor. The thin skin of my wrists. About how easy it might be. How I would do anything never to have to see him again. Anything except talk about it, because it was my fault.

I had let him touch me, all those times.

I hadn't spoken out.

I had let him sit beside me.

I had let him into my house.

The clinic was my first experience with a nasogastric tube, the pain of it, the stinging gag and choke. There were nine other women and girls in the program, the youngest just ten years old, and a single boy. We wandered the halls wrapped in blankets like homeless ghosts. Lining up for our pills, our weigh-ins, our carefully portioned meals. We huddled together in group therapy, talking about our families, about how we learned to starve. We sat in the TV room playing Scrabble, Uno, gin rummy, watching *Ellen*. I roomed with Maria, whose family still tried to bring her food, even though they weren't allowed. She was bulimic and had scars on her knuckles from where they hit the top of her front teeth when she stuck her fingers down her throat. She taught me how to curse in Spanish. It sounded better. She taught me how to cheat at weigh-in. She taught me how to smoke, because smoking makes you thin.

I taught her to chew and spit. We did our nails, the familiar sound of the bead rattling inside the bottle. I talked about everything except Jake. But he was there, watching me. Waiting. I could feel it. I stayed longer than most. The health insurance company wanted me discharged, but Mom fought them with all the fury she could summon.

One day Amy visited and brought me a card she and my other friends had signed. She didn't know where to rest her eyes;

they kept flicking around the room. She said I looked better. She filled me in on who was taking who to the end-of-year dance, and where everyone was going to high school. She told me Jake's dad had a new job and he was moving to Georgia at the end of the school year. I put the card down on the bed. My hand was shaking so bad the paper rustled.

'I'm sorry,' she said. 'I know you like him.'

'Yeah. Not anymore.'

I moved home and spent the summer under flickering fluorescent lights, at summer school. I finished eighth grade just in time to enter high school. I learned to eat enough to hover on the edge of things. Enough to run track and field, not too much to slow me down. I learned to surround myself with friends—to move in a pack of them—to always have someone to sit with. There was nothing as scary as an empty seat beside me.

I studied hard. I ran fast. I had the best times. The best grades. I learned to create a force field around me, like a spinning top. I whirled across the surface of high school. You couldn't get close to me if you tried.

CHAPTER 27

I sit beside her when they put in the tube, watch her clutch at the bed as they feed it through her nose, watch her gag, her face turn red and then pale again. They wheel the bed off for an X-ray to make sure the tube is in place, then bring it back to allow the feeding to begin. I suppose we are lucky they have these facilities on board, but all I can think of is how much it hurts her, and I know that it isn't the pain of the tube but the pain of eating. The loss of control. I know how much her stomach will hurt afterwards, how painful it is for that shrunken vessel to expand. I stroke her arm and begin telling the stories again, because she doesn't speak. Because if I don't say something the silence is unbearable.

·

The weather grew warmer, the trees began to bud, and Roy and I grew less tentative around one another. They planted the tobacco seeds in a small field near the house where they could cover them, protect them from late frosts, and just the beginning of these seedlings seemed to give us all hope. He tried, some nights, to talk to me before we fell asleep. He held me against his shoulder when I wept over Jack's death, my sobs dampening his laundered pyjamas. He picked the first of the wild violets which grew at the edge of the woods and put them in a jam jar beside the bed. Each flower had four purple petals, green leaves, a white stamen and a delicate pale stem. They didn't last long, wilting before I could make the beds the following day.

That morning I heard Mrs Jackson calling me from the kitchen downstairs.

'Sarah? Sarah!'

I came, holding the jam jar with the wilted violets.

'Fetch me the eggs, would you?'

There were none beside the icebox, so I went with the basket out to the chicken yard. The hens were sprawled in the dust, their feathers fluffed, lounging in the early spring sun. There were six hens and a single rooster, his shiny blue-black feathers a sharp contrast to the reddish brown of his girls. He strutted towards me when I entered the yard, making a low warning sound in his throat, but I swung the basket at him.

Inside the laying boxes were five warm brown eggs, two speckled and three single-hued. One of the hens was setting, and I didn't bother her, for there might soon be tiny yellow-brown chicks hatching from her pile. I wanted to sit in the sun and watch her, eager to see the chicks emerge sticky-feathered and scrawny pink from their fragile shells, skin wrinkled with newness, but I knew Mrs Jackson was waiting inside. For the first time since I'd arrived the truth of what Roy's condition meant hit me. There would be no small wrinkled pink babies to hold, no children to call inside when it grew dark, to hold to my chest when they woke in the night. It winded me, literally took my breath away, and I had to stand there in the enclosure, the rooster watching me out of one beady eye, waiting to be able to move again. After a few minutes I gathered myself and left, latching the gate behind me, holding the basket close so the eggs wouldn't jostle as I walked into the dim kitchen.

'Took you long enough,' Mrs Jackson said. 'You're not scared of that rooster, are you?'

'No, I thought maybe I saw a chick coming, from the one setting on her eggs.' I looked over to where I had left the jar with the wilted violets. It was gone.

'Oh, her. Broody, I'll wager. She's old enough for the pot, that one.'

'Will I go fetch her eggs then?'

'Leave her be. Now crack four in that there bowl and whisk them until they're pale.'

I did as she said, feeling the thin membrane inside each brittle shell tear from my thumb's pressure. The wet glistening innards fell into the bowl. Eggs made me feel queasy: the sliminess, the little red blotch of blood sometimes or the snot-like whitish trail, the chicken that had never quite been. I threw away the shells and began to whisk. The small blood specks and white trails disappeared as the liquid became pale yellow, frothy. I would do the same, I decided. Beat out my inconsistencies. Make myself part of this world. One day I'd fit, surely. One day I'd slide into place.

•

The seedlings took well and when they were big enough we all helped to transplant them into the ploughed fields. There were extra men and boys, most of them negroes, who travelled from farm to farm at this time of year, earning enough to last until harvesting. Careful with the roots, we dug out each small plant and placed them in large buckets, which two men lifted together into the back of the truck. These were then driven to the field, where each plant was tamped into the earth until there was row upon row of dark-leafed tobacco. It felt good to be out in the sun working. I thought of the Joads, of Jim's book which I'd left in my trunk. I wore a pair of old overalls, and the soil beneath my fingernails was thin and dry. Roy explained that tobacco plants thrived in poor soil, only the dirt mustn't be allowed to harden and cake along the young roots. Transplanting and harvesting were the two most labour-intensive times of the year—early spring and late summer. Harvesting could take up to a month, because leaves were harvested on each plant from the bottom up, individually, and then strung on a stick, hung in the curing barn and, once dried, graded leaf by leaf before being tied into hands and taken to auction. He told me about when he was a boy and they had to tend a fire in the curing barn—a fire that lasted four or five days. 'Now we use an oil heater, though Dad's always still in there, keeping an eye on the temperature.'

He told me more about his boyhood then, about Sally, the negro woman who had cooked for them and done their laundry, and how she had left when he was twelve, accused of stealing.

His ma swore then she'd have no more negroes working in the house.

'What was it she stole?' I asked.

'I can't recall,' Roy said. 'But Ma wasn't used to doing all the housework. It's too much for her to do alone, but she's stubborn. Once she's decided something, there's no going back on it.'

I was sad when we were done transplanting the tobacco and I had to stay in the house with his mother once more. If I had been able to work side by side in the fields with Roy, maybe we would have come to understand one another better.

Whenever there was a lull in the housework—often in the afternoons, between washing up after lunch and the preparations for dinner, when all the beds had been made and the floors swept, the laundry hung, the cupboards aired and the rugs beaten—I walked out to the horses in their paddock beyond the stables with a softened apple or carrot I had stashed in my apron pocket.

There was a spotted mare and a black gelding, both slow and old, their coats dull and patchy, their manes and tails tangled. The mare had a film of grey over her eyes, but her ears would prick up at the sound of me. They snuffed and stepped high towards the fence, which was soft with moss. They nudged me with their long, wet noses, finding the small treats I held out on my palm. They let me kiss their muzzles, scratch between their ears, run my fingers through the tangles in their forelocks. Once, they had been looked after, these two horses, and it made me sad that they weren't anymore. I could see their ribs, the sharp edges of their hipbones.

Roy found me out there one day. He'd finished work early, he said, and his mother had told him where I might be. I didn't like to know that she had been keeping her sharp eyes on me.

'Do they have names?' I asked, gesturing towards the horses, who had stepped back from the fence when Roy walked up. They were wary now, watching, the gelding's haunches quivering at an invisible fly.

'Him 'n Her, that's what Dad's always called 'em. We don't have a use for them any longer now we use the tractor to pull the plough. Don't know why Dad keeps them around. I would've sent them to the glue factory years ago.'

'That's an awful thing to say.'

'It's the truth, Sarah. You grew up on a farm. You know how it is as well as I do.'

I was silent, thinking of Big Bill, of Blackie, of the whole lost herd.

'Well, they're work if you're going to look after them right, and there's enough to do just planting a crop and tending it, harvesting, drying, everything else. I'm not being mean—I'm just saying rather than leave them here in this field half starved, with nothing to do, he ought to have shot them. Every time I see 'em it makes me sad.'

I squinted at him in the pale light, the faded freckles on his nose and the lines beside his eyes. Why was it I could no longer love him the way I'd thought I did?

'Show me their stables,' I said. 'Is that where they sleep?'

Roy limped ahead of me, opening the gate, leading the way into the shabby structure. It smelled of urine-soaked hay and mouldy feed, mouse droppings and damp.

'They probably do sleep in here to stay warm a little. It looks as though this stall has been getting some use.'

The light came in slatted through the boards, dust and fragments of cobwebs suspended in the still air. There was manure mounded on the hay-covered floor.

'Would your dad mind if I cleaned it out?'

'I wouldn't ask, if I were you. If it's what you want to do, fine. Just make sure it don't take away from the work.'

'Okay.'

Roy rested his hand on my shoulder then, and the warmth of his touch felt good in that dappled light, that place where his parents couldn't see us and stare.

'But why not ask?'

''Cause if he sees you care about something he might take it away. Better to act as though you don't care.'

I put my forehead against the dusty cotton of his shirt, the button pressing into my skin. 'He can't take away everything, Roy. You're a grown man now. You can do what you please.'

'I wish I could,' he said, moving his hand from my arm down to my waist. 'I need his help now. Haven't got money of my own.' His hand was travelling the curve of my hips to my buttocks, to the crevice between them.

'You can have what you want in other ways.'

'Like this?'

He lifted my skirt. His touch made me gasp, it was so cold between my legs. He tugged at my underclothes, pulling them to my knees. I fumbled with the buckle of his belt, the button and zipper of his heavy denim jeans. We were standing the whole time, his knees bent low, his hands on the stable post behind me. I was holding my skirt up with one hand, grasping his shoulder with the other. I watched his face contort, I was achingly full and still aware that it was not enough. Halfway through, as he gasped and thrust inside me, the horses appeared in the doorway of the stable. They did not flinch, but stood there watching me, silhouetted by the light, each fixing me with one wet, enormous eye.

•

So it was that when I'd finished my work in the house and kitchen I went to the stables, where I swept, shovelled and scrubbed the filthy old stalls. Once I had cleaned them I brought two bales of clean hay, spread them on the floor with a pitchfork, and filled the trough with clean water. On our trip into Roanoke that weekend I gave Roy money from the Red Cross lady which I knew I ought to save, and he bought a bag of grain for the horses from the Feed and Seed. We heaved it into the back of the truck while his dad was eating pie in the diner, talking weather and machinery with the other old farmers on their weekly jaunts to town, and his ma was at the five and dime. We covered it with the tarp and I sat on it during the ride home. Riding in the back of their truck was cold but there were blankets you could wrap yourself in, blankets which smelled of hay and mice. I didn't mind sitting there, wind whipping my hair across my face, watching the curves and corners of the road disappear behind us.

That afternoon we waited until Mr Jackson was having his Saturday nap, then we carried the feed between us to the stable. Him 'n Her followed us into their stall, and when I'd filled their food trough they gobbled as quickly as they could, as though if they didn't eat fast enough it would disappear. Afterwards I brushed their coats with an old brush I'd found, and with a pair of scissors cut the worst of the knots out of their manes and tails. They were gentle, strong creatures, more tetchy than cows but smarter too; if you did them a kindness they would not forget it, and the same if you did them a cruelty.

I found liniment for sores and rashes in the bathroom cupboard and rubbed it into the scabbed parts of their hides, the places where flies had laid their eggs and maggots had eaten away at the skin. I sat on the fence in the early spring sun, watching them pace the edges of their enclosure, imagining how they felt—trapped, longing for the days when they had known meaningful work. Still, I was happiest spending my time with them. They stopped me feeling sorry for myself. How sorry can you feel when a horse blows his warm, soft breath into your palm? When his ears prick up at the sound of your voice? Talking to the horses was a relief, because they would not comment on my strange accent or correct me, saying, 'We call them sweaters round here.'

I longed to let them out of their small field, for they'd eaten the winter grass bare in most parts, and just beyond their fence was more grass, thick in parts, with patches of clover. 'It won't do,' Roy said, when I asked him one night in bed, his breath reeking of the home-brewed spirit. 'Not unless you're going to tether them to a post. There's no fence there, and they're bound to run off and cause trouble.' He tried to caress me then but I told him it was my time of the month. This wasn't true, but it was close, I could feel it in the soreness of my breasts.

The next day was Sunday, and after we had been to church Roy came and helped me put on their halters and leads (I had cleaned and oiled the old, cracked leather). We picketed them beside the old apple tree, where the grass looked the thickest. We had already eaten Sunday dinner, and I had done the dishes. Mr Jackson sometimes 'read the Bible' in the sitting room after dinner on Sundays, but by now I knew that just meant taking a nap. The end of that everlasting church service for another week and the horses munching in the sun made me restlessly happy, and I swung myself up into the apple tree, climbing a few branches to sit in a fork, everything so close yet still beneath me. Roy grinned from where he sat beside the fence, licking his thumb and rubbing the dust off the toes of his polished Sunday shoes. Between us were the horses, ripping the grass in chunks from the damp ground, their lips smacking, their tails swishing against muscled haunches. We didn't talk but it was as happy as we had been since I'd come to America, together but separate, a brief moment of grace in which we weren't letting each other down.

After washing the lunch dishes the following day I went to the stables to feed Him 'n Her and brush their coats, which were just beginning to heal, to show some gloss and shine. They were not in the stall and I didn't see them when I first approached the paddock. They lay, side by side, near the western fence, each with a gunshot wound between the eyes. Their forelocks were matted with blood. Flies gathered around their open eyes, clinging to the wet surface of the dark, filmy irises. Their bodies were stiff when I crouched down to touch them. I stroked their long cold legs, their sticky blood-crusted noses.

He would have done it that morning before going to the fields. I wondered if Roy knew. If he'd tried to stop him.

I didn't go back inside then but walked into the woods at the back of the farm, only letting the hot tears spill when I was well out of sight of the house and fields. There was a creek which cut through banks of rhododendron bushes and I sat on a rock there, watching the water carry sticks and clumps of leaf litter past. My breath came in broken heaves. Water bugs skated on the surface in the eddies where fallen trees had blocked the flow and created small pools. The water was clear to the bottom, and when I put my hand in, the cold was enough to make my finger bones ache. The pain steadied me. I breathed in skunk, rotten leaves, distant wood smoke.

Walking back to the house in time to help make supper, I saw a truck from the slaughterhouse pulling out of the farm gates. The stiff, blood-heavy bodies of Him 'n Her lay in the bed of that truck, I was certain. At supper Roy avoided my gaze and no one spoke of anything except the crop and what the preacher had said the past Sunday and how the McAlisters were planting sorghum this year on half of their acreage.

He was already in bed with his back turned when I came from the bathroom that night, his light out, pretending to be sleeping.

'Did you know?' I asked, sitting on the edge of the bed, cradling my sharp elbows in my palms. My voice was hoarse.

'I was the one who pulled the trigger.'

I shut my eyes tight.

'Did you try and talk him out of it?'

'There's no use, Sarah,' he said, turning over. His face was blank. 'I told you in the beginning it was too much cost and work. And I was right. I tried to go along with what you wanted, but that ain't going to work. If you want to fit in here, you're the one who's got to change.'

He fell asleep a quarter of an hour later without speaking another word, and I sat there in the dark, listening to the rasp of his breath, thinking of what he'd said. The curtains let in the pale glow of a half-moon, and I thought of all the animals that would be out at night: the owls hunting mice, the raccoons and foxes searching for cracks in the henhouse, for warm bodies of sleeping birds in their nests. There is a point at which one fear can outweigh another. I made up my mind that night, lying in bed beneath the quilt his mother had sewn, on the bedframe his father had built, the mattress which Roy had slept on since he was a boy. Running away from my own family's problems, I'd ended up with his. Which were worse I wasn't certain, but I was determined not to find out.

In the morning I woke late, the sun high in the sky, the pillow beside me still dented where Roy's head had lain. I put some of my things in my suitcase, repacked my trunk and dressed in my travelling clothes.

Downstairs breakfast was finished, the dishes were in the drainer and Mrs Jackson was in the cellar, going through the shelves of canned stores—the pickled beans and canned tomatoes, the peaches in yellow juice, the beans like small pale seeds hovering in liquid.

'You sick?' she asked when she saw me at the bottom of the stairs.

'I'm leaving,' I said. 'I'd like a ride to the station.'

She put down the jar in her hands. 'Whatever for?'

'It isn't going to work out—me being here. I'm not happy, and I don't think Roy and I'll last.'

'Is it about children?' Her face was half lit from the high cellar window and for the first time I saw how she must dye her hair; the strands of grey were coming back in at the roots. It was odd, this vanity, on a woman so austere. I couldn't imagine her in the bathroom with a jar of black dye. Who did she get to help with the places in the back she couldn't see?

'More than that. Even if we could, I think it would be too hard.'

She sighed heavily and came to sit on the bottom step, smoothing her skirt over her knees and shins. I sat as well, keeping a decent space of six inches between us.

'You told Roy?'

I shook my head.

'Best you don't. He'll just try and talk you out of it. Tell you reasons why you're not to leave.'

'You sure?' I was relieved she didn't want me to tell him, but I felt guilt too. I pushed it down past my belly.

'You can write him a letter later, explaining. You'll go back to Australia?'

I nodded.

She stared at the shelves of jars, which glowed in the stream of sunlight from that high window.

'Sounds right. I told him it wouldn't work.'

'You told Roy?'

'Roy and Ronald. But they said it would. Ronald said it'd be good for me to have some help in the kitchen. Been doing it all myself for too long. But—no offence, child—you're different than us. It takes more time to teach you than to just get done with things the way I'm used to doing.'

'I tried,' I said.

'I do realise.' She leaned her head on her flat palm. Maybe for the first time I saw something soft in her face, a flash of vulnerability. But it was gone as quickly as it came.

'I've got to get back in time to make lunch, so come on then. I'll tell the men later. No use getting them all het up before a day's work is done.'

She stood and climbed the stairs, calling out behind her. 'Take the leftover biscuits from the pantry, now. And the coffee on the stove is still warm.'

I grabbed three of her biscuits and a napkin to wrap them in, swallowed a few mouthfuls of lukewarm coffee and rushed to the mudroom to put on my coat and boots. She had the truck keys in her hand. I hadn't even realised she could drive.

We walked out into the bright, cold air and I looked at the budding branches of the oak trees, the kittens curled sleeping on the porch swing. You don't really look at a place some-times until you know you're going to leave it. I thought of the stables, the apple tree, the smooth coats of Him 'n Her when I brushed them, the way they blinked and sneezed in the morning sun. I thought about how Roy had tried but it wasn't enough. I couldn't blame him for shooting the horses, but I couldn't forgive him either. I knew, deep down, that I ought to tell him I was leaving, and I nearly stopped her, but it was like stopping a log rolling down a hill. Once she got going you weren't going to stand in her way.

The truck had wooden slatted sides and a wide running board. It was hard to lift my trunk into the back with just the two of us, but we managed. I lifted my suitcase on my own. Mrs Jackson started the engine while I was still climbing in and I realised she was hurrying too, that she wanted to get me away before the men found out what was happening. Smoke billowed out of the exhaust and I had hardly sat down before she was reversing and pulling around, driving us down the steep hill of the driveway. I pulled my felt hat low over my eyes, rubbed my hands together and tried to slow my breath. The taste of coffee was still in my mouth, bitter and burned. I checked the side mirror, half expecting to see the men on their green John Deere tractor, waving us down.

She glanced at me, her lips flat against her gums, squinting so the wrinkles collapsed the skin around her eyes. 'You have anyone that can help you, child?'

'There are some friends I met on the boat. Other brides. But I'll go home. I'll just get the papers sorted, the divorce papers, so he can marry again if he wants to.'

Mrs Jackson stared out at the road ahead of her, her hands gripping the steering wheel tight. 'I've got a niece who lives in Maryland. I'll give you her name and such, in case you find yourself in need of a place to stay for a little while.'

'That's kind of you; I might look her up,' I lied.

She smiled with thin lips, proud of her Christian charity.

The rest of the trip to Roanoke and the train station passed in silence. Out the window the ridges of the mountains shadowed one another. I was certain that if I reached out a hand I could feel their bluish softness. The engine strained as we climbed between the granite-sided slopes, then flew downhill past pine and sugar maple into the valley. The windows were wound up but there was still the smell of manure from chicken and pig farms, strong enough I could taste it in the back of my throat. I wanted to wail for the chance I had lost: for babies, a cheque-book with his name and mine, arguing about the children, ironing his shirts. I was leaving behind everything I'd imagined for us, only it didn't exist; it had never existed outside my head. It was in the trenches of New Guinea, maybe, the jungle prison, the rotting wounds of men. In my mother's ear pressed to the radio, my father's gaze as his empty glass was refilled with beer. Roy in the dark park, kneeling before me in the damp grass. Useless hope, chances we'd never have. Instead it was the flies on the filmy-eyed horses, the knowledge that life would never seem so full of possibility again.

CHAPTER 28

Alex visits me on my second day in the infirmary. I know it is the opposite end of the ship from where he works. He is in his uniform, and he takes off his cap and places it in his lap when he sits, pulling up a chair. I have been either curled up in pain or sleeping, my body trying to adjust to the quantity of calories. They will let me go back to the cabin I share with Grandma tomorrow, as long as I keep returning to be weighed and checked, as long as I am showing progress.

I can tell that Alex doesn't know what to say, and he smiles at me, his eyes jumping towards the door. I pretend that things are normal. I know that he has been told otherwise. He isn't going to mention it directly though, and instead our words dance around the truth.

He says I'm missing the worst weather of the trip. That it is rainy and cold, that all the passengers are at the slots or playing bridge, and one of the engines flooded and failed. He talks about engine repairs and I clench my fists under the cotton blanket.

Then I say what I'm thinking. 'I have a boyfriend, you know, back home. I shouldn't have done what we did.'

Oddly, he smiles. 'Same! I was going to say something, but I thought it was wrong to tell you while you're here, in the infirmary. I'm engaged, would you believe it. So I should feel worse than you.'

I squint at him in the greenish light. He seems way too happy. 'Do you?' I ask.

He shakes his head. 'Do you? Feel guilty?'

'Yes. But I always do. It's a familiar sensation.'

I pull at a thread on the cotton blanket. My hair hasn't been washed since I've been in the infirmary and I can smell it, greasy and lank, like a half-open curtain I can duck behind.

He's still shaking his head, and I don't think he realises he's doing it.

'I wonder if there's something wrong with me for not feeling guilty. I probably shouldn't be getting married. But I love her. I just—'

'It's fine. You don't need to explain it to me.'

I don't actually want to know. I watch him smile, and feel a shudder as much for myself as him. At our mutual desperation to feel wanted.

He stands and brushes invisible lint from his pressed pants and I see the shininess of his shoes, the perfect half-moon of cuticle on his fingernails.

I am as blind to myself as I was to him.

CHAPTER 29

Where does sorrow bring you? Closer to home or further from it? The small city of Roanoke was suddenly before us: first the bleak brick and sprawling football fields of the high school, then the tall ornate courthouse and the Elwood Diner. The train tracks cut through the centre of the city like a gash. The smell of burning coal replaced that of hogs and chickens. Mrs Jackson drove right up to the train station and stopped the truck out front, cutting the engine with the same certainty she cut biscuits. She lowered herself out of the cab. 'You, boy,' I heard her say. 'Get that trunk for me and take it to the station agent's office. We need to get a ticket to Washington.'

A porter heaved my trunk out of the truck bed and Mrs Jackson bustled towards the ticket office, looking back just long enough to make sure I followed. Her purse slapped against her side as she walked, and the sleeve of her dress had a splotch of flour from breakfast.

Mrs Jackson rapped the glass window of the ticket counter, startling the young man dozing with his head on the desk behind it. 'One ticket to Washington DC.'

He mumbled something I didn't hear.

'Not return—she's goin' to visit a sick friend. She'll buy the return once she knows when she's fixing to get back.'

Which would be never, but she had to keep up appearances.

I pulled out my pocketbook, but Mrs Jackson was already paying him from her own. 'Here,' I said, trying to pass her a bill. She pushed my hand away, looking down her nose at me.

'Don't be a fool. You are going to need that money more'n I will. Now here.' She thrust the ticket into my hand. 'Platform two, and it's leaving in ninety minutes. I can't hang round and wait; I've got lunch to put on before the men come in from the field. You'll be fine?'

'Yes. Thank you.'

She patted my arm, her lips pursed, and a dimple showed in her cheek for just a moment, a sign of how glad she was to be rid of me. How quickly it all happened. I hardly realised what I'd done.

The porter appeared with my trunk then outside the station office. 'Platform two, boy,' she hollered. 'And don't you go bangin' it around like it's full of stones. She doesn't want to get there and have her things all smashed to pieces.'

'Bye now. Send a letter.' Those were Mrs Jackson's last words to me and I waved as she clambered into that big truck and drove off, not once looking back. She'd get home, make lunch and tidy the bedrooms as though nothing at all had changed. I would try my very best to forget that farm and Roanoke altogether. Roy's blank face, the flies gathered on the glassy dead eye of a horse. The mistakes I'd made, the way I left.

Memory is a strange creature, no doubt about that, for it can shove things behind the bureau for years and then suddenly they pop out like a jack-in-the-box, something lost suddenly found. They can still make you jump, and once you blow the dust off they feel like they happened only yesterday. I heard one of those brain doctors talking about it on the radio the other day. He was saying that you're more likely to remember something if you're in a similar place or state of mind, or the same piece of music is playing or you see the same kind of weather. I tried my best to forget Roy and his family, but there were things which always brought back those memories. The smell of fried ham in the morning or of Sloan's Liniment, which I stole from the medicine cabinet and rubbed on the horses. The sight of a man with a lump of chaw in his cheek, the smell of fresh-cut tobacco leaves, sappy and sharp. My time at the farm would come back to me when I least expected it, and always with a needle of regret—for my cowardice in running away without even saying goodbye.

•

Moving again, the past growing further away like a dot on the horizon. If I never stopped would it disappear? Couldn't I just keep looking out the window forever? The train, being regional, stopped in nearly every town it went through. The paltry offerings of the dining car (a soggy corned beef sandwich, weak yellow coffee) had to tide me over until Washington, and then I'd decide what to do next. It wasn't as though the Australian embassy kept a hostel for jilted brides. I walked up and down the cars, watching the restless children kicking each other while their mothers slept, the large negro family with their mouth-watering selection of food, the businessmen in dark suits and well-shined shoes. I wore my canary-yellow pencil skirt and jacket of light wool, with my best stockings and a pair of low-heeled black pumps. On top of my suitcase in the rack above my seat were my cream belted coat and matching hat and in the coat pocket a pair of black leather gloves. I wore my nicest things, for wherever I went I would be making an impression upon strangers, and I did not want them to guess the truth: that I was lost now. Far from safety; far from home.

After a few hours I pulled out a notepad and pen.

Dear Roy,
I know I should have said goodbye but your mother
thought it best I just leave.

No, I had to take responsibility. I crumpled the page and stuffed it in the seat pocket. I stared out the window at the rivulets of rain streaming across the glass, blown sideways by the wind and speed, and began again.

Dear Roy,
I want to say goodbye, and explain my leaving. I am sorry
that I wasn't brave enough to say this in person. Ever
since arriving at the farm I knew that I didn't belong—
and it seemed like the harder I tried, the harder it was
to fit in. When I married you everything moved so fast,

and I was desperate to get away from my family. I didn't think about what I was getting myself into. Did you? We didn't know what the next day would bring, so we weren't thinking about one, two years down the track. I can't see us ever being happy like we were in Sydney. We can't ransom our whole lives on that mistake. Maybe mistake's the wrong word. I did love you, Roy. I wish I still felt that way, or even the possibility of it. But instead I feel trapped by the past and dread the future. I hope you can forgive me, and that you can find happiness with someone else. Once I have an address I'll send it to you, so you can apply for a divorce. I'll remember our time in Sydney fondly, and think of you with the memory of our love.

Sarah

Good grief, I was harsh. *The memory of our love.* But I was honest too. I never did hear back from him. Just his signature on the papers his lawyer sent, and then silence. Fifty years of silence. And then one day a package in the mail from a Mrs Laura Jackson in Floyd, Virginia. Inside was a little card with neat handwriting:

Dear Mrs Rice,
My husband Roy Jackson passed away last Christmas after a prolonged battle with lung cancer. He asked in his will that these letters be returned to you. He told me about you when we first met, at church, and how it broke his heart when you left. But I think over the years he came to understand it was for the best, and we had forty years of

blessed marriage. His mother and father died in 1962 and 1963, leaving the farm to us, and we sold it to a housing developer and bought some land southwest of there, where we raised horses.

I do hope you found happiness as well and that these letters find you in good health.

Sincerely,

Mrs Laura Jackson

Horses. So he felt it too, that sorrow, and my regret then was big enough to eat my own heart. *Too late, too late*, it beat in my chest, the memories rushing back in no order: Roy in his uniform when we first met, the bruise on his cheek, the freckles across the bridge of his snub American nose. I had been young and foolish. The return of the letters did what I'm certain he intended. They made me realise how cruel I had been.

CHAPTER 30

I tell myself I'm crying for the horses. For Roy. For all that Grandma lost, and for what she was strong enough to leave. But I'm crying too because of the calories. The food I cannot control. The past that keeps coming back unbidden, because when I'm not hungry my thoughts are filled with things other than food.

New Zealand has come and gone; in two more days we dock in Sydney. I am out of the infirmary now, though I have to return twice a day to be weighed, to have my pulse taken and my blood pressure checked. Since he learned I'm in nursing school the doctor and I have found some common ground. He lets me take my own blood pressure, he gives me little tasks if I ask for them. He quizzes me about medications, conditions. Today he looks at me strangely after taking my blood pressure and vitals, and when I ask what is up he says he wants to understand why an intelligent person would knowingly cause their body irreparable harm.

'It becomes addictive,' I say. 'I know it doesn't make sense, but it is so tempting to take it the next step, and then the next—if I had three bites of a sandwich yesterday to try having just two today. At a certain point I can't shut it off. It's a compulsion.'

'Does it make you feel better than the rest of us mere humans? The ones who are always eating, always stuffing our faces?'

'It's not that. More that it gives me back a sense of control.'

'Do you want to talk about that, what makes you lose control?'

I shake my head.

'Okay, then, let me ask you this: where do you see yourself in ten years?'

I shrug.

'C'mon, answer the question.'

I look towards the window. This part of the ship is most often in shade, but just now light is coming in through the window, and outside there is the pale blue of sky meeting the darker blue of sea. A gull flaps past, carrying something glinting and silver in its beak.

'Working as an RN. Paediatrics, I hope.'

'Married? A family?'

I shrug. 'Possibly.'

'Still running?'

'Definitely.'

The doctor sits down on the chair behind his desk. He clicks the mouse to wake up his desktop and types some notes, adjusting his reading glasses, pushing them up the bridge of his nose.

'I'm not going to lecture you, Hannah. You've heard it all before. You know as well as I do that your goals will be impossible to achieve if you keep this up. Stress fractures, osteo-porosis, heart failure—anorexia has the highest mortality rate of any mental illness. Look at your grandmother: you could die before her. Look around you. There's so much you can do to help other people, but you can't do that if you can't keep yourself alive, if you don't get to the bottom of this—the real reason for your disorder.'

I look away as he says this, keeping my face as expressionless as possible. When he's finished talking I leave the room, saying I have to get Grandma for dinner.

She is waiting in the library, and as we walk arm in arm over to the restaurant she points out that we don't have many dinners left on the ship. We stroll underneath the lifeboats, along the deck. The sun is a bright orange ball dropping slowly, then disappearing all at once behind the horizon. The sky turns from orange to violet. I'd pushed away the doctor's words when he said them—I have heard so many speeches about how selfish I am that I immediately assumed this was his point as well. But now I think about what he said. I don't want Grandma to have to bury me. I want her to be proud of me. Like I am proud of her.

'You look thoughtful, poppet,' Grandma says. She hasn't called me poppet in years, and I grin at the quaint word, and the affection in it. 'Penny for your thoughts?'

I take a deep breath.

'I haven't been well for a long time, Grandma. There's so much I've been hiding.'

'I know, Hannah, I do.'

'Really?'

'Or I sensed it. It's why I wanted you to come with me on this trip. I can see now how selfish I've been; I've probably made you worse off. But I wanted you close. I guess I hoped you'd want to talk about it, one day. I suppose it's why I wanted to tell you about Roy. About the secrets *I* kept.'

'Is the divorce why you didn't come back earlier?'

Grandma stops and sits on a bench. She pats the seat beside her. 'When you've hidden the truth for so long it starts to seem normal. Coming back means facing all the lies I told. To Mum and Dad—even though they're dead now—to my kids, to you, to myself. I wish I'd been strong enough before. I guess none of us is perfect.'

It is that violet grey of dusk and the line of the horizon is nearly invisible, so close is the colour of the ocean to that of the sky. A flock of birds flies high overhead, their shapes black blurs above. They'll fly through the dark, all night. I've heard of birds migrating over the ocean that tire and—unable to rest—drop in the sea to die. I shut my eyes and wish these birds strength. I want more than anything for them to get where they need to go.

CHAPTER 31

'Ticket, please,' were the only words anyone spoke to me on the journey. It seemed we took on a new ticket-puncher with every stop—I had never seen such vigilant ticket-punching. By the time the train pulled into Washington DC my stub looked like a leaf munched through by a caterpillar; there were more holes than paper remaining to punch.

'Final stop, Union Station. All passengers will disembark the train here. Please take your luggage and personal belongings with you when you leave the car.'

It was night. I had travelled what felt like all day, and when I stepped onto the platform the air was a cold blast against my face. The narrow space was crowded with people, everyone dressed in dark colours, shouting above the noise of the trains. Though I stood out in my cream and yellow ensemble, I still felt the relief of being among a crowd again, the invisibility. I found a porter to help me with my trunk and asked him to take it to the Travelers' Aid counter. Wheeling my trunk on a small dolly, the porter led me into a huge hall with polished marble floors, white granite walls and ceilings inlaid with gold leaf. He helped me secure storage for my trunk and waited to make sure that I found a place in a hotel, then showed me the cab rank at the entrance to the station. I thanked him and gave him a five-dollar bill, which he seemed reluctant to accept. 'It's too much, ma'am.'

'Take it,' I said. 'Please.'

He tucked it in the breast pocket of his jacket, tipped his hat and gave a little bow. 'Enjoy your stay in the nation's capital.'

The way he said it made me feel like a tourist. It was a sham, but one I decided to play along with. I had procured a room in a small, slightly shabby hotel several blocks from the White House, in what the lady behind the desk at Traveler's Aid had assured me was a safe area for 'ladies travelling on their own'. At the front desk they asked for my passport and my reason for visiting.

'I'm seeing the sights,' I said. 'I would love some advice on what museums and monuments I should visit.'

The woman behind the desk nodded, droopy-eyed. She slid a map across the desk with my key. 'Breakfast is served in the dining room from seven to nine.'

•

I can still picture the tiny room in that hotel, the bare walls, the worn carpet, the narrow bed beneath a window that looked out to a brick wall. I nearly went home—I came so close. I began dozens of letters to Mum and Dad, explaining what had happened, but I never sent them. Pretending to be a tourist, I visited the National Air Museum and the National History Museum, walking for hours through rooms of flying machines, stuffed birds, insects stuck through with pins, forever suspended in a glass drawer. I walked through the cool marble interior of the Lincoln Memorial, down the National Mall to the Washington Monument, up the eight hundred and ninety-eight steps to the top and down again, my legs shaking as I descended. I walked past the green sloping lawns and white pillars of the White House, through the cobblestoned streets of Georgetown and along the banks of the Potomac River. It was a relief to be among so much history that had nothing to do with me. I only spoke to people to ask directions, and even then it was as though my voice was not my own. It came out croaky, dusty.

It came to me when I was standing in front of an enclosure that held two black bears, a male and a female, at the National Zoo in Rock Creek Park. Their fur was mangy and their eyes glassy; they slept in a patch of sun as though the place held no interest for them anymore. They were trapped, but I was free. And I would stay. To go back was to admit defeat. To pick up where I had left off: the heavy silence at the dinner table, the empty place where Jack once sat, watching Fred limp through his chores, hearing Mum's muffled wail behind a door.

•

The following Monday, after hours of waiting in a queue, I spoke to a woman at the Australian embassy. She said that to stay I would need to find work and apply for a new visa. She would give me a grace period of a few weeks in which to find work.

I had never heard that phrase before—a grace period—and I loved how it sounded. Grace was exactly what I needed now.

Between ten and eleven each morning—the lull between the breakfast and lunch rushes—I went into diners and small restaurants that served tourists near the Capitol and gave them my name and the telephone number of the hotel, saying I was available to work any shift they had. One owner brushed his short, stubby fingers on his grease-stained apron and said, 'How're you gonna be a waitress if no one can understand your accent?'

'I can speak slowly. I find most people do understand me.'

'It's cute, honey, don't get me wrong, you're cute, but we don't need cute. We need hard-working. We need experience.'

I walked out onto the street with my fists clenched.

'Hey,' I heard, and turned. It was the waitress who had been polishing the coffee urn, bottle-blonde with a liberal number of buttons left open on her shirt.

'My cousin's the bartender at a restaurant on G Street Northwest. The Olmstead Grill. Tell him Susie sent you. Better tips at that kinda place anyway. You'd be wasting your talent here.'

'Thanks,' I said, and she shrugged, returning inside and bumping the door shut behind her with her hip.

Susie was right about the Olmstead Grill. It was one of those low-lit places with soft music always playing and banquette seating, plush. Tables of dark polished wood, a menu stitched into a leather-bound book, a dessert cart. A bar with rows of coloured bottles sitting in front of a mirrored wall, a glass chandelier, a marble surface grooved from wear. I asked to speak to the bartender, and while I didn't hide my accent I tried to

say the r. Barten*der*. Not barten*dah*. A small man with a moustache came out from behind the bar, and straightaway I said
that Susie had sent me.

'How is that girl? I tell her to come work here instead of that
piece-of-crap diner, but she's got kids, don't want to work nights.
What about you? Can you work nights? What's your story?'

I didn't mean to tell him, but—whether it was the way he'd
asked, or maybe the friendliness, the first flicker of it I'd seen—
before I knew it I'd told him about Roy, about Roanoke, about
things not working out. About how I was staying in a hotel for
now, running out of money quick. About how I had decided
just the other day that I would stay. I wasn't going back.

'I can work any hours you like, and I'm reliable.'

'Alright, alright. Susie knows I'm a bleedin' heart. Tell you
what, we'll give you a week. Doesn't work out you're on your way.'

He put me on in the bar as a cocktail waitress, saying the
restaurant was harder than drinks, plus in the bar you made
better tips. But I had to learn, and fast, how any of it was done.
I'd hardly been inside a bar, and never one in America. I had
to learn what the drinks were, how much they cost, and what
they came with. I had to learn to smile and be friendly enough
without letting it go further, how to rebuff the customers when
they went too far too fast; men asked me out nearly every shift,
even though half of them had wives and children at home. I had
to learn how to remember who'd ordered what drink, and not
give the whisky sour to the gentleman who'd ordered a dirty
martini or the gin fizz to the one who'd ordered a glass of beer.
I learned to balance my tray on five fingers above my head as I
manoeuvred through a crowd. I learned which shoes I could

stand in for six hours without blisters, and how good it felt to sit and take them off at the end of the night. I learned that sleep came easier after those long shifts with a drink—or two. Charlie poured them for us at the bar while we counted our tips, and they were on the house. We always gave him twenty per cent of our tips, because a good cocktail waitress is nothing without a good bartender, and if you tipped the bartender well your drinks were quickest to hit the bar.

I worked with Maryanne and Jessamyn, with Esther and Ava. The friendly ones showed me how to use seltzer to get a wine stain out of a white shirt, how to make lipstick stay put longer by powdering your lips first. Maryanne taught me to watch my back in a crowded room; she'd snap up my tables when I wasn't looking—saying they were desperate for a drink—and take home tips which ought to have been mine.

Time took on a funny sort of quality then, it either flew past when I was working, or crept like cold honey when I wasn't. I left the hotel and found a room in a boarding house near the zoo, and sometimes I heard the lions roar late at night, a sound which made my hair stand on end even though I knew they were caged. I wrote letters home, pretending I was still in Roanoke with Roy. I got a PO box in DC for them to send replies to, telling them it was more reliable. Hoping they wouldn't look at a map and wonder at the distance between Roanoke and DC. I couldn't bear the questions they would ask if they knew the truth. Why did you leave him? Why, then, haven't you come home?

I polished my shoes and mended my stockings. I read books borrowed from the library, seeking out more Steinbeck: *Of*

Mice and Men, The Red Pony, Cannery Row. I read my way into America. *The Great Gatsby. A Tree Grows in Brooklyn. The Sound and the Fury. The Call of the Wild.* Once a week, on my day off, I treated myself to a matinee. The rest of my money I used, to pay the rent and to eat. I had never lived so close to the edge. Every week it was a matter of coins found between cushions in my room, at the bottom of my handbag, surviving on leftovers saved from the restaurant. My day off was something I cherished, but at the end of it I was always hungry, for I relied on the restaurant to eat and hardly bought a loaf of bread for myself.

After shifts I took the bus home—I couldn't afford a cab. It was only one and a half blocks between my boarding house and the bus stop, but I walked quickly along the badly lit street, eyes darting around, keys clutched in my fingers. I wanted to be fearless, unafraid of the dark shadows, but I'd read the newspaper stories about women attacked, bodies found floating in the Potomac. I'd heard stories from the women I worked with about customers finding out where they lived, showing up outside their doors, lingering in the alley where we smoked on our breaks. So it felt precarious, but so did everything, then. So did life.

I thought of Jim often and wondered why I'd kissed him, what it was I'd felt then: was it fear of what I was headed towards or did I have true feelings for him? Our conversations on board that train were the most memorable I'd ever had. He'd forgotten me, though, I was certain. One night when I couldn't fall asleep after a shift and I'd read all my library books I dug out *The Grapes of Wrath* and lay in bed rereading it. It made me remember the dining car of the train, the landscape passing in a blur, his earnestness and desire to get things right. Six months had passed since then—three months in Roanoke and three in DC. I read Tom Joad saying to his ma: 'The hell with it. There ain't no sin and there ain't no virtue. There's just stuff people do.' And by the time the sun was up and the book was finished, all the times I'd loathed myself for what felt like sin, and loathed my father for what felt like his sin, seemed just another waste of time and feeling. Finally I knew what stuff I had to do.

CHAPTER 32

'Hannah.'

'Mom.'

'Are you okay? I've been so worried.'

'I'm sorry, Mom. It's been back for a while. I still spend so much time fighting it.'

'I'm sorry, honey. I love you so much.'

I can hear her voice on the other end of the line, so far away, the creak of tears. My own eyes flood.

'I love you too. And it's good to be with Grandma. We dock tomorrow.'

'I can't believe it. After all these years, she's finally going to be back.'

'I know. And I nearly ruined it.'

'You didn't. You know she wouldn't have gone without you. Part of the reason she went is to take you. She thought it might help.'

It is hard to talk, my throat is so tight. I think about Grandma's Steinbeck. *There ain't no sin and there ain't no virtue. There's just stuff people do.*

'Has it helped?'

I nod, then remember that she can't see me.

'Yes,' I say. It feels good to be telling the truth.

CHAPTER 33

At dinner there is an announcement over the loudspeaker. We will be going through the heads the following morning around seven am and docking in Sydney by seven-thirty. Passengers are expected to disembark by eight-thirty. Suitcases need to be outside the cabins by six. Hannah and I go back to our cabin to pack, and I notice for the first time that she looks a little better; it's only been a few days, but there is colour in her cheeks again, some shine in her hair. I have been so busy worrying about her I've hardly thought about arriving, but as I think back over the letters Fred and I have exchanged I feel the nerves come on. When we started corresponding again he was cross with me. He accused me of doing some sort of disappearing act, said he couldn't believe I didn't at least come back when Mum and Dad were sick, when Dad and then Mum died.

I had my clinic then, I tried to explain, and we had a mort-gage, the kids' college educations to save for. I didn't tell him how terrified I was. How I'd run away from the past, and it made me feel sick to think of facing it again. Dad died quickly and we spoke on the phone before he passed away. He never said much, but when he went into the hospice they put him on high doses of morphine, and he grew quite talkative, though not a lot of it made sense. We spoke a week before he died and he asked me if I'd fed the poddy calves. I was going to say no—that was Mum's job—but I just said, 'Yes, Dad, I have.' He laughed and caught his breath; laughing winded him so fast.

'You love the cows, don't you, Sarah? More'n you love your old dad.'

'That's not true,' I said. 'I love you, Dad. I'm sorry I'm not there.'

'It's alright, Sar,' he said. 'I know you're just over in the shed. We've always been the most alike, you and me. Probably why we find it so hard to get along.'

He started talking about radio talk shows then and I lost the thread of where he was, but when Fred came back on the line I was still wiping away tears.

'It's like that,' Fred said. 'The drugs they're giving him. Hours of gibberish and then moments of the truest things he's ever said. He told me he was sorry he made me and Jack go to war. Said he always blamed himself for Jack's death.'

'Oh, Fred.'

'It's fine, Sar. I'll let you go.'

'Wait,' I said, but he'd hung up. I remember returning to the kitchen, where the kids were at the kitchen table with their homework spread out, and the rice had boiled over, starchy water pooled on the burner of the stove.

I took the tea towel and wiped at my face, thinking of my mum, whom I'd tried so hard not to become.

Caroline looked up from her maths homework, pulling her ponytail.

'What's wrong?' she said, scrunching up her freckled nose.

'Nothing. You kids need to clear the papers and set the table for dinner.'

•

Jim wasn't as hard to find as I'd thought he might be. Turns out he was right: Kilmarnock is a small place, and when you show up fresh from the bus station at the only diner in town at lunchtime and tell the waitress you're looking for a Jim Rice, naval officer, she'll not only tell you where he lives, she'll draw you a map on a napkin and offer to give him a call so he can come pick you up, since it's quite a walk.

'That's fine,' I said. 'I'll just walk over there now.'

'It'll take you an hour,' she said. 'Where are you from anyway? England? You've got the sweetest accent!'

'Australia.'

'Australia,' the waitress squealed. 'Did you have a pet kangaroo? What about the black people over there, what do you call them, Aborigines? What they like?' She grinned and then covered her mouth. 'Gwen, come here—guess where this girl is from. Say something,' she instructed me, as an older woman with her hair in an elaborate pile of grey curls walked over, tucking her notepad into her apron.

'What do you want me to say?'

'Well, honey, I don't know.'

275

'Come now,' said Gwen, 'leave her alone. How'd you like it if everyone told you that you talked funny?'

'Not funny—I told her I liked it.' The young waitress crossed her arms over her chest. 'So did you meet Jim when he was over there on R and R? He looked so handsome in his uniform. He told us how pretty the girls in Australia were; I bet he was talking about you.'

I looked at the door to the street, wishing that I could walk away from this conversation without making a fool of myself. 'Something like that,' I mumbled.

Gwen reached over and squeezed my shoulder. 'We hope we'll be seeing you again, now.'

She gave the younger waitress a stern look and I fled, thanking them as I backed out the door.

I walked down Main Street past a drugstore, a bowling alley, a hardware store and an oyster shop. When I turned off Main there were no footpaths, so I kept to the verge beside the painted timber homes with wide verandahs and lawns that flowed each into the next. The napkin clutched in my hand said it was the end of Cox's Farm Road, which the waitress had said was a few miles. I felt lightheaded, queasy in the stomach, regretting the hamburger I'd had for lunch. It was flat here, and humid. There was the back-of-throat smell of wood burning and a fishy sort of muddy smell of the bay meeting the river.

I passed a woman out in her garden cutting back rose bushes. 'Nice day,' she called out, and I nodded.

'Sure is,' I replied, walking on briskly before she could ask me where I was from. It seemed you couldn't walk past a person on the street here without saying hello.

It took about an hour to reach the end of Cox's Farm Road. Down the long driveway I saw a tall timber structure with porticos and a sharply pitched roof, a turret like something from a fairy tale. It was painted white with green trim, a recent paint job with no chipping around the sills and frames. I walked up, my purse banging against my hip, silently cursing myself for not thinking this through. What if he had a fiancée now, and she answered the door? But it was too late to turn back. I gritted my teeth until my jaw hurt, and stepped onto the creaking verandah, where a swing hung from a chain just like at Roy's house. What was it with the bloody swings in this country? And the rocking chairs? Did no one like to sit still?

Inside there was the muffled sound of a radio playing. I knocked—one of those brass lion heads, which needed a polish. There was a voice, female, 'Coming!' and footsteps. I stepped back a little, folding my hands in front of my waist. The door opened and there was the smell of baking, and the silhouette of a woman with sunlight behind her so I couldn't straightaway see her face. She was tall, like Jim, and her hair glowed kind of white.

'Can I help you?' Her voice had that soft, sugary sound of the American South.

'I—I'm a friend of Jim's from the *Mariposa*, and I'm in town for the day. I thought I'd stop by to say hello . . . if I've got the right place, that is. If he's around.'

The woman just stood there with her mouth open for a moment and then she grabbed my arm and pulled me inside. 'Honey, of course he is. That's my boy. Come inside now. You're one of them Australian girls, aren't you? He told me how y'all came over on that boat. Were you going to Roanoke? What's your name? I'll bet he told me about you.'

Once the words started flowing out of her they didn't seem to stop, and I was ushered into the kitchen and sat down and poured a glass of iced tea before she paused to catch her breath and ask me if she could get me something to eat. She was tall and slender, with a thin face and prominent teeth, her white hair pulled into a bun which frizzed out around her face. Her skin was lined and tanned, as if she spent a lot of time in the sun. I said I'd eaten, but she put a piece of pie in front of me anyway—strawberry rhubarb, she told me—and sat across from me asking questions and watching me eat. Since I'd come in she hadn't mentioned Jim again and I wondered if he was even home.

When I had finished eating and praised her pie, she took the plate to the sink and looked out the kitchen window. 'He's just coming in off the water now. Come on down to the dock and we'll say hello.'

I hadn't realised that their house backed onto the water, but as I followed his mother into the backyard I saw how the lawn dropped away to the brownish water of the river, and there among spindly trees and mangroves by the water's edge was a little timber dock. A small sailboat was angling up beside it and a figure leaped off, carrying a length of rope which he looped around a metal hook on the dock. As we got closer I saw it was Jim, but he was shirtless and his skin was brown, his hair longer, his face unshaven. He moved like a cat, graceful and easy, between the deck of his small sailboat and the dock.

'That boy just isn't happy unless he's on the water,' his mother was saying, 'and I tell him to wear a shirt but do you think he listens to me? You'll have to forgive him, Sarah. If we'd known you were coming . . .'

Jim looked up then at the sound of his mother's voice and squinted. I raised my hand in a half-wave.

'Aren't you going to come say hello? Sarah's dropped by for a visit, honey. Do you remember her? She says y'all met on the *Mariposa.*'

'Of course I do.' Jim shook my hand as a stranger might. 'Just hang on and I'll get my shirt from the boatshed. Did you offer her a cold drink, Mama?'

'Don't be a fool, Jim—who taught you your manners in the first place? We'll just wait for you down on the dock. I'll show Sarah the river up close.'

We sat on the soft, warm wood of the dock, our feet dangling over the side. My shoes were off beside me and my feet felt cool in the brackish water. There was the sound of it slapping the sides of the dock, and the rigging of the boat clanked in the breeze. The temperature had dropped a few degrees down by the water, and we waved away mosquitoes while she talked about boats and the crabbing and fishing they did all summer, and how nice it was to have a person to show around.

'How long can you stay for? At least till dinner, I hope. We can boil crabs for dinner.'

'I'm afraid my bus leaves at five.'

'Well, you'll just have to come for crabs some other time.'

Jim came over and sat beside me, wearing a yellow cotton shirt with the sleeves rolled up. 'Is she talking your ear off,

Sarah? Mama, isn't there something you need to do up in the house?'

His mother reached over and pinched his arm.

'Ow!'

She stood, brushing her skirt and smiling at me. 'You show Sarah round the place, now, won't you? I'll be up in the kitchen.'

'I like your mother,' I said, as she made her way back up the grassy hill, carrying her shoes in one hand.

Jim looked at me, his brow furrowed. 'You don't have to live with her.'

We were quiet for a moment or two and a heron flew low across the water on the other shore, landing in the bottom branches of a tree.

'I didn't think I'd hear from you again,' Jim said. He cleared his throat.

I looked down at my feet in the muddy water. 'I was ashamed of how I acted.'

'So what're you doing here?' He tossed a stick from the dock, arm brushing against mine.

'I brought your book back. I didn't want you to think I'd stolen it.'

'You came all the way here to return a book? I find that hard to believe.'

'I didn't have your address. And we never got to talk about how it ended.'

'Some ending, isn't it?'

'What do you think it means?'

'I don't know, Sarah. I don't know what much means. On

the train, I didn't mean to sound like I didn't want to kiss you; I just wanted us to talk about what it meant.'

I nodded and thought about what else I'd come to tell him. There weren't words yet for what had happened with Roy and the awfulness of everything. Instead I felt my throat close up, and I shut my eyes tight against the tears that were welling. They trickled out though, betraying me, and there was Jim's hand on my back.

'Oh, damn. I'm a disaster. I'm sorry, Jim. I thought I'd pulled myself together.'

'Hush, now, Sarah, it's fine.'

'I left Roy. I've been living in DC.'

'On your own?'

'Yes.'

'What happened?'

'It's a long story.'

'I got time.' Jim rubbed his hands up and down on his thighs and kept his eyes fixed out on the water.

I wanted to tell him, but not then. I didn't want Roy there between us.

When I didn't speak, Jim said: 'So what now? You go back to Australia?'

I shook my head. 'There was so much I wanted to get away from, so why leave now that I am? Away, that is.'

Jim stood up, stretching his arms over his head. 'Let's go out on the boat. You ever been sailing?'

'No.'

'Can you swim?'

'A little.'
'Well, you probably won't drown then.'

•

The boat was small; it wouldn't have fitted more than two. Jim told me where to sit and how to lean but he did all the work. He said there wasn't much of a breeze, but once we got towards the centre of the river it might pick up some. I dangled my fingers over the edge of the boat into the water as the wind ruffled the sail, making it slap and then catch taut, my fingers feeling the water heavy against them. I felt my hair pull loose from its pins and pushed what I could behind my ears. Jim looked over at me for what felt like the first time since I'd told him about Roy.

'It's nice to see your smile again,' he said. 'I've missed it.'
'You didn't tell me how pretty it is here.'
'Maybe I hoped you'd come and see for yourself.'
It felt so light, our banter, but unlike the talk in the bar it meant something. I felt like I'd been asleep for weeks and was just waking up. I shut my eyes and watched the sun draw pink and orange patterns inside my eyelids, and when Jim shouted, 'Duck!' I thought he meant the bird kind and opened my eyes, murmuring, 'Where?'

He meant the lower-your-head kind, I realised later, coming to consciousness in the sunroom of their house, a lump the size of an apricot on my forehead. The wind had changed course and with it the boom. It had swung straight into my forehead, knocking me almost out of the boat and unconscious at that. Jim sat beside me, describing how he thought at first he'd killed me, and his relief when he saw I was still breathing. I started mumbling as he carried me out of the boat, he said, but I wasn't making any sense.

'You kept saying, "Where's Mum? What's happened?" So I'd tell you and you'd just ask me the same thing again.'

Jim sat there with his cool hand holding mine while his mother fussed around and brought in a doctor.

The doctor's fingers were cold and dry on the inside of my wrist. Out of the corner of my eye I saw Jim's mother pull him into another room, and I heard the raised voices of their argument through the door they shut behind them.

'So I hear you met Jim on the ship over from Australia. You're one of them Australian brides our boys met over there?'

'I am.'

'This'll be a bit bright now.' He shone a little penlight into my eyes, and when he moved it away the bright spots lingered.

'Can you tell me what day it is today, Sarah?'

I shut my eyes, trying to think. All the days had lost meaning, but my day off was a Sunday.

'Sunday?'

He nodded slowly. 'And who's the president of the United States?'

That one was easy. 'Harry Truman,' I said. 'He took over when FDR died.'

'I'd ask you the president of Australia but I wouldn't know whether or not you were right,' he said.

'We have a prime minister, not a president, and his name's Ben Chifley,' I said.

'Well, you seem pretty certain on that one. I think you've

suffered a concussion but not a serious one. Your pupils are normal, your speech is fine.'

Jim and his mum re-entered the room, Jim looking chastened.

'I don't want her going anywhere until tomorrow,' the doctor announced. 'Can she stay here tonight?'

'Of course.' Jim came and kneeled where the doctor had been, fixing the blanket which had slipped down. 'She can stay as long as she likes.'

•

There are things in life which you realise like a flash of lightning which cracks and splits open your skin, and things which creep up on you slowly, like lines on your face, gradually creasing until they are just another part of you, until you would not recognise yourself without them. I woke up in Kilmarnock the next morning with sun slicing a band of light into the centre of the guest bedroom, and opened the curtains to see the river beneath me, rippling with light, the grey heron standing on an upturned rowboat on the opposite shore. The lump on my head was tender, throbbing a little, and my fingertips skirted its circumference. Somewhere downstairs the floorboards creaked. I heard the murmur of voices and a kettle whistle. I got back into bed, where the sheets were still warm from my body; they smelled like clean laundry and cedar shelves. There was a patchwork quilt on the bed and I traced the patterns of the different fabrics: the squares of tiny rosebuds in pink and white, the blue morning glories, the snaking ivy.

There was a knock at the door.

'Come in.'

Jim entered with a tray. His face crinkled in a smile. 'I had to fight my mama to bring this tray in myself. How's your head, Duck?'

'Oh no. You're not going to start calling me Duck . . .'

'Maybe I will.'

He set the tray on the bedside table and pointed at the contents. 'Hot coffee with cream; I told Mama you might not like cream but she said she's never known a lady to drink her coffee black. Toast with apricot jelly. Orange juice squeezed by my very own hand.'

I crossed my arms over my chest, feeling underdressed in the light cotton nightgown his mother had found for me. Jim squinted at my forehead then leaned in close, smelling like cut grass and citrus. 'You've got a helluva bruise.' I saw his eyes flicker to my chest and away, and his face flush as he looked out the window.

'Beautiful day. I can take you for a drive. I've got the day off. No use rushing back to DC just yet.'

'I've got to work tomorrow.'

Jim rubbed his jaw. 'Did you see that great blue heron?'

I nodded.

'I call him Henry,' he said. 'I can take you back anyway, so you don't need to take the bus.'

'I couldn't. You must have your own things to do.'

'Like what? I wouldn't ask you to stay if I didn't want you to. You can have a day of R and R. Looks like you could use it.'

'Okay, then. I warn you, though, you call me Duck and I'll think of something for you. Something worse, I promise.'

He grinned, backing out of the room. 'I'd like to see you try. Now eat your breakfast and there's a towel if you want to have a bath before we go. We'll want to get going soon if I'm going to get you to the city and come back today.'

'Hang on.'

Jim hovered in the doorway, his head flush with the top of the frame. 'What?'

'Why do you call the heron Henry?'

'He seems friendly, like a Henry would be. You know, like you could take the boat over and have a drink with him. He'd always give you the time of day.'

He was gone before I could reply, but it took until after I'd bathed and changed into my previous day's clothes to realise that my cheeks were sore because I hadn't stopped smiling. And to realise how little I'd used those muscles in the last months.

•

Jim took me back to the city in his Oldsmobile Series 60 coupe which used to belong to his father. There was a bench seat in the front and two jump seats in the back, and it was blood red, like a garnet.

'Know how to drive?' he asked, as we navigated the bumpy roads out of town and onto the busy highways which led towards the city.

'No. My dad had a truck, but he never saw the point of teaching me. He taught both my brothers, of course.'

'Well, do you want to learn?'

He spent much of the drive explaining the different dials, pedals and knobs to me. He was a good teacher, clear and patient, able to explain something without making it sound as though he thought you were stupid.

Finally, we pulled onto a side road, empty except for a few tired-looking mailboxes and trash cans with dented metal lids.

'You ready to try?'

We swapped places and I sat in the warmth of where he'd been on the cream leather.

'I can't reach the pedals.'

He reached over my lap to show me the lever and together we scooted the whole front seat forwards a few inches.

'Now, check you can see out of your mirrors. You can move them if you need to.'

I adjusted the mirrors and twisted around to get a better idea of how large the car was.

'What's the first thing you've got to remember?'

'Foot on the clutch and brake when I start. Then on the clutch and the gas. But not on the brake and the gas at once.'

'That's right, brake and clutch or gas and clutch. Easing on one while you ease off the other.'

Slow and jerking, I made my way down the dirt road, learning how much pressure was needed on the pedals, where to move the gear shift, how to check my side and rear-view mirrors.

'Go on, pick up some speed then,' Jim said, and I pressed the accelerator, the wind from the open window whipping my hair across my face. I hadn't felt this way in ages, this combination of control and freedom. It felt as though I could do anything. Behind the wheel, I could go where I wanted to be.

•

On the weekends or when I could get time off, Jim visited me in DC, sometimes staying overnight with family friends. We didn't write letters—he never was much of a letter writer—but he would call me on the shared telephone in the boarding house three or four times a week. There'd be a knock on the door and one of the sullen-looking girls would say there was a phone call for me. 'Don't hog the line,' she'd mutter. A few times he just showed up out of the blue at the Olmstead Grill, where he would wait at the bar until my shift was finished, chatting with the bartender and sipping from a glass of scotch so slowly the ice disappeared. He would walk me home and we fought when he told me he didn't like me working there, he thought I ought to quit.

'The way other men look at you makes me mad,' he said.

'Then don't come,' I replied, letting go of his arm, striding ahead.

He caught up and I stopped walking and tried to explain. 'It's a job, Jim, and I need a job. It doesn't mean anything, the way I smile at those men. They're just ordering drinks. It's not the same as the way I smile at you.'

He calmed down, and we agreed to go to a diner rather than say goodbye with our fight still fizzing in the air around us. We sat side by side in a booth, his thigh pressed against mine, the fan spinning above us as a drunk-looking man put nickels in a jukebox. We sat in the booth for hours, just to be beside each other. I can't remember what we talked about but I knew that we could talk forever, that hearing his slow deliberate way of speaking, watching the smile begin to crinkle the corners of his eyes, would never grow old.

He walked me home when the sky was the old-penny colour of early dawn, the keenest of the sparrows chittering in the trees. My feet ached and my head felt light from too much coffee but still I didn't want the feeling of his hand on my waist to go away, for him to go away. I thought of ways to sneak him into my room. I thought of slipping in myself and unlocking the back door, telling him where to find the gate. But then I pictured Roy on the floor at Mrs Mulligan's, his pants around his ankles. Instead I stood on my aching toes when Jim bent down to kiss me where the front lawn began, while the dark house still slept.

Jim breathed a sigh when we parted. 'I'm tired, but I don't think I'll sleep,' he said.

'Me neither.'

'I'll come on the weekend. What's your day off?'

'Sunday.' I turned to walk up the path to the front door of the house, and when I turned the key and opened the door I looked back to see him standing there, still watching me, and raised a hand in farewell. He did the same, his silhouette hazy in that half light of the beginning day.

•

Next Sunday we hired bicycles at the tidal basin and rode around the monuments of the city, across the flat stretch of the Mall and circling the obelisk of the Washington Monument. It was August, and our clothes stuck to our skin with sweat, the handlebars of the bicycle slippery. The heat was swampy, thick like egg cream, bordering on sweet. My straw hat kept the sun from my face but my arms were turning red and finally we

collapsed beneath a tree beside the basin. Children were swimming in the muddy water. I thought of the surf back home,
the way my skin felt cool to the touch after swimming at the
beach. I would never find that here.

'What's going on in that head of yours?' Jim said, fanning
himself with his hat. His whole shirt was dark with sweat, and
there were splotches of red on his face.

'Did you swim in Sydney?'

'Did I ever. Those were some beaches.'

'Where did you go?'

'Bondi,' he said, saying it like every American I ever met:
Bondee. 'You must miss it.'

'Days like today, what I wouldn't give.'

'Well, I can't help you with an ocean today, but we'll go to
the beach soon. It'll be nothing like you're used to; still cools
you off though. Meanwhile, I've got good news.'

'What's that?'

'I've been offered a desk job with the navy here in DC. So
I was thinking I'd move here, rent a place, get to see more of
you. How's that sound?'

He looked up from where he lay in the grass, sprawled, grinning up at me. I leaned down and kissed him, and his lips were
salty against mine. Almost as if he'd been swimming in the sea.

•

After he moved to DC we saw each other daily, meeting for
lunch if I was working or for dinner or a movie if I was off.
We got to know things about each other—how he got short-
tempered if he didn't eat regularly, how I didn't like queues

or crowds. We drove up to Ocean City before the summer ended. I tried to hide my disappointment at the beach. It was enough, I told myself, to walk arm in arm along the boardwalk with Jim, eating ice-creams, feeling the sea water dry tight on my skin. The waves were not the kind you can catch but we swam anyway, and he wrapped his arms around my legs beneath the water, lifting me up like a child, laughing. With the ocean hiding our bodies I felt free of my self-consciousness, unhinged with glee. I darted around him, I slid my hand in the waistband of his swim trunks, feeling the smooth skin ridged by elastic. He kissed me and pulled me under, and I opened my eyes in the green light, his face before me, bubbles rising from his mouth as he said words I didn't catch. I didn't need to. I understood him; I felt understood.

We were staying at his cousin's beach house—the key had been hidden beneath a brick behind a magnolia—and Jim put me in a bedroom that looked out through a small high window to a stretch of sea. After dinner at a hamburger place near the beach we walked back to the house and collapsed on the deck-chairs outside. We could hear the small waves breaking against the sand, and there were pinpricks of light—fireflies—flickering like messages, like tiny airborne lighthouses. We stayed up and talked for a long time before Jim yawned and kissed me good-night. He wasn't even going to try, I realised, with a thorn of disappointment. I brushed my teeth and my hair, ran a bath and lay in the lukewarm water, watching my fingers turn pale and pucker. The bedroom where I towelled off was hot from the sun shining in the windows all day. The air was still and I lay in bed awake. I kicked off the musty-smelling sheet and slapped at the mosquito buzzing around my ear.

I heard a noise downstairs and my heart thudded. There it was again. I tiptoed to the top of the stairwell. I imagined a burglar searching through my purse, stealing the keys to Jim's car. Creeping to the landing, I leaned over the banister. There was Jim, standing in the yellowy light of the refrigerator, drinking milk from the bottle. A feeling of foolishness flooded me, mixed with relief. He hadn't heard me and stood oblivious, swigging the milk, pausing, swigging some more.

'I'll pretend I didn't see that.'

He grinned and turned towards my voice. He wiped his lips with the back of his hand. 'Can't sleep either?'

'Not with someone thumping around like a burglar downstairs.'

'Sorry. I tried to be quiet.'

I went down and opened the cupboard, handed him a glass. He set it down. With the fridge door shut the kitchen was dark other than the light from the hall bathroom, which gave it a faint glow. Enough to see outlines but not much more.

'Can I ask you a childish question?' Jim said.

'Go ahead.'

'Did you love Roy?'

'Is that what's bothering you?'

Jim cleared his throat. I hopped onto the counter, crossing my legs, leaning forwards on my hands.

'Don't answer if you don't want to.' He was looking at the fridge still, though he'd already put the milk back and shut the door.

'No, I want to answer.'

'Okay.'

The only sound was the high hum of the refrigerator's motor, and beneath that what I imagined to be the susurration of distant small waves against the shore, though it might have just been the breeze, or the water running through the pipes in the ceiling above us.

'I thought I did, but you know yourself how things were. I wanted to be with him, no question about that. But I don't think I did love him. Not enough, at least. Not like the way I feel about you.'

The words were out of my mouth before I could spool them back in and Jim blinked, mouth open. He walked across to the countertop where I sat and it felt as though time were thick. As though he might never reach me. Then his stomach pressed soft against my knees. I opened them and he fitted between, his chin sharp on the top of my head.

I can't remember anymore what he said, how he replied, only how his breath caught and jolted later that night (and so many nights after) at the precipice between awake and asleep. How his body seemed too long for that tiny room, feet dangling over the end of the mattress, and how the sunlight travelled to his head on the pillow in the morning, waking him gradually. His dark hair against the white cotton pillowslip. How his smile was slow when he opened his eyes and recalled where he had spent the night, and what had happened there. How he already felt like a part of me, his skin an extension of my own. I knew how to touch him. There was some benefit to experience.

I did not regret, this time, knowing what it was I might do.

•

Eight months after I returned *The Grapes of Wrath* we drove over to Great Falls one Sunday, planning to go for a hike. I had packed a picnic in the boot of the car (which I was learning to refer to as the trunk) and he had insisted I drive along the winding roads which led there. The parking area was nearly full, and once I'd pulled the car into a spot, rather than leap out and stretch his legs, he started shuffling through things in the glove box.

'I was going to wait till we reach the falls but I'm feeling too nervous. And then I thought—if—we'll have to walk all the way back.'

'What on earth are you talking about?'

He passed me a clamshell, ridged with brown and pink.

'It's so pretty. Where did you find it?'

'Near the dock behind our house. It had washed up in the grass, the two halves still attached.'

'It's beautiful.'

'Open it up.'

Inside was a little nest of grass, and on top of it a gold and garnet ring. My chest felt tight to bursting with joy and terror.

'I want us to marry, if you would.'

'It's not official yet, the divorce with Roy.'

'Well, we can wait till it is.'

I put my hand on his leg and felt the shaking there, the way my own hand shook too. Just because you mess up once doesn't mean you can't get it right. But the quantity of happiness seemed out of my reach—something I didn't deserve.

'Where will we live?' I asked.

'Well, I've got the job in DC now. But we can talk about living somewhere else one day.'

'Will we have children?'

'I hope so.'

'I'd like that.'

'Does that mean . . . ?'

I didn't trust myself to speak, so I nodded, and we didn't even make it to the falls that day. We sat in the car, talking about the future we might have together. Wrapped up in each other, in the chance we were taking, the possibility of hope where there hadn't been any.

Less than a year later we were married, and six months after our wedding we had the first of two children, a boy, and then eighteen months after a girl. Andrew and Caroline. I knew that anyone who wanted to could do the sums and try to shame me, but they couldn't mar our happiness—we'd fought too hard for it.

It wasn't always easy, no question of that. His mother came to stay and interfered, as was her way, and some days life seemed an endless drudge of diapers and bottles, grubby fingers and crying in the night. I quit the waitressing job as soon as I realised I was pregnant, and it came as a surprise how much I missed it: the smell of cigarettes and booze and the clink of glasses on my tray, the jingle of tips in my apron, the hoarseness in my throat after a night of shouting orders at the bar.

But there were other joys: the babies sucking their toes in the dappled shade of our backyard, the smell of their clean skin, the reassuring squeak of the swing as I pushed them in the park.

There were the dogs, beginning with the collie Jim brought home as a puppy when Andrew was starting school, and that feeling I got—that memory—watching him bound low across the park. My heart was in his chest, it was all I could want, as close as I would get to that past which was gone.

Jim was good to me. There were parts of ourselves we didn't speak of often and we each respected that—there was just the present, the future. The money he made with his desk job in the navy was more than enough to live on, but I could see as the children grew older that he smiled less, he was always tired. He was in the navy, but so far away from water. We bought a sailboat and he spent weekends fixing it up, sanding the splintered timber decking, stitching tears in the sails. Sometimes we all went out on it together, the four of us, and the children complained of getting wet or cold, of the hard ropes on their hands, of being hungry or thirsty. So he went on his own, or with others from the sailing club, and it became another of the things we didn't share. And I made friends with the other mothers at the children's school and became involved in their committees, their tennis doubles, their bridge clubs, their ways of filling the empty hours between eight o'clock and three.

I wrote letters to Mum and Dad—not mentioning the divorce, not mentioning Jim by name—and sent photographs of the children, pictures they had drawn. As Caroline and Andy learned to write they sent letters themselves, the kinds of empty words you send to people you've never met. In return I received letters in Mum's neat and tiny hand, news of the land, of the droughts and floods, the disease and death, the grandchild my brother had given her and how she wished she could meet the ones who lived so far away. If I visited I'd have to tell them Jim wasn't Roy, and then all the lies would unspool around me, like when the kids were little and spun the toilet roll so fast there were piles of white on the floor.

Finally, when the children were eleven and ten, just before I turned thirty-five, I had the realisation on the tennis court that I was merely bouncing a ball back and forth. We had moved for what was meant to be only a few years to Ithaca, New York, where Jim was teaching Naval Reserve Officer Training Corps to young men at Cornell University. The winters were brutally cold, snow the likes of which I had never seen, and moving out of my familiar circle I came to realise my days were filled with nothing. Without Jim and the children I was just that— nothing. I loved them but I also needed them, they were my only sense of purpose, and there would come a time when the children no longer needed me.

My collie Sunny was dying; she had developed a tumour on her leg. Some mornings I had to carry her outside so she could relieve herself. The trips to the local vet clinic were an exercise in frustration. The veterinarian was an old, crotchety man with terrible breath who cared little for animals and less for their people. When the tumour was still small he hadn't wanted to remove it, and now it had spread and it was too late. Eventually I had him put Sunny to sleep, and he fumbled the needle so she was frightened in her last moments of life, her paws quivering against my arm, as her breath and then her heart stopped on the cold metal table. I stroked her while she was still warm and soft, the tears streaming down my face, past the corners of my mouth, down my neck to the collar of my shirt, and the man turned away, embarrassed by my emotion.

'Do you think you'll get another collie?' he asked, wiping down the table once the nurse had taken Sunny's body away. 'I know a good breeder about twenty miles south of here.'

I shook my head, not trusting myself to speak.

Jim was at work and the children were at school. I went home to an empty house, and it seemed as though it were an extension of myself, hollowed out inside.

Weeks later I had lunch with Jim at Cornell. We sometimes met in the dining hall during the week, we called it our lunch date, and he would tell me about work and we would watch the college students with their schoolbags and trays, flirting and laughing, guessing which ones would end up with each other. Afterwards I walked the campus; the first buds were finally on the trees and I felt the restlessness of spring in my bones. On my way to Beebe Lake I walked past the School of Veterinary Medicine as I usually did, but this time I stopped, retraced my steps and walked inside. I took an admissions booklet from a stand and a copy of their newsletter and, sitting on a bench beside the lake, I read both from cover to cover.

I didn't notice the time and was late home so the children had to let themselves in and make their own after-school snacks, but I hardly cared. That night, as Jim and I changed into our pyjamas for bed, I told him of my plans to become a veterinarian. Cornell was one of the only schools in the country to take women as vet students. He laughed first. And when he saw I was serious he took off his glasses and rubbed his eyes.

'How'll you manage that and the children, looking after the house?' he said. 'It's too much, Sarah. My job is too demanding. I need you home to take care of things.'

'We can make it work, Jim. It's what I need, it makes sense to me. It would make me so happy.'

'You need a hobby. Volunteer at the church. Let's get another dog.'

'I'm not ready for another dog. And I have hobbies—tennis, bridge. I'm sick of keeping busy for the sake of it. I need a purpose. My whole life I've been looking for something like this.'

He shook his head, turning over in our bed, his back to me. I watched him pull his book off his nightstand, get up and walk into his study to read. He didn't return to our bed that night. I stayed awake for hours, looking at the booklet again, the newsletter. I fell asleep thinking of the way udders had felt in my palms as a girl, the press of a wet nose against the back of my knee.

For two weeks I didn't speak to him. I cooked the meals, cleaned the house and looked after the children but a smile didn't cross my face and no lighthearted words left my lips. I asked Caroline and Andy about their days before he came home from work, helped them with their schoolwork, vacuumed the house and ironed his shirts. I did not kiss him goodbye in the morning or hello in the evenings. I turned off my light and pretended to be asleep before he came to bed. I began to work on my application in the empty hours of the day, forgoing tennis, skipping bridge. One afternoon after school Caroline asked me what was wrong, folding her long skinny legs beneath her on the sofa beside me. She was all elbows and knees, narrow-faced with big eyes. 'Why are you mad at Daddy?' she asked matter-of-factly, twisting a strand of brown hair around a finger so tightly the skin whitened.

'What do you mean?' I was hemming one of her skirts, and the needle was too blunt for the stiff fabric. I jammed it through and pricked my index finger. 'Ouch!'

'You seem mad at him,' she replied. Caroline was so similar to Jim, both in colouring and in temperament, and the two had a connection that went beyond words. There were times I felt they could read each other's minds. 'Do you want me to find you a thimble?'

'I want you to learn to do your own hemming, is what I want,' I snapped. Immediately I felt awful. She looked up at me through her thick brown lashes, blinking back the tears pooling in her eyes. I put down the hemming and pulled her in close, kissing the top of her head. It smelled like sun-dried leaves at the tail end of summer. Her body curled against me, and I shut my eyes tight.

'Don't worry,' I said, thinking of my own mother. 'There's nothing at all the matter.'

The booklet and the newsletter went in the bottom drawer of the hall table, with the paid bills and Christmas cards from last year. I started thinking about getting another dog. I bought patterns and fabric at the store to make summer clothes for the children. It would give me something to do.

I went to bed on the Friday of the second week while Jim was still watching TV. But when I came out of the bathroom, still wrapped in a towel, he was sitting on the edge of the bed.

'I miss you, Sarah.'

'I know. I'm trying. It's hard to get over disappointment.'

'Maybe you shouldn't have to.' He sighed.

Neither of us said anything for a moment and I realised I was holding my breath.

'I've always known how smart you are. And I can tell how much you want this. It won't be easy, but I hate to be the one who doesn't let you try.'

With a gasp I let go of the breath I'd been holding and embraced him, my towel falling to the floor. Neither of us minded one bit.

•

I had never gone to college so I needed to do that first, a pre-vet program at Cornell University to give me a solid base in biology, chemistry and mathematics. For my admissions interview I sat across the desk from a pre-vet adviser, a middle-aged man with thinning blond hair and the broken capillaries of a drinker on his cheeks and nose. He didn't look at me but at the papers on his desk.

'The problem with vet school,' he said, 'is that they don't really take girls. I don't want you to waste your time doing pre-vet when you won't get in.'

'But there are two women in the graduating class this year,' I replied. I'd done my research. I was sweating in my smartest skirt and jacket, the pile of papers which he hadn't even asked to see threatening to spill from my lap.

'They graduated top of the class in pre-vet.'

'What's to say I won't?'

He shrugged and stood. 'I'd suggest you reapply for a different program. What else interests you? Music? Books? Art? We have a nice art appreciation course.'

The interview was over. I went home convinced I would not get in, but the following week I got my acceptance in the mail. I would do pre-vet, and I was more determined than ever to do well.

Being an undergraduate at college at my age took some adjusting to. I wasn't just a girl, I was a married woman, not worth even the scarcest amount of attention from the young men. I moved through the campus as if I was invisible, and in the classes the professors rarely called on me when I raised my hand—perhaps because some were younger than me. There were two other girls in pre-vet in my year, and while they lived on campus and spent their social hours dating or going to coffee houses, the three of us studied together and commiserated on the lack of assistance we received from professors and fraternities. After two years of pre-vet I had enough credits to apply for veterinary school. My grades were some of the highest, but still the interview committee sat me down and asked me *why* exactly I wished to be a vet. 'You're married with children?' one committee member asked.

'Yes, but they all support me,' I said.

'It's fairly late in life to enter the profession,' another said, as though I was hobbling around on a cane.

'By the time I graduate I figure I'll have at least twenty good years of practice ahead of me. And there's not much else I'd rather be doing.'

The men looked at me over their spectacles. I didn't look away.

That autumn I began my first year of veterinary school, in a class with three other women. By now the children were used to making their own school lunches, to coming home to an empty house, to helping me fold the laundry, chop the vegetables for dinner and cook simple things—tomato soup from a can; macaroni and cheese—when I was busy studying. I worried about their nutrition sometimes but they didn't stop growing weedy and tall, Jim's height in their genes. They spoke longingly of mothers who made cookies for their children when they came home from school, mothers who helped with science fairs and volunteered for the PTA. I told them, then, about my mother. How she sometimes took to her room for days with headaches. How when I was a girl there were times I couldn't go to school because the farm work had to be done.

'I wish you'd at least come to the Christmas concert,' Caroline pleaded. 'I have a solo on the violin.'

'I'll try my best,' I said, feeling terrible. Of course I had heard that solo two hundred times over the past month, but surely it would sound better in the context of the entire orchestra (I hoped). In the end I skipped ambulatory clinic to go, and missed out on a visit to a farm where three cattle had tested positive for TB. Still, it was worth it to see the smile on my daughter's face when she spotted me in the audience. She sat straight-backed and proud on the stage, her pale bare knees vulnerable. The children were at the age where I spent equal amounts of time wanting to hold them close beneath my wing and longing to push them out into the world like fledglings from the nest. Without trying they'd never learn to fly, but I couldn't bear to see them fail.

Jim and I still met for lunch in the campus dining hall, but now I was often the one who had to rush off for a class or a study group, a practicum or a lab. Sometimes he grew short-tempered when dinner was late, when the house was a mess, but I could still manage to find a way to make him smile or laugh. We could still laugh at most things.

There was so much to learn: respiratory, digestive, vascular, diagnostic. Anatomy and cell biology, nutrition and physiology, virology and immunology, bacteriology and dermatology, parasitology and pharmacology, pathology and epidemiology, dentistry and ophthalmology, neurology and toxicology, endocrinology and urology, cardiology and oncology, animal behaviour and anaesthesia, surgery and post-operative care. It was like learning an entirely new vocabulary, a new language. Sometimes I doubted that I could—I was too old, too weary, I had wasted too much of my life. I could read the textbooks until my eyes ached but so much was practical too—how a tumour felt, how a cow's ovaries changed when she was pregnant, what a blocked intestine felt like and a swollen spleen. I quickly lost any squeamishness I'd had; when your arm is up a cow's vagina there is no pretending to be dignified. Thankfully, even when I forgot the names of things I knew how they felt; my hands found things which my mind sometimes couldn't.

When Caroline was sixteen and Andy seventeen I walked in the graduating procession at the Cornell University College of Veterinary Medicine; the year was 1964. They were all there to watch, my family, and it was worth the arguments to see how proud they were of me.

There was one practice in Ithaca which was known to hire women, and I applied there straightaway. Nothing came of it for six months, during which time I moped around the house, doing all the housework I had neglected over the past six years, refusing to consider that my work would come to nothing. Then, just before Christmas, I had a telephone call from the practice. They wanted to know whether I was still available to work; one of their vets was retiring in the new year. Large animal and small. It would mean farm call-outs, the owner said, and he wanted to know whether, as a woman, I would be up to it.

'I grew up on a farm,' I replied. 'I love large animal work.'

Believe it or not, the vet retiring was the one who had been so terrible when Sunny died, and I thought how funny life was that now, seven years later, I would be the one to replace him. Those first years were the steepest learning curve of all. I performed a tracheotomy on a horse. A caesarean on a sheep. I amputated limbs from dogs who had been injured by cars, spayed thousands of pets and resuscitated a pet parrot.

But the humans tested me more than the animals. There was the farmer who, when he saw me step out of my car, said, 'I told them not to send the broad.' The dog owner who thought I was the nurse and asked when the vet would arrive. The owners who refused to pay for treatment and let their pets suffer needlessly because 'it was just an animal'. The pets rescued from homes where they were neglected or abused, the fear which never quite disappeared from their eyes.

Two years later, when we moved back to Virginia to look after Jim's mother, I opened my own practice. I learned that purpose might come late in life, but lateness does not mute its strength. At forty-four I knew how to save a cow with a prolapsed uterus, how to tell by feeling a dog's stomach if he had an obstructed bowel, how to extract a terrified cat from the corner of her cage without being scratched. The children spent their summers home from college working in the clinic, cleaning cages and hosing runs, walking dogs, feeding those who weren't too sick to eat. Caroline and Andy seemed to inherit my love of animals. I would find Caroline sitting beside the cages of the loneliest animals, singing top-forty tunes. Andy loved nothing more than coming on the farm calls, standing knee deep in cow muck helping me to pull a calf from a birthing cow.

Strange how life is a circle, how that which filled my girlhood gave me purpose later in life. Strange to be drawn back to that steady silent language of animals; the ways their eyes and your hands could speak when human language failed.

I made enough in my practice that Jim could retire from the navy and start a business repairing old sailboats. Meanwhile my practice saw a steady stream of pets and livestock, and I hired other vets as I grew older and wanted to spend more time in the garden or with my granddaughter (who came as a surprise when Caroline was in her forties) or out on the water with Jim. Sometimes Jim and I would sit on the dock as the sun set over the river, slapping mosquitoes, and talk quietly about the children and grandchild, the tides, the foot and mouth at the Wilkinses' place. He was stooped with his years but still handsome, and he still listened carefully to every word I said. I would retire for good in two years, we decided, and we would go on a cruise together. To Australia, he suggested, and I looked at him, surprised.

'Isn't it time?' he said.

'I thought it was too late.'

'Oh, Sarah, I should have made us go twenty years ago.'

'It's not your fault,' I said. 'We've been busy.'

'Don't you think it's time we told them the truth?'

I took his hand, calloused from rope and brown against my own, spotted from the sun. As familiar as my own hand now, only dearer. We watched without speaking as a heron dived for a fish then flapped off triumphant, silver glinting in his long beak, to roost in a mangrove and eat his dinner as twilight fell and the stars began to poke their needles of light through the fabric of sky. Jim turned to me and smiled—there was so much we didn't need words for—and arm in arm we walked up the hill through frog song and crickets chirruping, through damp grass which needed mowing, to our house which needed painting and our lives which were full to overflowing, though we hardly paused to see.

CHAPTER 34

Grandpa was a bristly grey moustache kissing me on the cheek, the smell of bourbon, the twinkle of kind eyes. When I was just a girl he took me out on the water, his gnarled fingers on the ropes, showing me knots that I promptly forgot. The clank of rigging and the unfurling of a sail. He died of prostate cancer when I was twelve. I never knew that they were planning to travel. I think of how many years it has taken after his death for Grandma to see their plan through. How long this journey has sat in the back of her mind, tempting her but also terrifying her. I have never seen her so vulnerable. At work, in the clinic, even as she aged I thought of Grandma as a person with sure hands, with a steady strength.

I had forgotten until she began telling me about going to vet school how she had encouraged me in my desire to go to nursing school. The time I spent in her clinic in Kilmarnock, the smell of disinfectant and alcohol swabs, the confidence with which she gave needles, snipped stitches, bandaged wounds.

I was with her once, during a high school summer vacation, when a kitten who had been hit by a car was brought in. I had been cleaning out cages when she called for towels. The kitten was bleeding on the operating table. Mewling, shaking in pain. Grandma gave it a shot of a sedative and staunched the bleeding. The person who had dropped the kitten off wasn't its owner, and it had no collar, no ID.

'The internal injuries are too serious; I'm going to have to put him down,' Grandma said. 'You don't have to stay for this.'

'I'll help,' I said, swallowing my cowardice. 'Tell me what to do.'

I sat with the kitten in my lap, wrapped in a towel, and stroked his little head as Grandma got the pentobarbital. She had shaved his foreleg so she could better see the vein.

'He won't feel pain now, but he might jerk or gasp before his heart stops. It's a natural reaction. You're doing great.'

I murmured to the kitten and stroked him, and he looked up at me, let out a meow that went straight to my heart. Grandma, with steady hands, found the vein, inserted the needle, injected the solution. The kitten half closed his eyes, as though in sleep. He twitched, the little body stiffened then softened. He had stopped breathing. Grandma listened for the heartbeat. He was gone.

'You did well, Hannah,' Grandma said. 'Think of how much easier you made the last minutes of his life.' She took the little bundle from me.

Blood had seeped through the towel onto the leg of my jeans, leaving a dark stain I didn't want to get rid of. It reminded me of that brief life and the pain I had helped to ease. It reminded me that I could be strong, too.

CHAPTER 35

It's hard to believe I am here. That I have finally returned. As the ship came through the craggy cliffs of the heads and into Sydney Harbour at dawn, I saw before me the distant arch of the Harbour Bridge, the small islands whose names I still recall: Goat Island, Garden Island, Fort Denison. The sandstone pylons of the bridge as we drew closer, the linked triangles of steel. The leering clown mouth and Ferris wheel at Luna Park, the green-and-yellow painted ferries cutting through the water. There was the light bouncing off the water, the little pilot boat ahead of us leading the way. The ship berthed beside Circular Quay, which had far more buildings of a far greater height than I remembered, but most startling were the solid white sails of the Sydney Opera House, which I had seen in photographs but never in person. It sat between the Quay and the Royal Botanic Gardens like tips of cuttlebones poking out of the sand, or a tiled lily. It looked as though it had always been there. I thought it was beautiful.

It took ages to get off the ship, navigating queues of people and luggage and paperwork and passport checks. We were exhausted by the time we caught a taxi to our hotel in The Rocks. I decided to splurge on separate rooms for the night we are in town. Hannah needs her space. Once I have unpacked I call Fred from my room, which has a view out over The Rocks and the harbour, North Sydney beyond.

His voice is familiar from our more frequent conversations these days, rough and crackling with age.

'Is it really you, Sar? You're really here?'

'I am. I'm really here.'

'I'm on me way. There's been some traffic, but I'll be there for lunch. Will I pick you girls up from the hotel?'

'That'd be perfect.'

'I'll call when I'm in the city.'

'Okay.'

'Hooroo.'

Fred will stay in the city for a night, then we'll all head south. He stayed on farming—said the country was the only place his mind was quiet after the war. He even did well, better than Dad ever managed, and bought back the farm Dad had sold so many years ago. Said he did it for Jack.

'I liked being in the city, but Jack never did. This was where he spent the best part of his short life,' Fred wrote in one of his emails. There were photographs attached. A new dam. The same wide verandahs. The creek swollen with rain. The wattle blooming yellow in spring. He and his wife—Sharon—had a son, whom they named Jack. Jack was driving Fred up to Sydney, since Fred was in his nineties. Jack had three children—one of whom also lived, with his family, on the property with them.

I'd told Fred in emails about leaving Roy, about marrying Jim, and he wanted to know why I'd kept it from them so long. 'Mum and Dad wouldn't have minded, just as long as they knew you were happy.'

I'd wept when I read this, because I knew it was too late. And true.

I pull the drapes and ease myself down on the bed, unlacing my shoes. I need to sleep. It is all too much, even just hearing the familiar accent, the lady at reception calling the elevator a lift. I am taut to bursting with the present and past, all of it mixing within me, every sound and smell bringing up what it was I left behind. I shut my eyes and doze, dreaming of Dad's hummingbird-wing hat, the pub across the road in Forest Lodge, the smoke of a cigarette deep in my lungs.

CHAPTER 36

I look through the fridge and the drawers of the mini bar. There are tiny packages of M&Ms beside chocolates I've never heard of (Cherry Ripe, Coconut Rough). There are nuts and potato chips, miniature bottles of liquor. I run a deep bath that is too hot at first, but I flinch into it, my forehead beading with sweat. The bath gel smells lemony and grassy—lemon myrtle, it says on the label. I use the entire bottle. Underwater my ears and nostrils fill and the light through my closed eyelids is pinkish-orange. I hear my heart beating in my ears. I shampoo and condition my hair and shave the spiky growth from my legs, careful over the bone of my shin, which is easy to nick. I look down over the flat plane of my stomach, the hairs at the V between my thighs, the jut of my hipbones. There is excess flesh because I'm eating again. The voice saying *fat, fat, fat* is humming at the back of my brain. I go underwater again, just to shut it up, to hear the thud of my own heart.

It is nice to be alone in this room. I've shut the drapes and I walk around naked once I'm out of the bath. I turn on the TV but it is mid-morning, there's nothing on. Only old sitcoms and what looks like an American morning show—the same loud voices and semi-hysterical laughter, bright clothes and shel-lacked helmets of hair, only the voices are Australian, and they call each other by weird-sounding nicknames. Donno and Di, Gaz and Shaz. Grandma always told me that Australians like to shorten things, but I thought it was another remnant of the past, like short-wave radio and iceboxes, outdoor loos and chip-heater baths. I turn off the TV and think about lunch. I think about seeing Alex on the deck above ours when we disembarked; he was squinting into the sun but spotted me and waved. He mimed a phone to his ear. I nearly gave him the finger, but instead forced a smile and waved. I turn my phone on, log in to the hotel's wi-fi and download my emails. There are several from Ash. I turn the phone off again, shut my eyes. I've started a letter in my head, telling him the truth about me. I don't know how he will respond, but I want to give him a chance—or give us a chance. I want to tell him all of it—about Alex and the clinics, about the lists of food I keep and the real reason I run. About the bus, even, and Jake, and how part of me is stuck in that bed still, speechless with terror. Still seeking the right words.

•

Grandma and I meet in the lobby at noon. Grandma looks tired and puffy-eyed; she says she slept too long. Her pants are wrinkled where she lay on them and I feel a pang of guilt for not helping her get ready. Her lipstick is straight, though, and she tells me I smell nice.

'It's lemon myrtle,' I say. 'Have you heard of it?'

'Heard of it? The bushes are everywhere. When I was a girl they were common as weeds.'

'Your accent's gotten stronger just since we've arrived, Grandma.'

She winks at me. Her hands are twitching in her lap though—she's nervous—and I ask how long it has been since she has seen her brother, my great-uncle. She concentrates for a few seconds then looks up at me. 'Sixty-eight years.'

Two men walk through the revolving doors then, one older than the other, and it is immediate, the recognition, though I have never even seen a photograph. My great-uncle is a few inches taller and about twenty pounds heavier than Grandma, and his skin's been wrecked by the sun, but they have the same face. The same eyes.

I help Grandma out of the chair and we walk towards them. Grandma's arm is trembling in mine, and when I look at her face there are tears streaming down her cheeks. She lets go of me and holds out both arms to her brother and he is wet-eyed too. His son is holding him up, and I am on the other side, and it isn't until they've parted that we greet one another. Fred is wiping his eyes.

'I'm getting silly in my doddery old age,' he says. 'Look at you, dear girl, you must be Hannah.'

He kisses my cheek with his spiky whiskers, and then ruddy-faced Jack kisses me too, both men looking embarrassed and out of place in the shiny, sharp lobby of the hotel in their buttoned-up short-sleeved shirts and shorts with socks and orthopaedic shoes.

We walk to a nearby pub for lunch in the touristy part of the city—what's called The Rocks. They explain the difference between a schooner and a middy of beer, and Grandma orders a shandy.

'What's that?'

'Half beer, half lemonade,' Fred replies. 'The ladies fancy it.'

'Not the lemonade you're thinking,' Grandma says, patting my arm. 'Lemonade here means Sprite or 7 Up.'

'Thank God I've got you here to translate for me.'

'What'll it be, then—shandies for both the ladies?'

'I'll have a glass of wine. House white. Let me pay.'

'Not on your life. If I can't buy my niece a drink the first time I meet her this is a sad world,' Fred says, as his son counts out the brightly coloured bills and lays them on the bar.

'Grand-niece, and we'll shout the next round,' Grandma says, and her brother grins at her.

There is a menu on the wall in the corner of the pub and a counter where we order food. There are pies, and fish and chips, and all the deep-fried things you could imagine, and I feel my stomach clench into that familiar panic of how to manage. I take a deep breath and look up at Grandma, who is laughing at something Fred has said, gripping his arm.

'Let's find 'em a seat,' Jack whispers. 'Then we can sort the food.'

I nod, and we find a table, then order the fried things and the burgers and meat pies, and Jack and I trade different words we have for things, and why, and I laugh at the beetroot and egg and pineapple on the burger and he says how much he would like to travel to America one day, before he gets too old. And with those words we both look at Fred and Sarah in the corner, their heads together, their faces wreathed in wrinkles and their eyes on the edge of wetness. And I think about how Grandma seems different here, as if she has slipped right into place; the veneer of trying is gone. And I think about what it is to be too old and how I don't want to get there and wish I had spent my life feeling happier with what I'd had, rather than always feeling bad about what I'd done.

CHAPTER 37

I was hoping for a nap after lunch, as I'm not used to drinking in the middle of the day, but Jack has planned to drive us past some of the old sights. In Forest Lodge we sit with the engine idling outside a block of flats where our house used to be. There is still an oleander vine across the neighbour's fence, and one of the pubs where I would fetch Dad in the evening is still standing, but everything else has changed. Everywhere now there are cafes and convenience stores, SUVs parked with their tyres up on the kerb on the narrow streets. There is a yoga studio where the milk bar was and a hairdresser at the corner shop where I bought cigarettes waiting for Dad. There are hoardings up where people are knocking down the tiny semis and weatherboards and turning them into four-bedroom houses that extend right up to the edge of their properties. Even the weeds have to fight to survive amid the concrete and bitumen; gardens are reduced to a few spiky ornamental plants in pots.

'Changed, hasn't it?' Fred says, rolling his window down. The air is warm and smells of star jasmine. I feel infinitely tired, as though if I shut my eyes now I would fall asleep for a year.

We drive past the dogs at Wentworth Park, and Jack tells us they're closing soon, the land has been sold to a developer. Hannah puts her hand on my shoulder. I think of climbing those stands, watching for Dad and seeing him—without Mum— happy, handsome even. For so many years I blamed myself for not telling Mum what I saw, but I think now: what would have changed? I only wish I could have tried to know him then. I only wish I tried to understand.

CHAPTER 38

Grandma is quieter than usual when we drive south the next morning. She sits in the front seat looking out the window as Jack points out landmarks and Fred dozes beside me. We leave the sprawling suburban network of Sydney behind and head south on the Princes Highway heading through the Royal National Park and then a string of small coastal towns, the road winding past surf beaches and rolling green hills. The day is overcast. When we stop for gas I help Grandma to the restroom, balancing the key tied to a plastic spoon on the edge of the sink. She uses the cubicle first and I hear her groan as she lowers herself onto the seat.

'You okay?' I ask.

'I didn't sleep well last night. As much as I love to see this, as good as it is to be here, I'd just love to sleep in my own bed.'

The toilet flushes and she comes out, washes her hands with lurid pink soap from the dispenser.

'It'll be good to see the farm again though,' I say, keeping my voice light.

She puts her hands under the dryer and there is just the high blast of air, the roar of sound.

CHAPTER 39

Driving along the road to the farm—still dirt, I notice—past the familiar curves and properties, I feel my pulse quicken. We roll down the windows; the air is sharp with eucalyptus, a mossy smell of rain. Jack slows as a wallaby ducks out of the underbrush, leaping halfway across the road and then turning back the way it came. Hannah gasps in the back seat.

She gets out to open the gate and waits for Jack to drive through before closing it behind him. Here is the drive down into the valley, land which is ours once more. Where I learned that you can work hard and still lose what you love.

How is it a place can speak to you? The way the bark on the trees catches the light, the sound of kookaburras laughing at dusk, whipbirds high in the trees. The snap of branches beneath your feet and the rustling sound they make above when the wind blows through. How is it that all these things can still wrap around you like a blanket?

They are all there to greet us as we drive up: Jack's wife Ellen and their son and daughter-in-law, tall and tanned, with a baby and a toddler; Fred's wife Sharon bent over, leaning on a cane. They kiss our cheeks then stand back shyly, the silence suddenly awkward. We all wipe our shoes on the mat and walk into the kitchen for a cuppa. The old house is gone, long ago replaced by a large, more practical place. It still has a wraparound verandah, but the windows are double-glazed, and there's insulation and air con.

'I hope you like lamb,' Ellen says. 'I've got a leg in the oven for dinner.' And that's the smell again, of Mum's roast lamb on a Sunday, and my hunger is deeper than I knew possible.

Sometimes there aren't words, once a story is told, for what it means. There aren't words for this—because you're there, you're here, and as much as you love both you don't fit in to either place. Because of the love of both. In spite of it.

I excuse myself to lie down, and in the dim bedroom a fly buzzes again and again into the window above my head. I open it. I miss Jim more intensely than I have missed him in years—here, of all places. I fall asleep thinking of the way he looked in the nursing home when he was dying of the cancer, the way the bones of his face stuck out from his skin but his eyes still laughed even when his voice couldn't. I never brought him home. Our plans for a cruise fell apart like our lives when he was diagnosed only a few months after suggesting it. He died before I had the chance to show him where I was from. Is it too late now?

•

I wake not knowing where on earth I am.

They take me to see the milkers, the sheds of equipment, the glistening industrial machines. Jack leads me proudly past cows that are little more to him than the numbers tagged in their ears. I realise, running my hand across the rump of one, watching her jump and quiver, that they no longer know human touch. We talk vaccinations and disease. It's a healthy herd, but they are used to cold metal, the hum and pinch, the whirring machine. I smile and nod for Jack's sake, for Hannah's, telling him how fine it is, how much sense it makes. But I walk from the shed through the paddock back to the house thinking of the naked udders in my hands, the sound of milk hitting a tin bucket, the sweet frothy smell of grass and hay.

Hannah skips up beside me. 'You should try again, Grandma. Milking by hand. Should I ask?'

'No, love. It's enough to remember.'

I think, then, how much I've forgotten. How bloody hard it all was, how tired we would be by the end of the day. Every single day. No break, not even for Christmas. The past seems prettier than it was. I ought to tell Hannah. I've given her the wrong impression.

•

The lamb is delicious, so much like Mum's used to be, and there are so many voices over dinner. Laughter, stories. They can't get enough of Hannah. My glass of wine keeps being refilled and my face is hot, the room is too hot. I stand and say I need some fresh air, go outside for a moment. Inside they are all still at the table, and I watch them in the light, their voices muffled by glass. Watching it all is mesmerising, until I see my own reflection, shadowed against the light. An old woman looks back at me, bent by the years. For so long the past has called to me. I have watched it from the outside looking in, so bright sometimes it hurts my eyes. I turn away from the doors, from the voice of my father, the radio, the lamb sliced paper thin.

The air is cool and the sky is huge, the frogs at the dam chirrup and there is the hum of the generator. Above me are hundreds of stars; I can pick out the Southern Cross among them. The wind brings the sharpness of wood smoke, eucalyptus leaves, the tea trees that line the banks of the creek. Something rustles in the leaf litter beneath the pepper tree.

Hannah steps outside to join me. She clasps my arm.

'You okay, Grandma?'

I don't know. I can't say.

'It must be strange to be back.'

I nod.

'Will we go back in? They're waiting for you, to serve dessert.'

I let her lead me, one hand gripping mine, the other gentle on my back. Inside there is the warmth of the fire, the golden light on my brother's face. To see him is to see how old we are. I sit among them, at the head of the table, where they have placed me. I lean towards their faces, and watch the young ones clear the plates, their eyes sparkling with their secret jokes, their faces full of unlived life. I try to recall what it is I wanted to say, what I have come back for.

I remember the book of photographs, and Hannah fetches it for me from my suitcase. I show them Jim and me at our wedding, at my graduation from vet school, at his retirement party. Blurry snaps from family vacations. Andy and Caroline, Hannah as a little girl. They pass the book around and echo each other's words. *How lovely. How handsome.*

'Better lookin' than that first Yank you got hitched to,' Fred says in his laconic drawl.

The room is silent for a second before exploding into laughter. His wife gives him a smack on the arm.

It's not too late.

CHAPTER 40

In the morning I lace up my running shoes as the first light appears on the far horizon, the red of it spreading like pancake batter. Last night Jack told me which would be the best way to run. I leave my watch behind. The house is quiet, and our glasses from the night before are crowded beside the sink, ringed with red wine stains and lipstick marks. I find a clean glass and drink; the water comes from their rainwater tanks and the cold travels down into my chest. I walk down the driveway from the house. The smallest kelpie, Friday, is at my heels. 'She's likely to follow you,' Jack had warned me, 'but you can tie her up if it bothers you.'

She looks at me with amber eyes, pleading. 'Okay,' I say, 'you can come.'

I latch the gate behind us and together we run up the steep driveway to the edge of the property, past the paddocks of cows heading to the sheds to be milked, the grass shimmering with dew. My legs burn with the steep climb and my heart thuds.

I slip through the last gate and Friday bounds out with me, her paws hardly touching the rocky clay beneath. We run along the dirt road as the sun slowly rises, and unfamiliar birds call out in the trees above. There are grey-green leaves, trunks of silver-white and mottled grey. Light pierces the canopy, flashing across my vision. The breeze makes the trees rustle and sway. Ahead of me Friday leaps in and out of the underbrush, chasing invisible wallabies, birds, kangaroos. I think of Grandma last night, out beneath the stars, and how hard it is to align memory with the past, how you imagined the world with how it has changed.

The trees stop then for a strip of power lines and everything converges into a field of light, blazing like fire. So bright that I cannot look away. I stop and stare at the open fields either side of me, the lines above buzzing with life. I call Friday and we turn back in the direction we came. Her tongue hangs pink from her open mouth and her eyes stay fixed on me as she careens past.

There is so much trust in her gaze. So much she seems to think I can do.

I follow her home, the wind whistling me through. With each breath I let the world in.

ACKNOWLEDGMENTS

This book would not exist without a visit to my late great aunt Marge Fogel in 2013, in San Diego. Her 90-year-old boyfriend Bert recalled his visit as an American GI to Sydney during WWII and all the 'beautiful girls' he met and danced with. The following year, in 2014, a conversation with Helen Mckay in the Byron Bay Hinterland intensified my interest when she told me her aunt, a war bride from Sydney, moved to the small (and familiar to me) town of Kilmarnock, Virginia after WWII. These conversations planted the seeds, and my curiosity watered them.

Along the way, I had help from so many people. I'd like to thank:

- Dr Robyn Arrowsmith for her detailed social history of Australian war brides who went to the US during WWII, *All The Way to the USA*, and for making time to talk to me and generously introduce me to Australian war brides in America.

- War bride Dorothy Pence Berry and her daughter Beverley Sollars in San Jose, California—particular thanks to Dorothy for her stories of her wedding dress and her ship leaving early (cancelling her Christmas with family), which I borrowed for my character Sarah.
- The WWII War Bride Association and President Robert Pence (son of Dorothy Pence).
- War bride Joann Patterson and her family in Portland Oregon, who welcomed me and told me wonderful stories which brought the past to life.
- Jill Koenigsdorf, the daughter of an Australian war bride I met at Tin House Summer Workshop in 2016 who shared her mother's experience and her own as the daughter of a war bride.
- My dream agent Grace Heifetz for believing in this book and taking it on, and for always being willing to talk dogs.
- At Allen & Unwin: Jane Palfreyman for her enthusiasm and brilliance. Siobhán Cantrill for all of her work and thoughtfulness. Ali Lavau for making me kill my darlings. Clara Finlay for her eagle-eyed proofread.
- Sandy Cull at gogoGinko for the stunning cover.
- The Australia Council for the Arts for the grant that allowed me to write this novel.
- The Copyright Agency Limited for the grant which allowed me to travel to the US.
- Dana Spiotta and the workshop group at the 2016 Tin House Summer Workshop for helping me hone my focus, Dana particularly showed me how not to be scared of trying a different structure.

- The RMS Queen Mary in Long Beach, California and my very fun research companions on board the ship: Beth, William, and the yet to be born Nisora.
- Kyle Day on the *SS Jeremiah O'Brien* in San Francisco.
- Director of the Royal Brisbane and Women's Hospital Eating Disorder Service, Dr Warren Ward.
- Varuna and the Eleanor Dark foundation for the alumni residencies that helped me complete this book, and for the chance to meet other writers and the conversations and friendships which have resulted.
- Laurie Comings Turner for her expertise as a nurse and having put up with me for all these years.
- Jenna Crawley, who brought me to Kilmarnock and let her house there be my second home during college years. Her welcoming, generous father John C Wilson and his book *The Northern Neck: A Pictorial History*, which helped me imagine Kilmarnock in earlier days.
- Vanessa Rae Many for the dog who eats bananas and for coming to Portland and waiting for my train which took forever (thanks Jenna too). And Evelyn Thornton and Jessica Arends for their long-distance friendship over the years.
- My running group who put up with my long rants on long runs: Bridget, Antonia, Sylvia, Juliet, Vix and Yasmin. Sharon for always making me laugh and for full to brim. Rose for Thursdays. Rachel, Carl, Sam and Callum for the dog named Friday. The Sweetapple-Moss clan and Sally (particularly for Conjola Creek).

- Writing friends and mentors Debra Adelaide, Poppy Gee, Ashley Hay, Bianca Nogrady, Ashleigh Synott, Sunil Badami and Annabel Stafford.
- My mother, Nancy Limprecht, for always reading my work and not holding back on the criticism, or the praise. My sister, Alma Klein, for her brilliant blurb writing.
- My wonderful children Eliza and Sam for forgiving my frequent distraction and being the best distractions of all. And finally, my husband, Simon, without whom I never would have left the comforts of my homeland and stretched myself into the shape of a writer. For your support, love and laughter over the years.

FURTHER READING

War Brides

Robyn Arrowsmith, *All the way to the USA: Australian WWII War Brides*, 2013.

Rebecca Britt, *Stories of Love and War*, New Holland, 2010.

Dyson, Catherine, *Swing by Sailor*, Hodder Headline, 2007.

Annette Potts and Lucinda Strauss, *For the Love of a Soldier—Australian War-Brides and their GIs*, ABC Books, 1987.

Ann Howard, *You'll Be Sorry: How World War II changed women's lives*, Big Sky Publishing, 1990.

Peter A Thompson and Robert Macklin, *The Battle of Brisbane: Australians and the Yanks at War*, ABC Books, 2000.

British War Brides Club, *Journey to a new life—WA War Brides Stories* 2002.

Women in Veterinary Medicine

A biography of and interview with Patricia Thompson Herr, DVM, ecommons.cornell.edu.

Jeanne Logue, *The Wonder of it all*, Harper Collins 1979.

Eating Disorders

Marya Hornbacher, *Wasted: a memoir of anorexia and bulimia* Random House, 1998.

Roxanne Gay, *Hunger*, Little Brown, 2017.

Wright, Fiona, *Small Acts of Disappearance*, Giramondo, 2015.

Courtney E Martin, *Perfect girls, starving daughters*, Simon & Schuster, 2007.

Works cited:

'Floating Creche Coming for US War Brides', *The Argus*, 28 January 1946.

'A Bride's Guide to the USA', British *Good Housekeeping* magazine in conjunction with the United States Office of War Information, 1945.

'When Your Man Comes Home', *The Albury Banner and Wodonga Express*, 28 September 1945.